Readers Love
Kim Fielding

Good Bones

"The energy between Dylan and Chris is quirky and interesting. Both men have secrets in their pasts that could derail any long-term relationship. Fielding slowly reveals the complexities of these characters, peeling away layers with a fine skill and poignant imagery."

—Creative Ink Reviews

Brute

"Fielding does an excellent job with layering her characters, making them so accessible in their personalities and actions that we are engaged in the storyline and their futures immediately."

—Joyfully Jay

Night Shift

"…remarkable and a fresh breath in the choice of character."

—MM Good Book Reviews

By KIM FIELDING

Published by DREAMSPINNER PRESS
http://www.dreamspinnerpress.com

BURIED BONES

KIM FIELDING

Dreamspinner Press

Published by
Dreamspinner Press
5032 Capital Circle SW
Ste 2, PMB# 279
Tallahassee, FL 32305-7886
USA
http://www.dreamspinnerpress.com/

Buried Bones

Cover Art by Christine Griffin
alizarin_griffin@yahoo.com
http://christinegriffin.artworkfolio.com/

ISBN: 978-1-62380-710-8
Digital ISBN: 978-1-62380-711-5

Printed in the United States of America
First Edition
May 2013

For Dennis. Cheerleader, accountant, and fan: what more could I ask of a husband?

CHAPTER 1

DYLAN scrubbed furiously at the wall in the spare bedroom, as if the dirty yellow paint had offended him personally. He was scowling, his hair hanging in his face a little. He looked like he wished he could kill something.

Chris put down the scraper he'd been using to peel away the floral wallpaper border and walked closer to Dylan. "Dude. You don't have to lift every molecule of those fingerprints. You're gonna paint over it anyway."

"Paint won't cover right if the wall's not clean."

"Sure it will. We can slap on a few extra coats if we have to."

Dylan didn't even bother to look at him. "I want to do the job properly."

"Whatever." Chris took a few more steps so that he was close enough to touch Dylan. But he didn't. Instead, he stood at the curtainless window, looking out at the line of poplar trees that separated Dylan's property from his own. It was the first day of July, so the leaves masked most of his view. But there was a little break in the tree line—one or two of them had fallen, or maybe they'd been chopped down at some point—and through the space, he had a glimpse of his ugly back deck. As usual, it was littered with empty bottles and cans. Maybe soon he'd borrow Dylan's pickup truck and carry a load to the recycling center. There were probably enough empties to fill the bed.

It wasn't a great view, not even with a couple of birds circling far overhead and the leaves rustling slightly. Dylan's bedroom, the master bedroom, had a better view. It was at the front of the house, over the living room, and it looked out at a broad field of wheat with green hills as a backdrop.

"You really should've redone *your* room first," Chris said, his gaze still focused outside.

"That's going to be a bigger job. We're going to have to tear down that wall, and the flooring under the carpet in there is shot to hell. We'll have to sleep somewhere else in the meantime, and I'm not going to be comfortable sleeping in here until this room looks halfway decent."

Dylan's tone was gruff, but Chris couldn't help a small smile. *We,* Dylan had said. *We'll have to sleep somewhere else.* The foundation of their relationship seemed solid—God, Chris could hardly imagine life without Dylan now—but the structure was still a little shaky. Well, that was what happened when a backwoods hick like Chris tried to hook up with a city boy like Dylan, with his fancy degrees and fancy job. And that was what happened when a guy found out that the man he'd been working beside and fucking for months—the man who'd pretty much stolen his heart—was a goddamn werewolf. Dylan's sister-in-law had said something the other day about how Chris and Dylan should try relationship counseling, but Chris was pretty fucking certain no shrink on the planet was prepared to advise a couple on what they should do if one of them turned furry once a month.

Dylan swore under his breath, bent, and retrieved the cleaning fluid. He sprayed a lot of it on the wall. He must have used up half the bottle already. Then he started scrubbing again, putting his weight into the action.

Chris could have helped, maybe, but he figured the fingerprints were Dylan's own damn issue. Chris would've just painted over them. They were a little creepy, though—he had to admit that. They belonged to his great-uncle Frank, who'd lived in this house his entire life. Died here, in fact, of an aneurysm, seven or eight years back. Well, he hadn't died in the house, actually, but rather in the middle of the gravel road out front. On his way to Christ knew where, and the old guy just keeled over. Chris probably would have been the one to find him, the next time he ventured out of his own little shack next door, except Chris had been up all night drinking and was passed out on his ratty old couch. It was the man who rented Chris's fields who'd stumbled upon the body. Poor old Bill Gorman just wanted to plant some seed, and instead he'd ended up almost running over a corpse.

But before Uncle Frank died, he used to spend a lot of time looking through the same upstairs bedroom window that Chris looked through now. Staring through the trees at Chris's house. Chris used to catch sight of the old man's face in the window now and then, pale and indistinct. Used to scare the shit out of him. But now Chris smiled again, remembering the first time he'd seen Dylan—standing at this very window and thinking about whether to buy the place. Watching Chris take a piss off the side of his deck.

"I'm gonna go make dinner," Chris announced.

Dylan sighed and tried to swipe his hair back from his face. It fell right back into place. "Yeah, okay. I'm almost done here anyway. We're not going to get to painting yet today."

"Walls'll still be here tomorrow."

"Yeah." Dylan stood up straight and twisted his shoulders a little, like maybe they were itchy. Chris reached up and gave Dylan's upper back a nice scratch. Would've been better without the sweaty T-shirt in the way, but Dylan still seemed to enjoy it. "Thanks, Chris. Maybe I'll shower while you cook."

Chris waggled his eyebrows, which was a waste of effort since Dylan wasn't looking his way. "Could join you."

"Nah. It's getting a little late."

Peeking out the window at the sun, which was still high, Chris shrugged. "Whatever. Guess I'll just go slave over a hot stove."

Dylan spun around, dropped the rag he'd been holding, grabbed Chris around the waist, and dragged him close. "I like it better when you smell like this anyway," he said, snuffling under Chris's ear and at his neck.

Chris's heart thudded a little faster. "Stinky?"

"Mmm. Manly." Now Dylan actually licked Chris's skin, which made Chris shiver. "Salty and a little musky. And you smell like that beer you had with lunch, and cigarette smoke and… and plaster and maple syrup and grease from that engine you were swearing at this morning."

"Hmm," said Chris, trying to hide how pleased Dylan's words made him. Because before Dylan, nobody had bothered to sniff him— well, okay, maybe that part was just a little weird—and nobody had noticed him much either. But Dylan noticed him a lot, and he could map out Chris's entire day with one inhalation.

Chris swatted Dylan's ass hard enough to make Dylan give a small yelp. "Dinner," said Chris. "Unless you'd rather screw right now." Which wasn't a bad idea, now that he'd thought of it. He squeezed a handful of Dylan's firm butt.

But Dylan pushed him gently away. "It's getting late," he repeated.

"Didn't know we had a goddamn schedule," Chris muttered. But he was already turning away, heading to the door. He *was* kind of hungry.

Dylan's kitchen was a beauty, like something straight out of a magazine. Chris was still faintly surprised he was even allowed in such a swanky place, let alone given the run of it. Not that Dylan was going to get much use out of his own pricey stove and expensive cookware. As far as Chris could tell, Dylan could manage sandwiches, soup, and anything nukable, and that was about it. It was a wonder he'd survived on his own.

The previous day the two of them had driven to Scappoose for paint and supplies, and while they were at it, they'd stocked up on groceries. So Chris had some nice thick T-bones, a couple ears of sweet corn, and the makings of a decent salad. If the weather stayed warm, pretty soon they'd have tomatoes from his garden. Chris would sprinkle them with a little fresh basil and Dylan's obscenely overpriced but tasty

4

olive oil. But tonight there was salad, and peaches and raspberries for dessert. Some ice cream would go nice with that.

Chris whistled softly to himself as he filled a big pot with water and set it on the flame, rinsed the veggies, and tore the lettuce into a blue ceramic bowl. He liked cooking. He'd learned mostly out of self-defense, because his mother had usually been too wasted to remember to feed him at all. At best she'd throw some Ritz crackers and American cheese his way, or plop a jar of peanut butter in his lap. Sometimes Chris had lived with his grandparents instead, but after Gram died, Gramps could manage burned burgers, burned grilled cheese, half-raw roasted chicken, or canned beans heated slightly and poured over toast. Even when he was little, Chris had watched cooking shows and done his best to copy them. He wasn't exactly Julia Child, but he didn't go hungry.

He husked the corn and set the butter out on the kitchen table to soften. The water was beginning to bubble just a bit but wasn't yet boiling. He quickly chopped some mushrooms, a sweet red pepper, and an egg he'd hard-boiled that morning, then dumped everything onto the lettuce and placed the big bowl next to the butter.

The frying pan was a really good cast iron job. It had been practically new when Chris took over Dylan's kitchen, but now it was nicely seasoned. Sure beat the cheapy Teflon skillet that lurked in Chris's particleboard cupboards.

As a little drizzle of oil heated in the pan, Chris seasoned the steaks with some freshly ground pepper and sea salt. He wasn't convinced that sea salt tasted any different from the kind in the familiar blue canister, but of course Dylan didn't have ordinary condiments. Hell, the pepper was probably free-range, free trade, organic, and non-GMO.

Chris snorted and tossed the meat into the pan. It sizzled deliciously.

"Make mine rare."

Chris jumped a little; he hadn't heard Dylan enter the room. "Could just give you the thing raw," Chris said, looking back over his shoulder.

5

"I'd eat it that way." Dylan's hair was damp and slicked back a little; the curls hadn't had a chance to reassert themselves yet. He was wearing an orange T-shirt with a picture of the Tin Man screen printed on it. The shirt was tight enough to show off his strong but not overly bulky muscles and his flat stomach. His jeans were a little on the snug side too. Chris licked his lips.

"Tastes better cooked," Chris said, turning his attention back to dinner.

"I guess."

Chris heard the fridge open and close, and the little *pop* as Dylan pried the cap from a bottle of beer. Then Dylan sighed heavily and sank into one of the kitchen chairs. Chris didn't know what was bothering his lover, and he hadn't quite worked up the balls to ask.

As soon as the steaks were seared, Chris transferred the pan to the preheated oven. Then he dropped the corn into the briskly boiling water: *plop plop*. A droplet or two splattered onto his hand, but he ignored the tiny burns. He pulled a couple of plates down from the cabinet. "We need knives and forks," he growled.

"Yeah, okay." Dylan hauled himself upright with another sigh and plodded over. He paused as he passed behind Chris, and for a moment Chris was positive Dylan was going to touch him, but then he continued forward to the cutlery drawer.

Neither of them said anything as Chris served the food and then sat opposite Dylan. The steak was really fucking good, though. Dylan inhaled his almost faster than Chris could watch, and followed up by slathering about half a stick of butter over his corn and gnawing busily at the ear. Only when the corn was gone did he look over at Chris with a little smile. Dylan's lips looked buttery, and there was a little smear of grease on his chin, where his soul patch used to be. Chris wanted to lick it off.

"That was great, Chris. Thanks."

Chris craved a cigarette—he was feeling a little unsettled—but Dylan didn't allow them indoors. He stabbed his fork at his lettuce instead. "Was just meat."

"It was good meat. Everything you do is good." Dylan wiped his mouth with a paper napkin—a shame, Chris thought—and jumped to his feet. He carried his dishes to the sink and dumped them in, and Chris expected him to start washing up. That was their deal: Chris cooked, Dylan cleaned. But Dylan didn't turn on the water. He stood there for a few moments instead, twitching his upper body, drumming his fingers on the granite countertop. It was his turn to stare out a window. This one looked out at the grass and weed patch that served for a backyard, then past a couple of small outbuildings to the blackberry-brambled slope leading down to his pond. Berries would be ripe pretty soon.

"I have to go into the office on Friday," Dylan said to the window. "Stender has a new project for me."

"Is that what's got you all on edge? You're worried you ain't gonna be able to handle what he throws at you this time?"

"No. I mean, yeah, I guess I'm a little stressed over it."

"Come on, Dyl. He practically wet himself over that house you designed for the futon queens, and you told me yourself he's got people lining up for you. He ain't gonna throw you to the curb." Chris pushed away the empty salad bowl and stared at Dylan's broad back.

"I know. It's just... I don't know. Now everyone has high expectations and I have to live up to them."

"And you will."

Dylan shrugged. "I guess." He spun around to look at Chris. "You want to come into town with me Friday? I could drop you off at a bookstore or something for a couple hours. And we could have lunch together. If I don't introduce you to Matty pretty soon, she's going to kill me."

So Dylan was finally willing to let him meet someone outside the immediate family. Chris grinned. He'd heard some stories about Dylan's office mate and had been wondering whether his lover would ever acknowledge him a little more publicly. "Didn't realize Matty was so scary," Chris said.

"She's maybe five two and can't make it up a flight of stairs without huffing and puffing. But if I really pissed her off, she might poison my coffee."

"Sounds like someone I'd like to meet."

"So come with me Friday."

"Okay," said Chris, even though the idea made him a little nervous. Like Dylan, Matty was an architect. She was probably really smart and cool, and she was one of Dylan's very few friends. What if she hated Chris?

Dylan nodded and then glanced out the window. "Good. But, um, I need you to go home now."

Chris felt like he'd been punched in the gut. Here he was, rejected again. Cast aside. He opened his mouth to say something caustic, but then he noticed the expression on Dylan's face. Dylan didn't look like a guy who was trying to get rid of a pain-in-the-ass fuck buddy—he looked anxious, worried. Antsy.

"Full moon tonight, ain't it?" Chris asked quietly.

"Yeah."

"Sorry. Didn't realize."

"Why would you? Doesn't matter much to anyone but astrologers and me."

Chris stood and walked across the kitchen. He stopped only when he was very close to Dylan, so close he could feel the puffs of Dylan's breath on his face. "So now it matters to me too."

Dylan looked more pained than relieved. He ran his fingers through his hair, which by now had dried into untamed waves. The fingers didn't help matters any. "You need to go to your place, Chris. And lock the door. I know that didn't keep… didn't keep Andy out…. Fuck. Maybe we should have bought you a gun."

"With silver bullets?"

"I don't…. I'm not sure if that myth is true."

Chris shook his head. "And whether it is or not, do you really think I'd shoot you?"

8

"If I was coming after you."

"You won't."

"You don't know…." Dylan bit his lower lip. "When I change, I'm a wolf, Chris. A real wolf. I don't think like a person. I'm a predator. I want to chase things, and when I'm even a little hungry, I want to kill them. I want to feel my jaws tearing into their flesh and I want to lick their blood from my muzzle."

"Yeah, I get it, dude." A note of irritation had crept into Chris's voice. "You're not Fluffy the poodle—you're the Big Bad Wolf. I seen what you can do, remember? Saw you kill that other wolf. You ripped him to fucking pieces."

"Then you understand why you need to be safe."

"I am safe!" Chris yelled, making Dylan flinch a little. "You were right there in my living room and you coulda tore me up even easier than you did Andy. But you didn't. You saved me from him, in fact. And the months before that, before I knew what you were, you never tried to hurt me."

"But I could!"

"You could but you won't."

Now Dylan was raising his voice. "All it would take is one bite, you know that? I wouldn't even have to kill you. Just one little goddamn nip and… and then you're like me." His eyes were anguished. "I couldn't live with myself if I made you a monster too."

Chris closed his eyes and tried to frame his next words just right. Then he looked at Dylan and settled his hands on Dylan's tense shoulders. "You're not a monster, Dyl. You've… okay, you kinda got a little monthly problem, and all the Midol in the world ain't gonna help. But you *protected* me. I been… I been hurt before. Sometimes by folks who were supposed to care for me." He swallowed and forced himself to go on. He didn't talk about those parts of his past, didn't fucking think about them—but right now it was important. "They were just ordinary humans and they hurt me, but you didn't. Never have. I trust you, Dylan."

9

He reached up with one hand to trace the scar high on Dylan's forehead, the scar that was usually hidden by hair but that Chris knew was there. One of the scars Dylan had gotten when he rescued Chris from Andy the werewolf. "I trust you," Chris repeated.

Dylan looked like he was trying not to cry. Hell, Chris *felt* like he was trying not to cry, and that pissed him off. Crying wasn't his thing. Hadn't cried when his mother died of cancer when he was fifteen, and he wasn't about to start blubbering now.

So he glared at Dylan instead. "Look. I'm tryin' to make this thing with us work. We both are. And if it's gonna work, you need to stop freaking out and sending me away every twenty-eight days, and I need to see what I'm dealin' with. The whole thing, I mean. Didn't really get to see much that time, just a lot of blood and fangs and fur. I want to see you. Need to." And he meant it, because he was pretty sure that if they didn't get this thing cleared up, everything was going to break down. Secrets eroded good things.

After a few moments of thought, maybe Dylan came to the same conclusion. "Okay," he said. "Next month. We'll get you a gun, and I don't know, maybe we can see about the silver bullet thing—"

"*This* month. Tonight." Chris crossed his arms and put on his most stubborn face, which clearly expressed his resolve. He wasn't going to move. If Dylan wanted him gone, he'd have to pick him up and fucking carry him. He might be strong enough to give it a try, but Chris was going to put up a fight.

"No. I feel… something feels really weird this month. Don't know why. But it's like—I don't know. Creepy-crawly, like someone's watching me. Like I can almost see something moving, just out of the corner of my eye, but I can't quite catch it."

"How do you know you ain't gonna feel even weirder next month? It's all in your head, Dyl. You're just an ordinary, run-of-the-mill werewolf. Nothing unusual about that."

"You're impossible," Dylan said, his shoulders slumping a little.

Chris grinned in triumph.

BuRIED BONES

CHAPTER 2

ALTHOUGH sticking around while Dylan turned into a wolf had been
Chris's idea, at the moment he was having serious second thoughts. But
he wasn't going to let Dylan know about the misgivings. No way.
Instead, Chris joked lightly as Dylan did the dinner dishes, and then
Chris headed out into the backyard. It wasn't quite dusk, though the sun
had already dropped behind the nearby hills, and the air was still
pleasantly warm. He shook a cigarette out of the pack he kept in his
shirt pocket, flicked his blue plastic lighter, and inhaled. Dylan had
been giving him the stink-eye lately over his smoking habit. It made
Chris happy to know someone cared enough about him to nag.

But the nicotine didn't calm his nerves. In less than half an hour,
the sun would set for real and Chris would watch his lover turn into a
wolf.

Fucking A. The world was a really strange place.

He lit a second cigarette and puffed thoughtfully. Until recently,
his world had been a pretty small place. He wasn't stupid—uneducated,
yeah, but not ignorant. He read a lot, watched TV, listened to the radio.
Didn't have much use for the Internet and hadn't bothered with that.
But he knew there were all kinds of people in the world, all kinds of
strangeness. He just hadn't interacted with any of them very much,
preferring his own corner of the universe where he might not be
important or respected, but in which he had a pretty good idea where
the next blows would come from. The devil he knew, right?

Only now it turned out life was even more extraordinary than he'd suspected. Werewolves really existed. And so did men—well, one man, anyway—who wanted Chris for more than a quick fuck. A man who was smart and kind and sexy as hell. Who could be a good friend and, most miraculous of all, could fall in love with Chris. Who would risk his own life to save Chris.

It all made Chris wonder what other surprises the universe might have in store for him.

He took one last drag, ground out the butt under his heel, and went back inside.

DYLAN paced the kitchen, unable to stand still. His eyes were wide, his breathing was fast, and his muscles were a little spastic. He reminded Chris of someone tweaking on meth—not a very nice memory.

"Go home, Chris. I mean it."

"No."

Dylan reacted with resigned exasperation. He paused his walking just long enough to dry-scrub his face with his hands. "This is a really bad idea."

"Maybe." Chris had acted on a lot of bad ideas in his life. Some of them had landed him in deep shit. But some of them—like hitting on the hot but totally not-his-type guy who'd just moved in next door—had turned out pretty damn well. Chris wasn't going to move from his spot near the doorway that led from the kitchen to the hallway.

Dylan growled and stomped across the room, loudly, despite his bare feet. He yanked open one of the drawers and pulled out his biggest blade, an eighteen-inch sashimi knife he'd apparently acquired under the delusion that he might someday make sushi. "Then take this," he said, striding quickly in Chris's direction.

A little alarmed by the way Dylan was waving the blade around, Chris backed up against the wall. "I don't need a weapon," he said.

"Take it anyway." Dylan held it out in his direction, mercifully handle-first.

Chris hefted the knife. "So if you go 'All the better to eat you!' I'm supposed to filet you? 'Cause I saw the way you went after that other wolf. I don't think a foot and a half of pointy metal would have slowed you down all that much."

"I'll feel better if you have it."

"Whatever."

Dylan nodded and peeled off his orange T-shirt. He folded it neatly and set it on the counter.

"What do you do once you're… changed?" Chris asked. "Howl at the moon?"

"I run. Smell things. Hunt. I hunt things, Chris. Kill them." He looked more than a little wild, and his voice seemed just a bit rougher than normal.

"Gramps liked to hunt. Took me with him a couple times. I never killed nothin', but I saw him take down a deer once."

"I've killed deer. Rabbits. Raccoons. Caught a fish once. I use my teeth, not a gun. I can crunch through a deer femur the way you munch on Kay's sugar cookies."

Keeping his face neutral, Chris nodded. It was strange to hear his lover saying these words. The same man who listened to the Decemberists while posting things to Instagram—who could be such a tender lover that Chris sometimes had to badger him into going a little rougher—and here he was in his fancy kitchen, looking eager and excited as he discussed mayhem. The experience was a little scary for Chris, but also kind of thrilling. It was like biting into a chocolate and discovering that the center was liquid chilies.

"How far do you run?" Chris asked.

"Far. Miles. I'll be out all night." Dylan unbuttoned and unzipped his jeans and pulled them off. He was wearing a pair of gray boxer briefs, the heavy outline of his cock and balls clearly visible. He traced the scars that swirled across his belly, but his thoughts seemed far

13

away. The scars looked as if they'd been there for years instead of months. Chris liked them. When they were in bed, he liked to lick them, to feel the little indentations against his tongue. A reminder of the sacrifice Dylan had made to save him.

"Fine," said Chris. "I'm gonna sleep in your bed tonight." He'd been sleeping there every night, lately. It was much better than his own.

"'Kay," Dylan replied a little absently. He stepped out of his underwear and stood in the middle of the kitchen, magnificent enough to steal Chris's breath away. The kitchen wasn't especially warm, but Dylan's skin wore a light sheen of sweat. The hairs on his chest— usually sparse and pale—seemed lusher and darker, and his fingers kept flexing as if he were a boxer getting ready for a fight.

"Is it dangerous out there?" Chris asked quietly. "For you, I mean."

"Not really. I stick to the state forest land. I don't think hunters are an issue, I stay far away from roads, and I don't have any predators. I'm the top of the food chain." He grinned, well, wolfishly.

But then his face grew more serious again. "Look. When I… change… it hurts. A lot. So I might scream a little. But it's kind of… kind of a good pain, because I want it so badly. And it's over with pretty quickly."

"Like a speedy fuck when you're all hot and horny and don't want to screw around with a lot of prep work."

Dylan looked a little skeptical. "I guess. Just, don't come near me, okay? It probably looks really ugly, but I'll be fine."

"Got it."

They both just stood there after that, silent except for Dylan's noisy breathing. Come to think of it, Chris was breathing pretty heavily too, and his heart was thudding. He realized his grip had tightened painfully around the knife handle, and he forced himself to relax his hand a little. He was just considering going to the fridge and fetching himself a beer when Dylan gasped.

As Chris stood rooted to the floor in fear and fascination, Dylan's body began to change. It reminded Chris of watching someone reshape a ball of clay, only there were no giant hands prodding at Dylan, and he was groaning a lot more noisily than any lump of clay. His lips pulled far back in a grimace and his teeth lengthened, growing sharper. His joints warped. He dropped to all fours, but not before Chris noticed that his lover's cock was fully erect.

"Guess it does kinda hurt so good," Chris mumbled.

Dylan didn't pay him any attention. And he didn't look like Dylan anymore. The hair on his head had spread across his face, down his shoulders and back and haunches. And as it grew, the curls disappeared and the individual hairs turned a tawny gray, lighter under the belly and across the muzzle. Because Dylan had a muzzle now, his lips and nose a shiny black. His ears stood upright atop his head, pointed, swiveling slightly in Chris's direction when Chris made a small noise.

Wide, furry paws had replaced Dylan's hands and feet. Even more remarkable, a tail had sprouted from his hind end. It was bushy, tipped in black.

And Dylan's eyes. Usually they were a warm amber near the pupil and sea-glass green near the edges. Now they were yellow. But the first time Chris had seen Dylan as a wolf—when Dylan was half-dead, covered in his own blood and Andy's—and Dylan had swung his head to look at him, Chris had seen something familiar in those eyes. Couldn't have said what, certainly not then, not even now. But he'd recognized something in that gaze, so he hadn't been half as shocked as he should have been when the wolf collapsed and then morphed into his lover, naked and torn to shreds. Now he saw Dylan in the wolf's eyes again, and although Chris was wary as hell, he wasn't frightened.

The wolf stretched the way a dog does after a long nap, then lifted his head to scent the air. He trotted over to the stove, where maybe a few spatters of steak grease had escaped Dylan's cleanup, and licked his jowls with a very long pink tongue. Maybe Chris should have bought an extra T-bone.

The wolf shook his body from nose to tail. He was a beautiful creature with thick fur, long legs, and heavy muscles. If there were a Werewolf Westminster, he'd have taken Best in Show. Then he seemed to notice Chris, who was still squished up against the wall, stupid knife

15

in hand. Looking not remotely like anyone's pet, the wolf sauntered over.

"Uh, hi, Dylan," Chris said, keeping his voice soft. He wasn't terrified, but he wasn't exactly calm either. He knew the wolf could probably hear his racing heart and smell the sweat dripping down the back of his collar.

The wolf seemed neither threatening nor alarmed. He came up close—so close Chris had to restrain himself from petting the thick ruff of fur around his shoulders—and sniffed at Chris's shoes. Then he poked his nose at the hand without the knife, snuffling loudly. His nose was cold and wet. That meant he was healthy, right?

His ears perked slightly forward and his upright tail slowly waved. Chris decided discretion was best: he slumped his shoulders a little and dropped his gaze, trying to appear as submissive as possible. "Don't mean you get to boss me around when you're human. And you better not try to hump my leg."

The wolf made an odd sort of chuffing sound but didn't seem upset. And then he did something that shocked Chris so much that he dropped the knife with a clatter: the wolf rose up on his hind legs and rested his front paws on Chris's shoulders. He wasn't as tall as the human Dylan, or as heavy, but he was still plenty big. And my, what big teeth he had! His tail was still moving gracefully back and forth, and Dylan was still in there, deep in those feral eyes.

With another chuff, the wolf pushed away and landed back on four paws. He turned to the back door—which Dylan had earlier instructed Chris to keep open—and slipped outside into the darkness.

Chris slid down the wall until he was sitting on the floor. The knife blade had nicked the floor a little; Dylan was going to be pissed.

"Holy shit," Chris said to the empty room. His boyfriend had just turned into a wolf.

CHRIS tried to keep himself busy that evening. He ran over to his house—pretending he wasn't scanning the darkness for signs of wolf—

and searched his overstuffed bookshelf. When his eyes fell on his battered copy of *The Call of the Wild*, he dissolved into a laughing fit that sounded slightly hysterical. He chose something by John Grisham instead.

But back in Dylan's living room, seated in the really comfortable leather armchair Dylan always let him appropriate, Chris couldn't concentrate on the plot. Who gave a crap about lawyers anyway?

Chris dimly remembered his mother yelling about some damn attorney back when Chris was very small, after his father had taken off for good. And then Chris had to deal with lawyers himself when his gramps died. There had been even more legal maneuvering—long letters on official-looking letterhead showing up in his mailbox—when Uncle Frank died. Frank had left his house and fairly useless acreage to some distant relatives, and for some reason the third cousins twice removed had feared Chris would contest the will. They'd offered him a little cash to keep him quiet. Chris had been tempted to take the will to court and tell them to screw themselves—just for the pleasure of being ornery—but he was short on funds at the time, so he'd signed their paperwork. Seeing as how he lived next door, he'd been a little worried about what they were going to do with the property, but as it turned out, they'd done nothing. The place sat empty for years before Dylan came along and snapped it up.

Dylan. What was he doing right now, Chris wondered. Had he hunted something down already? Chris was dimly aware that there were real wolves in Oregon—the 24/7 kind, not the once-a-monthers— but he didn't know if any were nearby. What if Dylan met up with some of them?

Giving up on the novel and tossing it onto the end table, Chris stood and walked to the window. He couldn't see anything but the reflection of the living room, and there was really nothing much to see outside anyway, other than the distant hills and the wheat fields he rented to Bill Gorman. Possibly a coyote or two—they came by pretty frequently—but most likely no prowling wolves. Still, he couldn't help the creepy feeling that someone was watching him, so he doused the lights, leaving the living room lit by only the full moon.

He wandered into the kitchen, thinking he might have a beer. But he stood in front of the open fridge, staring at the contents without seeing them, wondering how the night forest smelled to a wolf.

Dylan owned an old TV but had never bothered to unpack it. It was probably down in the basement somewhere, along with his sister-in-law's grandmother's furniture, a bunch of tools and home improvement supplies they weren't currently using, and some boxes full of old school records and family treasures Dylan couldn't quite bear to part with. When Chris and Dylan wanted to watch the idiot box, they traipsed over to Chris's house and squished together on his lumpy sofa. But Chris didn't want to be in his own house tonight, not by himself.

Dylan's laptop was sitting on his drafting table in the other downstairs room, the room he'd lately been calling his office. Chris thought about booting it up—Dylan had confided his password weeks ago. Chris could see what Wikipedia had to say about wolves. Or maybe surf some porn. But as soon as he sat down, he got that itchy feeling in his back, like someone was staring at him. Nobody was, of course, but still he gave up on the Internet and headed back to the kitchen instead.

He ended up making bread. He liked making bread because all the kneading was physical work—he ignored Dylan's fancy mixer—and because it smelled so damned delicious while it baked. One of the best smells in the world, along with coffee, bacon, and gasoline. Homemade bread tasted far better than anything you could buy in the stores too. Well, except maybe in Portland at one of those snooty bakeries where they went on about artisan this and stone-ground that, but Portland was an hour away.

As soon as the bread was cool enough to slice, he had a thick piece slathered in butter. It was good. He left the dirty dishes for Dylan to deal with the next day, gave the carefully folded clothes on the counter a long look, and sighed. He stuck his head out the back door and heard nothing but leaves rustling in the breeze. He made sure to leave the door open a bit, then trudged upstairs.

He and Dylan had already redone the master bathroom. They'd installed a shower stall big enough for two, but the bathtub attracted Chris's attention tonight. He didn't have a tub at his own place, just a crappy plastic shower. Dylan's tub was a huge claw-foot affair, probably original to the house. Dylan had paid to have it refinished; now it gleamed whitely, pristine and tempting. A basket of bath oils and salts perched nearby—one of Dylan's sister-in-law's crafting projects, which both Dylan and Chris pretended was far too girly for them but secretly enjoyed.

Chris started the tap, waited for the water to heat, and then plugged the drain before adding a healthy drizzle of Kay's citrus oil. "With vitamin E and almond oil!" she'd announced happily. "To moisturize your skin."

The men had grumbled, but the truth was that the stuff did feel really nice. Plus when Chris bathed with it, Dylan liked to lick him all over afterward.

Not that there would be any licking tonight.

Chris soaked until his skin felt wrinkly and the water had cooled. He thought about Dylan the entire time. Worried. Wondered. But then he thought he heard a noise, which startled him from his reverie. "Dylan?" he called.

There was no answer.

Chris climbed out of the tub and dried off with one of Dylan's organic bamboo towels. "I'm not a goddamn *panda*," he liked to grumble to Dylan, but in fact the towels were a lot softer than anything Chris owned.

Chris usually slept nude, whether in Dylan's bed or his own. But for some reason he felt compelled to wear something tonight. He dug through Dylan's dresser drawers until he unearthed a pair of plaid flannel lounging pants, which he put on. He crawled into Dylan's big comfortable bed and turned off the light. The sheets smelled like Dylan and sex, and Chris considered jerking off but didn't. He fell asleep surprisingly fast.

He woke up some time later when the bed shook. He was a little disoriented at first, then alarmed when he heard heavy panting and felt something heavy moving across his legs. "Dyl?"

The wolf moved to the empty space beside Chris, circled two or three times, and settled down. Even Chris's human nose could smell mud and pine sap on him, along with a faint odor of wet dog. Very slowly, very cautiously, Chris moved his hand over until his fingers were buried in soft, warm fur. The wolf gave a noisy, contented sigh.

"Night, Dyl," Chris said with a smile and soon fell back asleep.

CHAPTER 3

DYLAN woke up to the smell of frying bacon and felt ravenous. He was curled up on top of his comforter, but with a spare blanket thrown over his nude body. He wrinkled his nose at the smell of forest and blood, climbed carefully out of bed, and stretched. He had a few little scratches on his torso—probably those damn blackberries again—but he felt great. He always did after a good run. But he was going to have to wash the bedding again.

"Finally awake, sleeping beauty?" Chris's voice made its way up the stairs and down the hallway to the bedroom. He must have been bellowing. Instead of shouting back, Dylan stomped his foot on the floor a couple of times.

He should probably shower, but the smell of breakfast was too tempting. He noticed his favorite pair of lounge pants tossed in the corner, smiled a little, and pulled them on. They smelled like Chris. He didn't bother with a T-shirt or socks; the morning was already pretty warm, and he tended to run hot around the time of his change.

Chris was standing in front of the stove, wearing boxers and the previous day's shirt: an old black one with the ZZ Top logo almost entirely faded away.

"Did you cook all the bacon?" Dylan asked, walking close to him.

"There's another package in the fridge."

Dylan gave Chris's shoulder a quick squeeze before going to the refrigerator and pulling out the plastic package. He tore it open with his teeth and slid a few slices of raw meat into his mouth.

"That's disgusting, dude."

After chewing and swallowing, Dylan shrugged. "Tastes better this way sometimes. I didn't cook my meal last night either."

Chris looked slightly wary. "What'd you eat?"

"Possum."

"Bleh."

Dylan shrugged again and ate more bacon. He would really have loved to go after bigger game, like the elk he could smell in the woods, but he probably couldn't manage it on his own.

Chris shook his head. "There's toast on the table, if you wanna eat somethin' civilized. And I was gonna scramble some eggs."

"I like the eggs raw too." To demonstrate, Dylan cracked a couple of eggs into a mug. He slurped the contents noisily, enjoying the expression on Chris's face. Then he filled another mug with coffee from the pot Chris had brewed, and he crossed to the table. He was smearing butter onto toast when Chris joined him.

"Wow! This bread is amazing! Did you make it?"

"Yeah. I'd probably be more flattered if the food critic didn't just eat a half pound of raw bacon."

"Hey, you should be happy that I'm easy to please. Rick says that Kay's been craving smoothies, and they have to be a particular *kind* of smoothie that they sell at this place all the way across town from them. Plus she won't let him cook anything stinky or she threatens to puke."

Chris snorted. "But Kay's only gonna be pregnant for, what? Six more months? Your deal is permanent."

"But only a day or two a month." Dylan could tell by now that Chris wasn't really annoyed—it was only the good-natured snark that was one of Chris's favorite conversational gambits.

They ate and drank in silence for a while. Dylan was replaying little flashes of memory from the previous night. His wolfish recollections were always a little fragmentary and confused, he supposed because the wolf's senses and mind were so very different

22

than the human's. But he knew he'd enjoyed himself and that he'd be satisfied for another twenty-seven days.

When his food was gone—he'd gobbled four slices of toast—he looked across the table. "You didn't... didn't freak last night. It took a lot of balls to stand your ground."

"Told you. I trust you. And you didn't eat me."

Dylan scratched his chin. Maybe he should grow his soul patch again. "I didn't want to. I feel... the *wolf* feels that you... that you're mine."

Chris beamed. "That's 'cause I am, dope." His smile turned slightly evil. "But maybe I oughtta get you a collar. A leash. Sign you up for some of them obedience— Ugh!" The remainder of his sentence was lost as Dylan darted around the table and tackled him, sending them both tumbling to the floor.

The floor was cold and hard. But Dylan didn't care because Chris was underneath him and very little fabric separated them. And when he kissed Chris, he tasted delicious, without even the taint of the morning's first cigarette.

Chris slid his hands beneath Dylan's waistband and grabbed his ass. When he spoke, his voice had gone low and rough. "Full moon do this to you too? 'Cause it's way better than sucking on eggs."

"*You* do this to me," Dylan replied, undulating his body a little so their hardening cocks rubbed together nicely.

"Fuck."

"I hope so."

Chris chuckled and so did Dylan. It felt so good to have someone he could do this with. Not the sex—well, the sex was great too—but the intimacy. The companionship. The *fun*.

While Dylan licked at Chris's slightly stubbled jaw, Chris wrestled the lounging pants past Dylan's hips and ass. That left Dylan hobbled around his thighs, but it wasn't as if he intended to go anywhere. Chris bucked a little and rolled them both over so he was on top. Dylan reached for Chris's boxers, but Chris laughed and jumped up, scooting out of reach. "Hold that thought," he said.

Dylan watched as Chris impatiently tugged off the ZZ Top shirt and threw it across the room, then climbed out of the boxers so quickly he almost fell on his butt.

"Jesus," Dylan groaned. He could never get enough of seeing his lover's body. Hard muscles. Light-brown skin that, without the aid of tanning beds and no matter what time of year, always looked like Chris sunbathed nude. And his beautiful cock, which now jutted proudly from black curls.

Chris leered and struck a few poses he might have stolen from porn magazines and then, for good measure, licked his lips and gave his hard-on a few long, slow strokes. Dylan groaned again and reached for his own groin, joining in with Chris's torturously wonderful rhythm. Dylan might have been the storybook monster, but Chris was the one who looked positively evil just then. Dylan wouldn't have been at all surprised to see his lover sprout a long red tail and a pair of pointed horns.

And Chris's wicked glee only increased as he sauntered the few steps to the kitchen table, still fondling himself. He reached over and, using two fingers, scooped a healthy glob of softened butter out of the green glass butter dish Dylan had bought at that 1950s retro place over on Hawthorne Street.

"You're kidding," Dylan said.

"Don't tell me the dude who scarfs raw bacon and eggs is gonna get squicked by a little dairy-based lube."

"But… it's messy."

Chris waggled his eyebrows. "You can lick it off when we're done." Then he rested one foot on a chair and began to work the butter into himself.

"Oh, God…," Dylan said and had to move his hand away from his dick before things ended way too soon.

Chris's answering chuckle would have done the most malevolent demon proud. But he was obviously turned on by what he was doing to

24

himself—and what it was doing to Dylan—because a bit of fluid glistened at the red tip of his cock. Dylan wanted to taste it, so he was pleased when Chris swaggered back toward him.

He was even more pleased, however, when Chris straddled him on his knees, rubbed a buttery hand up and down Dylan's cock a few times, and then guided the slippery organ to his ass. Slowly and with a look of intense concentration, Chris impaled himself.

They'd been using condoms, but after Dylan was outed as a wolf and they reconciled, Chris had growled something about trust and they'd both had themselves tested. Dylan had worried that his blood work would turn out weird on account of his supernatural infection, but apparently everything looked pretty normal. He was still concerned that Chris might catch werewolfism from barebacking, but Chris had been stubbornly adamant on the subject, and Dylan had to admit that impromptu sex without worrying about a rubber was pretty damn nice.

Dylan now blasphemed at the sensation but then couldn't manage even swear words as Chris flexed his thick thighs, moving himself up and down.

"Always... Christ!... always wanted to be... a cowboy," Chris panted.

"Yee-haw?" Dylan reached up and wrapped his hand around Chris's bobbing shaft, which made Chris throw his head back and squeeze his eyes shut but didn't slow the movements of his body at all.

"Chris... shit, Chris—"

And then Dylan yelped, pushed Chris off, and tried to jump to his feet. But the pants were still bunched around his legs, and he and Chris ended up tangled on the floor in a painful heap.

"What the fuck—" Chris began furiously.

"Someone's in the house."

Dylan had seen a movement in the hallway, past Chris's shoulder. He managed to get upright successfully this time, yanking his pants up as he ran for the hall. Chris was right behind him, still bare-assed.

There was no one in the hallway, and the front door was closed. They both raced into the living room—nobody there—and then the office. No sign of anyone. Dylan went to the front door and rushed onto the porch, Chris hard at his heels.

They scanned the gravel road, the field with the young wheat, the scrubby front yards of Dylan's house and Chris's. There was nobody there. Only a short time had passed since Dylan saw the person in the hallway, and the intruder couldn't possibly have made it very far.

"Dyl, are you sure—?"

"Positive. I *saw* someone."

"Who was it?"

"Don't know. Just had a glimpse of him—I think it was him—as he went past the doorway."

"What'd he look like?"

"Dark hair. Light clothes." Dylan knew that wasn't a very useful description, but it was the best he could do. He was absolutely positive he hadn't been hallucinating.

To his credit, Chris stopped questioning Dylan's credibility. He rubbed his ass, which had probably been bruised when Dylan dumped him so unceremoniously. "Maybe he went upstairs."

"Maybe," Dylan replied.

They trooped back inside and up the stairs, but a quick survey of the rooms revealed nothing but a very large spider on the master bedroom ceiling.

"He must have made it out back," said Dylan. "Down the hill towards the woods."

"Must've. He kinda killed the mood," Chris said, unhappily looking down at his wilted hard-on.

"Sorry."

"Not your fault. Why the hell would anyone break into your house? And how'd he get here? I didn't see no car."

"I have no idea." Dylan looked around uncertainly. "Should we call 911?"

"Nearest cop's twenty minutes away, and they ain't gonna find nothin' when they get here. Can you— Maybe you could play bloodhound, dude."

That wasn't a bad idea, actually. They ran down the steps again and stopped at the kitchen doorway. Feeling slightly ridiculous, Dylan inhaled very deeply. He smelled coffee, bacon, toast, butter, and Chris, all of which were very distracting scents and not at all useful under the circumstances. So he sniffed again, and then again. And he caught... something. Just barely.

"What is it?" asked Chris. "Can you smell someone?"

"No.... There's something kind of... earthy. Probably just something I dragged in on my paws last night." He sighed. "I guess maybe I was seeing things."

Chris came closer and embraced him. "When I ride you, you should be seeing stars. Fireworks. Maybe God and a heavenly choir. Not guys running down the hallway."

Although he was still a little shaken by the experience, Dylan laughed and cupped Chris's buttery ass. "You were pretty good."

"Good? Dylan, I am fucking *spectacular*."

DYLAN still felt a little uneasy later that morning as they worked on the spare bedroom. He kept turning around quickly, as if he might catch someone staring at him, but there was nobody there but Chris. It didn't help Dylan's mood that those damned fingerprints wouldn't come off the wall, no matter how hard he scrubbed at them.

"What the hell did the old man have on his hands?" Dylan groused as he tossed the cleaning rag aside.

Chris was wearing his overalls and had a smudge of beige paint on his cheek. He looked sort of adorable. "Told you to just paint over it."

"That's not how you're supposed to do it."

"Nobody's gonna revoke your architecture diploma over it, man."

"I guess not."

Chris waved the paint roller. "C'mon. Let's get this done and then we can pick up where we were interrupted this morning."

That was an appealing thought, but Dylan said, "I think I want a nap. I'm wiped."

"That's what happens when you spend your nights skulking through the wilderness."

"I do *not* skulk."

Chris laughed in that infuriating way that made Dylan want to strip him naked and fuck him through the nearest mattress. "Fine. *Loping* through the wilderness, then." He thrust the roller into Dylan's hand. "So let's finish paintin'. We can nap and then we can fuck. Or the other way round. Or maybe fuck, nap, fuck. I could go for that."

"*You* have a crappy work ethic."

"Just got my priorities straight, is all."

Dylan dipped the roller in the tray and began to paint.

They made a good team. Chris did the corners and edges with a brush, while Dylan swiped the broad expanses of wall with the roller. When one of them was working near the ceiling and was perched on the ladder, the other helped out by refilling the paint tray. With, truth be told, a little gratuitous groping.

Dylan's mood gradually lightened as they worked. He liked working with Chris. He always did, but today was especially good, the banter between them fond and relaxed. They'd been getting along well since their reconciliation, but never as well as this, and Dylan's heart felt light and strong.

Part of the reason for his happiness was the fact that he hadn't attacked Chris the previous night. Hadn't remotely wanted to. The wolf's emotions were somewhat different from the man's, simpler and not tinged by uncertainties. But they weren't *that* different. Wolf or human, Dylan loved Chris, would never harm him, would do anything in his power to protect him. Dylan needed no longer fret over Chris once a month, because now he knew Chris was safe.

So Dylan was relieved to be able to trust himself, but he was equally thrilled with Chris's reaction. When Dylan had shifted last night, he'd opened himself up wide, revealing the last of his dark secrets to his lover's eyes. Chris would have been fully justified in being horrified or disgusted at what he'd witnessed, not to mention scared out of his wits. But he'd been none of those things. Chris had watched Dylan turn into a beast, had slept with a goddamn wolf in his bed, and in the morning he'd greeted Dylan with breakfast and enthusiastic—if interrupted—sex.

And now Chris was humming off-key and getting paint in his hair, and every so often he'd throw Dylan a blinding smile. The morning not-hallucination had been really weird. Dylan couldn't help but feel that there was something he was missing, something really important that had escaped his notice. But at the moment it didn't matter because Chris Nock loved Dylan Warner, architect and werewolf, and Dylan loved Chris right back.

CHAPTER 4

"IT'S time to unplug yourself, Dyl."

Dylan didn't look up from his laptop screen. "But I have these plans to finish and that meeting at work in two days."

"And you've been click-clackin' away since dawn."

That was true. Despite a pretty vigorous completion of their kitchen-floor activities—this time on his much more comfortable bed—Dylan hadn't slept well. Maybe he shouldn't have had that late-afternoon nap. He'd tossed and turned and woken up every time the old house made a small noise, and finally he'd crawled wearily out of bed. He'd left Chris snoring loudly and padded downstairs to get some work done on a house he was designing for the semiretired lead singer of a grunge band and the singer's tattoo-artist girlfriend.

"Just give me another hour," Dylan said. "Maybe two."

"Nope. It's the Fourth of July. Independence Day! You shouldn't be workin' at all."

"That's what I get for taking yesterday off."

"Well, you're gonna take the rest of today off too." Chris snapped the laptop shut.

"Hey!" When Dylan tried to reopen the computer, Chris grabbed his arm and dragged him out of the chair.

"Go get dressed," Chris ordered. "I got plans."

30

Dylan was immediately suspicious. "What kind of plans?"

"Get your ass in gear and you'll find out."

Begging, threatening, and a big dose of puppy-dog eyes didn't drag any additional information out of Chris, so Dylan went upstairs. "What am I supposed to wear?" he yelled down to Chris.

"What am I, your fashion consultant? It don't matter. Wear your regular shit."

Looking at his open dresser drawer, Dylan tried to decide what his regular shit was. Jeans and a tee, he supposed. He pulled on one of his nicer pairs of jeans and the vegetarian zombie T-shirt Rick and Kay had recently bought him. Socks and sneakers finished the ensemble. He gave his hair a quick comb—he really needed to get it cut—and trotted down to the kitchen, where Chris was waiting.

Chris took one look at Dylan's shirt and snorted. "Yeah, that's gonna go over well."

"Why? Where are we going? Should I change?"

With a roll of his eyes and a sigh, Chris grabbed Dylan's keys off the counter. "Let's go."

The sun was out and the weather was absolutely perfect. Chris steered Dylan's Silverado down their bumpy lane and onto the county road, whistling to himself as he drove.

"You're not going to give me even a tiny hint?" Dylan nagged.

"We're headin' somewhere I ain't been since I was a little kid. I mean, real little. Used to go with my mom and dad."

Dylan turned to watch his lover, who was focused on the road. Chris rarely spoke of his mother and never his father. "You have happy memories of this place?" Dylan asked softly.

"Guess so. I ain't even thought about it in years, but yesterday when we were— Well, somethin' brought it to mind." He grinned.

Now Dylan didn't have any better idea where they were going and his curiosity was really piqued, but Chris refused to say another word on the subject. He took them onto the highway but, to Dylan's

31

surprise, did not continue all the way into Portland, instead turning onto Cornelius Pass Road.

"So our destination isn't in civilization," Dylan prompted.

Chris bopped him in the bicep—not very gently—and turned on the radio. They sang along together, not achieving anything approaching harmony and only accidentally approximating the right tune. They discussed the house Dylan was finishing and speculated on the project Stender had waiting for him next. They calculated how many blackberry pies they could cajole Kay into baking once the berries were ripe, and wondered whether her pregnancy would make her more or less willing to bake. Dylan told a couple of stories about his office mate, Matty, and Chris had a long and funny tale about how he'd acquired the flatbed truck he occasionally managed to get up and running.

They made a few more turns, heading generally south. Dylan still didn't have a clue what their destination might be.

Finally they came to a little town with a whole lot of traffic. People walked alongside the road—precariously close to the cars— carrying seat cushions and coolers, and wrestling with strollers and backpacks and hyperactive kids. Some cars were parked at an alarming slant where the road shoulder met a ditch, but Chris drove into the town proper and pulled into a high school parking lot, where a pair of wholesome-looking kids in cowboy hats charged them five bucks to park.

Chris and Dylan got out of the truck and joined the crowds moving toward downtown. But Dylan still didn't know what the big draw was, not until they turned a corner and there was a big banner strung over the street.

Dylan stopped in his tracks. Chris stopped too when he realized Dylan had halted. "What?" demanded Chris.

"We're going to a *rodeo*?"

"Yep. One of the biggest, in fact." Chris walked closer to Dylan, pulled the phone out of Dylan's shirt pocket, and checked the time before shoving the device back in place. "We got almost an hour 'til the show. We can go pick up the tickets at will call and then grab somethin' to eat."

"But—"

"Come *on*, Dyl. I bet they got them giant corn dogs."

Well, who could say no to giant corn dogs?

Dylan followed Chris down the main street, across a parking lot, and through the entrance to the rodeo. But long before they got to the fairgrounds, he could smell their destination: fried foods, popcorn, hay, horse and cow shit, beer, human sweat. Despite his trepidation, he found the scents exciting. What did horse taste like, he wondered, and then shook his head to clear it.

They entered near the arena but had to walk halfway around it to get their tickets. The middle-aged lady behind the counter wore a red-checked shirt with a bandana around her neck. "Have a good time, boys," she said as she handed over the little envelope.

Chris grabbed one of the free bumper stickers and shoved it in his back pocket. "You need one on your truck," he told Dylan with a wink. Then he led the way to the food stands.

As it turned out, there were giant corn dogs, along with nearly anything else that could be deep-fried and/or shoved on a stick. Most of the booths seemed to be fundraisers for various local organizations, and they were all doing a brisk business. Dylan had a surprisingly great burger, a huge cone of curly fries, a giant sausage that made Chris leer like a twelve-year-old, and a funnel cake with powdered sugar. "Maybe this was a pretty good idea after all," Dylan admitted, eyeing the place that sold deep-fried Oreos.

"Maybe someone should just serve you up one of them steers on a paper plate."

"Sounds good to me."

But Dylan eventually filled his stomach, and they spent a little time wandering the carnival games and the booths that sold cowboy hats, jewelry, T-shirts, wooden signs, and beer cozies. "Maybe I'll buy you a hat before we go," Chris said. "Might be a good look on you."

"I don't know if I'm a Stetson kind of guy."

"So we'll get one for me. And maybe a pair of chaps." He leaned in close and lowered his voice. "Picture me in that and nothin' else the next time I go for a ride."

Oh, Dylan could picture that very well, thank you kindly, and he probably had a dazed look on his face as they walked back to the arena.

The bleachers were hard, but they had good seats, only a few rows up and near the center, with a good view of the grandstand. At least, Dylan assumed the location was good. He had only a very vague impression of what he was about to witness and didn't know where in the ring the action would take place.

The stands were packed with talking, laughing, eating people of all ages. Closest to Dylan and Chris were a family with small kids, an older couple holding hands, and a group of eight or nine men and women in their twenties. A little girl in a pink cowboy hat was eating deep-fried Oreos and talking a mile a minute. A lot of the people wore fancy boots, and they all looked like they could converse intelligently about calving pens or brands of herbicide.

The show began with the national anthem, which Dylan probably should have expected based on the ample red-white-and-blue bunting and banners. He wondered if rodeos were always patriotic or only on the Fourth of July. A bunch of high school girls rode horses into the arena—rodeo princesses and their queen, he gathered—and impressed him by galloping very fast. Next came the rodeo clowns in a fake fire truck. Dylan might have enjoyed their fooling around if it weren't for the announcer, whose commentary included conservative political jokes that made him cringe.

But it was a particularly lame faggot jest that made Dylan turn to Chris and say, "You've got to be kidding."

Chris shrugged. "They been sayin' the same shit since 1870, probably. Ain't discovered political correctness yet."

"It's like being transporter-beamed to a red state."

"Consider it a cultural experience. Like the time you went to Barcelona. Which is in Spain."

34

That was a snide reminder of an insensitive comment Dylan had made to Chris months ago, back when they were first getting to know one another and Dylan still assumed his new neighbor was an ignorant redneck. The comment must have really stung for Chris to remember it so clearly. Dylan considered apologizing, but he'd already said he was sorry, and he wasn't all that happy with Chris for unexpectedly raising the subject. He opened his mouth to say so, but then the show began in earnest.

An enormous animal—a bull—came thundering out of the chute, and on its back was a man who looked very small in comparison. The bull immediately began to buck, and the cowboy flopped around, one hand holding onto a rope and the other waving wildly in the air. First the guy lost his hat, and then he lost his seat. As soon as he tumbled to the ground, the rodeo clowns dashed forward to distract the bull. The cowboy sprinted for the fence and climbed over it.

"Ow," Dylan said.

Chris laughed.

Several more men on bulls emerged in turn. All the men—who seemed to have names like Colby, Cody, Corey, and Dustin—were certainly impressive athletes. And every one of them was insane, as far as Dylan was concerned. Some managed to stay on the bull for eight seconds, at which point a horn sounded and they rolled themselves off the animals and away, and then their scores flashed on the big scoreboard.

"I bet it's really hard for these guys to get decent health insurance," said Dylan.

"Some of 'em make some good prize money."

"I'm sure that's a lot of consolation when they spend the rest of their life in traction."

After the bull riding was bareback horse riding—Chris snickered every time the announcer said *bareback*—in which the cowboys were again whipped back and forth and then thrown to the ground. At least they had a shorter distance to fall. Then came the broncos, who wore saddles, although that didn't slow them down.

"How the hell do they stay on there at all?" asked Dylan, who'd never ridden anything but a carnival pony.

Chris grinned. "Strong thighs."

Barrel racing was the next event. The competitors were women, and they were no less amazing than the men as they raced their horses around big plastic bins at speeds that took Dylan's breath away.

Still, Dylan was happy to see that the next event—team roping—involved men again. He had to admit, strong men in cowboy gear were damn sexy. He decided he'd definitely buy Chris those chaps.

The team roping competition involved pairs of men working together to catch a steer. It must take years of practice to work so smoothly with a partner—even without horses involved. He got to wondering whether any of the cowboys were gay. At least some of them had to be, right? And when they were practicing the roping and the bucking, maybe—

Chris shook his shoulder. "Eyes're kinda glazed there, dude. Your mind replaying every cowboy porno you've ever watched?"

Dylan actually blushed. "No."

"Told you you'd enjoy it."

But Dylan's reaction to the next event had nothing to do with sex and a lot to do with amazement—maybe with a little terror mixed in. It was steer wrestling, which involved the cowboy riding his horse alongside a running steer, leaping off the damn horse, grabbing the steer's horns, and wrestling it to the ground. All without getting trampled, gored, or otherwise killed. The horses in this event were as impressive as the riders, although Dylan couldn't help but wonder how the steers felt about the whole thing.

"Who wakes up one day and decides he wants to do this for a living?" asked Dylan, waving his hand in the direction of the arena.

"Dunno. Guys who like some excitement."

"I like excitement but you're not going to see me trying this."

"Dylan, running your car a couple miles after the gas light goes on is not excitement. Neither is putting your garbage bins out at the curb the morning of garbage day instead of the night before. Or eating lunch meat a day past the sell-by date."

Dylan tried to hide his hurt and probably failed. "I'm sorry I'm so boring," he grumbled.

So Chris socked him in the arm—right in the same spot where he'd punched him before. "Less than twenty-four hours ago you were goddamn Fenrir, Dyl. I don't think that counts as boring in anyone's book."

"Fenrir?"

"Giant wolf from Norse mythology, college boy," Chris replied smugly. "I been doin' some reading lately."

Dylan probably should have been angry, except he had the sudden realization that Chris wasn't put off by his werewolf status; he actually considered it interesting. Exciting, even. Worthy of research. Dylan smiled.

They watched a few more events after that and sat through more stupid and offensive attempts at humor from the announcer. Dylan's ass began to hurt from the hard seat, but he was otherwise having fun. "Just don't expect me to go to a tractor pull next," he said to Chris, which made Chris laugh.

When the show was over, they let the crowds dwindle before weaving their way out of the arena. They waited in line to use the Porta-Potties and then stood for a few minutes, watching little kids try a bucking bronco ride.

"I'm kind of hungry," Dylan said after a while.

"I think you ate all the food already."

"You're just jealous of my metabolism."

"I do like your girlish figure."

It was Dylan's turn to sock Chris.

This time he had a grilled turkey leg, which he waved around while doing a bad impression of King Henry VIII. He followed it up with an ear of corn and a caramel apple, and even considered a bag of cotton candy before deciding on a beer instead. Chris just watched, a look of frank admiration on his face. "You can really put it away."

"I think the whole wolf thing burns a lot of calories."

"Guess so."

Dylan wiped his hands on a paper napkin, ducked around a large man in an NRA T-shirt, and tossed the napkin in a big metal bin. "Want to go look for that hat?" he asked Chris.

The crowds were heavy, and it was difficult to proceed past the food booths toward the people selling nonedible items. It didn't help that Chris stopped twice, once to admire a glass beer stein engraved with a cowboy on a bucking horse, and once to play with a plastic lightsaber.

But eventually they made it to a stand where a grizzled man with a mustache was selling cowboy hats of a variety of shapes and descriptions. "Do you think I'm a white hat kinda guy or black?" Chris asked.

"I think either would suit. Let's just skip the one with the camouflage print, okay?"

Chris found a mirror and started trying on hats. Dylan watched for a while, but then his attention strayed to the booth next door, which sold jewelry and similar items.

He wandered over, nodded absently at the proprietor, who was helping another customer, and examined the goods. He saw a fancy cigarette lighter—silver and turquoise—and even though he disapproved of Chris's smoking, Dylan thought he might buy it as a little gift. But then he saw a heavy silver ring with the silhouette of a running wolf, and he smiled. He picked it up and examined it. He was no expert on such things, but it looked to be well made. He wondered what size Chris would wear.

He replaced the ring on its holder and waited for the salesman's attention. But then Chris came up behind him, startling him a little.

"No hat?" Dylan said.

"Couldn't decide. Need your input. It's for your enjoyment, after all."

"Yeah, okay, Chris. I was just—"

The salesman interrupted him. "Can I help you?"

Dylan looked at the guy—really looked at him for the first time—and almost gasped. It was Chris—well, an image of Chris with an additional thirty years on him, hair gone mostly gray, some of his teeth missing, and a not very healthy sheen to his skin, but with the same startlingly clear blue eyes. He wore an old plaid shirt and faded jeans.

"I… I…," Dylan stuttered.

But the man had shifted his gaze to Chris, who was scrutinizing a shark's tooth pendant and was totally oblivious.

"Christian?" the jewelry seller asked hoarsely.

CHAPTER 5

CHRIS had been enjoying watching Dylan at the rodeo. Dylan was way out of his element, which was amusing; but he was also having fun, and that made Chris happy. Plus, he was pretty sure he'd be getting cowboy-themed nookie for the foreseeable future.

In fact, they were both having such a good time that once they'd purchased the cowboy hat, Chris was going to suggest they try out some carnival games. Maybe they could win a stupid stuffed animal or two and donate them to Kay and Rick's kidlet-to-be. But first he had to choose a hat. He was having trouble with that because, to his own eyes, he looked like a dork no matter which one he tried. In desperation he looked around for Dylan and found him at the next booth over, bending over a tray of jewelry.

And then the salesman came over and called him "Christian," which no one had done since his mom died fifteen years earlier.

For several heartbeats, nobody moved. The sounds of the rodeo—laughter, music from the carnival rides, a crying kid—seemed dim and far away. The jewelry salesman cleared his throat. "Christian Nock?" he said.

Chris grabbed Dylan's arm. "Let's get the fuck out of here," he said and tried to drag Dylan away.

But Dylan was rooted to the spot with his mouth hanging open, and the salesman darted around the table full of jewelry until he was standing almost close enough to touch. "Chris. Jesus Christ, Chris!"

Chris gave Dylan's arm a really hard yank, almost pulling him off balance. But Dylan regained his footing and blinked dazedly at Chris. "He smells like you, Chris. Not exactly the same, but… really similar."

Which was way more than Chris could stand to hear at the moment. He let go of Dylan, whirled, and began to stride toward the rodeo exit. But the dense crowds made quick movement difficult, and Dylan and the salesman were right behind him, Dylan reaching for Chris's shoulder.

"Fuck!" Chris spat and halted. He turned around to face the other men and was surprised and more than a little pleased when Dylan placed himself between Chris and the salesman.

Dylan didn't actually have any hackles to raise at the moment, but Chris could practically see the lifted fur anyway, and he heard more than a hint of a growl in Dylan's voice when he demanded, "Who are you?" The answer to which was probably patently obvious to all of them, but Chris appreciated his boyfriend's attitude anyway. He'd never before had anyone care enough to be protective.

The salesman took a half step backward because Dylan was fucking scary when he got like this. "James Nock. Jimmy. I'm Christian's—"

"The fucker who's listed on my birth certificate," Chris interrupted.

Jimmy nodded. "Christian's father. Shit. Christian, let's… let's go find someplace…." He looked around as if searching for a quiet conversational corner.

"Got nothin' to say to you, asshole."

"Please, Christian. I just want to—" He moved slightly forward, but Dylan put out a hand to stop him.

"Stay back," Dylan warned. He sounded like he meant it.

They were attracting a small crowd, curious onlookers who were probably hoping for a good fight. Dylan sort of snarled at some of them too, and the closest ones moved several feet away. With his hand still almost touching Jimmy's chest, Dylan turned his head to look at Chris. "What do you want to do, Chris?"

"I want to go home," Chris replied, realizing he sounded like a little kid. He sort of felt like a little kid at the moment, scared and confused and overwhelmed.

Jimmy held his hands up. "Look, Christian, just give me a few minutes. Please. I didn't— Fuck. Just tell your buddy here to stand down, okay?"

"He's not my buddy—he's my goddamn boyfriend! The man I fucking love."

Jimmy blinked and several members of their audience gasped. One guy—a young man in a mullet—muttered, "Faggots," but Chris heard him and so did Dylan, who bared his teeth and looked terrifying enough that the homophobe paled and slipped away into the crowd.

"That's right," Chris said loudly, addressing Jimmy. "I'm a fucking faggot. How do you like that, Jimmy? The fruit of your goddamn loins takes it up the ass and *likes* it. Goddamn rolls over and *begs* for it." His hands were balled into tight fists and his chest felt too tight.

Dylan settled a hand on Chris's upper arm. "Let's go home, all right?" He kept his voice pitched very low and calm.

But Chris wrenched himself away. "Fuck off!" He turned and lurched toward the exit, and Dylan let him go. On top of all his other whirling emotions, Chris was ashamed of himself for yelling at Dylan like that—Dylan was only trying to look out for him—but Chris hated his own weakness, his need to be looked out for. Next thing he knew, he'd be wearing ruffly shirts and fainting when he saw a mouse.

He didn't know what Dylan and Jimmy did after he left. All he knew was that somehow he made it back to Dylan's truck, and then he unlocked it and climbed into the driver's seat, where he leaned his arms on the steering wheel and buried his face in them.

He didn't look up when the passenger door opened, when Dylan slid in beside him and eased the door shut. They sat there like that a long time, neither saying a word.

"You didn't get your hat," Dylan said gently

"Fuck you," Chris said into his arms, equally softly. He was suddenly very tired.

"I bet we can find you one somewhere. We live out in the sticks—there must be cowboy hats somewhere in our neighborhood. Or at least baseball caps with John Deere logos."

Chris snorted and rolled his head to look at his lover. "You're an asshole, you know that?" he said with affection.

Dylan grinned. "But I'm *your* asshole." He reached over and gave Chris's hair a tug. "Want me to drive this time?"

"Yeah. Okay."

They climbed out of the truck and swapped seats, and Dylan piloted them out of town and back onto a county road lined with fields and tree farms. Dylan didn't say anything, didn't ask any questions. That was something Chris loved about him: Dylan wasn't the type to force anyone to talk about his feelings, to drag painful words out of someone who just wanted to sit for a while and let things settle. And okay, the downside was that Dylan himself wasn't exactly forthcoming about what was going on in his head, and sometimes Chris had to be a fucking mind reader, but that was all right.

"Thank you," Chris said in a near whisper.

Dylan reached over and squeezed his shoulder. "Thanks for the rodeo. I never would have thought of going to one on my own. It was fun. A cultural experience." Chris could hear the smile in Dylan's voice.

WHEN they got home, Dylan started fumbling around the kitchen as if he intended to make dinner. Chris wasn't especially hungry, but he had no intention of exposing either of them to Dylan's approximation of a meal. He grabbed the frying pan from Dylan's hand—what the fuck Dylan thought he was going to do with the cookware, Chris had no idea—and said, "Go work on your house. I'll cook."

"You're sure? I was thinking I could probably manage to make some burgers or—"

"I ain't in the mood for food poisoning tonight." Which was a little harsh. Dylan's cooking wasn't quite fatal; it just tasted really horrible. "Go on. I'll find us somethin' worth eating."

Dylan nodded and wandered off to his office. Chris rooted through the cupboards and the fridge before deciding on a stir-fry. He poured rice into the cooker—of course Dylan had a rice cooker, an ordinary pot wasn't good enough—and started chopping veggies and slicing some chicken breasts. He could have improvised with one of the cooking sauces in the fridge but decided to make some from scratch instead. Preparing food like this took just enough concentration that he didn't have to think about anything else.

Over dinner, Dylan made a few awkward attempts at friendly conversation. But Chris was pissed off at him, mostly because Dylan should have been pissed but was being really nice instead—sort of walking on tiptoe, as though Chris might erupt any moment. God, maybe he *would* erupt. His emotions certainly felt molten.

He went outside for a smoke while Dylan washed the dishes. Something was moving around in the darkness, watching him—he was sure of it, even though he couldn't see anything. Raccoon, maybe. Chris wasn't frightened, especially with his werewolf boyfriend only a few yards away, clearly visible through the open back door. Chris went back inside just as Dylan was putting away the wok.

"I'm gonna head over to my place," Chris announced.

Dylan frowned at him. "You sure?"

"Yeah. I know you wanna work on those plans. Don't wanna be in your hair."

"You won't be. I mean, you can sit near me and read while I work." Dylan gave a funny little shrug and looked away. "The company's nice."

It was so good to hear those words that Chris wavered a little. But deep in his heart, he knew that if he stuck around he'd end up acting like a jerk, and they'd probably end up in a fight. Dylan didn't deserve that.

"Nah. Gonna go watch TV. If you get a lot of your shit done, we can work on the flooring in that bedroom tomorrow afternoon. Come get me when you're ready, okay?"

"Okay," said Dylan, although he didn't sound very certain. He took a hesitant step in Chris's direction, but Chris just waved at him and ducked out the back door.

Chris's house seemed smaller and shabbier than ever. And it was almost as if the place was haunted, because he kept picturing his gramps sitting on the sofa, taciturn as usual, beer can in his hand and sandwich plate balanced on his lap. Gramps was in the crowded kitchen too, sitting at the Formica table and tapping his cigarette into the brown plastic ashtray, and he was sitting in his threadbare armchair in the living room, leafing through *Reader's Digest*. Maybe Gramps had been happy at some point in his life, but Chris remembered him as perpetually disgruntled, disappointed with everything and everyone around him. He hadn't been a cruel man, although he'd hit Chris a few times, usually when Gramps had been drinking and Chris did something wrong. But he also hadn't been the kind of man to comfort a boy whose father had abandoned him, whose mother was too wasted or too worried about her next high to pay much attention to her son.

"Fuck this," Chris said out loud. And fuck Jimmy Nock for popping into his life long after Chris had stopped wishing he'd reappear.

He turned on the TV and watched some stupid sitcom about an improbably perky family, then a cop show where everyone was attractive and well dressed. When that show was over, he flipped the channel and ended up watching the last ninety minutes of *Forrest Gump*. Usually he liked that movie, but tonight it annoyed him.

He went to bed earlier than usual. His bed was narrower than Dylan's, the mattress way too old and lumpy. His sheets were a lot scratchier than the zillion-thread-count ones Dylan used. And he couldn't sleep. He tossed around for a while, trying to find a comfortable position. He tried jerking off, because sometimes that helped him sleep, but his dick wasn't interested and he gave it up. He fetched a book instead and lay in bed reading until his eyes felt grainy, and then he turned off the light.

He was still wide awake when he heard the soft click of his back door and then a muffled grunt and a curse as someone collided with a piece of furniture in the dark living room. Chris lay very still as someone entered his bedroom. There was the rustle of clothing against skin. And then the blankets were lifted and his mattress dipped as someone climbed in next to him.

Dylan spooned his bare body against Chris's back and wrapped his arms around Chris's middle. "I finished the plans," he said against the back of Chris's neck. He was very warm.

Chris sighed and moved his butt backward a little so that Dylan's groin was nestled firmly against him, the wiry hairs tickling a little but the soft cock feeling really nice. "You should get some sleep."

"Can't. Bed's too empty."

"I don't want goddamn comforting, Dyl. Don't need it."

"I assure you, my motives in coming over here were entirely selfish. I was lonely."

"And horny?" asked Chris, wiggling his ass a little bit.

"We can just sleep if that's what you want."

Suddenly, and very urgently, what Chris wanted was Dylan. He wiggled around in Dylan's arms until they were face-to-face, tugged him a little more tightly against himself, and plastered their lips together. Dylan seemed willing to go along with the program. He opened his mouth for Chris's tongue and threaded his fingers through Chris's hair, and they made out until they were both breathless.

Chris pushed at Dylan until Dylan was flat on his back, and then climbed on board. Chris nipped and licked at Dylan's collarbones, at the junctures of his neck and shoulders. He felt Dylan's hard cock digging into his belly, Dylan's hands kneading his back, while Chris sucked on Dylan's nipples and dragged his nose through the hairs on Dylan's chest. God, he loved the way Dylan felt beneath him, long bones and lean muscles. He loved the noises Dylan made—groans and growls and gasps—and the way Dylan clutched at him as if afraid Chris might go away.

Chris was not going to go away.

What he did do was slither down Dylan's body. He pushed the covers down as he went, but the night was warm and they were generating plenty of their own heat. He dipped his tongue into Dylan's bellybutton, making his partner laugh and squirm, then licked at the crease where Dylan's leg met his body. Dylan tried to guide Chris's head to the side a little, but Chris wouldn't let him. He tortured Dylan for a while instead, using his tongue and fingers everywhere except where Dylan obviously wanted him the most.

He only gave in because Dylan was begging incoherently, and because Chris's own body was demanding more. Moving quickly, he squiggled back up the mattress, fumbled a bottle of lube from the nightstand drawer, and shoved the bottle into Dylan's hand.

"What do you want?" Dylan asked.

"Want you so deep inside me I can fucking taste you."

Dylan's breath hitched a little. They repositioned themselves, Chris on all fours with his ass in the air, Dylan on his knees behind him. But maybe Chris had teased Dylan a little too long, because now it was Dylan's turn to be cruel—and he *was* cruel, in the most goddamn wonderful way. He squeezed, spanked, and fondled Chris's ass, then bent over and licked delicately down the crease, behind Chris's balls, all around the edges of Chris's hole. When he actually stuck the point of his tongue inside, however, Chris swore and his arms buckled—his chest now against the mattress, his face half-buried in his pillow.

Dylan had long fingers, like a pianist. He slicked them up and slid two of them into Chris, then probed carefully for the bundle of nerves that made Chris swear. "We missed the fireworks tonight," Dylan said. "Going to have to make our own."

Chris would have laughed at the lame humor, except he was too busy whimpering as Dylan withdrew his fingers, traced around the outside of Chris's opening, then glided them back in.

47

"Ready?" asked Dylan.

"If you don't start fuckin' me now, I'm gonna kill you."

"I guess that's a yes."

A certain amount of maneuvering and repositioning followed because Chris wanted the greater intimacy of skin-to-skin contact, and Dylan seemed to feel the same way. They ended up on their knees with Dylan behind. That position didn't allow for the deepest penetration or the most vigorous movements, but it meant Chris could lean back against Dylan's chest, and Dylan could nuzzle at Chris's neck and jack his cock, all while swinging his hips in a steady and spectacular rhythm.

"Fuck… fuck, Dyl, like… God!"

Dylan wasn't even trying to talk. Too much multitasking already, maybe. He was panting heavily, though, right into Chris's ear, his breaths warm and moist.

There was a particularly nice little twist to Dylan's wrist and an extra swivel to his hips. "Gonna…," Chris choked out. "Gonna come."

"Do it. Let go. Let *go*, Chris."

And Chris did. Dylan was probably taking Chris's entire weight now and could barely thrust, but that didn't much matter to Chris, who was shouting and convulsing and, for Christ's sake, seeing those fucking fireworks after all.

It took several minutes for Chris to come back to himself, at which point he realized he was lying on his side in Dylan's arms, and Dylan was slowly smoothing a hand down Chris's bare flank.

"Holy fuck, Dyl. I couldn't even tell if you—"

"Oh, I came too. Don't worry about that. You were spectacular."

"Told you." Chris gave a satisfied little wiggle. His muscles felt melty, and it was as if all the hard and pointy edges of his world had been softened for a while. Dylan's arm was pleasantly heavy around him.

"Sorry," Chris said after a while.

"Okay. Um, for what?"

"Today. I kinda outed you in front of the entire rodeo."

Dylan made a dismissive noise. "I'm not exactly in the closet to begin with, and I don't care what a bunch of strangers think of me."

"But maybe you don't want half the state to know you're sleepin' with me."

"Jesus, Chris! Are you kidding? I'm tempted to brag about you everywhere I go. Erect a billboard or two on I-5. 'Hey everyone! Look who *I* have! Look who lets me in his bed!'"

"Dork."

"I prefer *geek*."

There was more nice silence and even nicer petting. "Sorry about my d—about Jimmy. About him showin' up like that, out of blue."

"It kind of shook you up."

"Yeah. I didn't expect it, that's for sure. I hardly ever think of him. Don't really remember him all that great. I don't think I saw him that much even when he was around, and by the time I started first grade, he was gone. Mom didn't talk about him either, except to complain that the bastard wasn't payin' no child support."

Dylan's response was a little hesitant, as if he weren't sure how Chris would take it. "Do you have any good memories of him at all?"

"A few. That damn rodeo, for one. I remember sitting next to him in this crappy trailer we were livin' in, and it was morning and Mom wasn't around. Maybe she was still asleep. Me and him were both in our underwear and laughin' at cartoons, and he was lettin' me eat ice cream for breakfast." He sighed. "I think he used to laugh a lot. Really loud."

"I don't remember either of my parents laughing," Dylan said, reminding Chris that Dylan's folks were both dead. "I guess they must have, sometimes. But in my head they're always really serious. Lecturing me about responsibility and things like that."

"I don't think Jimmy ever lectured me about nothin'. Certainly not responsibility. He wasn't exactly an expert on that."

"Hmm." Dylan was tracing little shapes on Chris's belly with his fingertip. Chris wondered if his lover was creating new house designs right on his skin.

"What'd you say to the old man after I left?" Chris asked.

"Not much. He wanted your phone number but I told him no. Said it's totally up to you whether you ever speak to him again."

"Dunno... dunno if I want to."

"I can understand that. You don't have to decide tonight, or even tomorrow. Or, well, ever." Dylan pulled away slightly to kiss the spot between Chris's shoulder blades. "I will say one thing for the guy—he didn't seem to care that you're gay. He told me to take good care of you."

Chris snorted, but Dylan's words were a small relief. "Can take care of myself."

"I know. But now you don't have to."

Chris sort of dozed off after that, but Dylan kept wiggling behind him. Finally, Dylan sat up. "Your bed sucks, Chris. Let's go sleep in mine instead."

They didn't bother with clothes or shoes, just tromped bare-assed out of Chris's house, off his deck, through the line of poplars, and into Dylan's kitchen. The joys of country living. When they got inside, Dylan wrinkled his nose. "I'm going to have to search the basement and the attic tomorrow. I keep smelling something weird."

"Weird like how?"

"Like... I'm not sure. Like the ground smells when you dig a big hole. I like—the, um, wolf likes to dig sometimes. After rodents."

Chris grinned at the mental image of wolfy Dylan pawing at the ground, clods of dirt flying behind him. "What do you think it is?"

"No idea. Maybe squirrels or something building a nest? Or... you tell me. You have a better idea than I do what kinds of creatures to expect around here."

"We'll go critter-searchin' tomorrow." Chris yawned hugely. "I'm beat. You wore me out."

Dylan slung an arm around Chris's shoulders, and Chris's arm fit nicely around Dylan's waist. Side by side, they walked slowly through the kitchen, down the hall, up the stairs. They didn't turn on the lights as they went, but Dylan made a pretty good guide dog.

At the top of the stairs, Dylan said, "I was thinking maybe tomorrow—" And then stopped.

Straight ahead of them at the end of the hall, a floating figure lightly bounced, like a balloon on a breezy day. It glowed slightly and resembled a slender dark-haired man in light clothing. The features and details were indistinct, as though he were a pixilated photo. He looked at both of them and raised his hands… in threat? In supplication? Dylan and Chris remained frozen as the apparition floated toward them—and then disappeared.

CHAPTER 6

CONSIDERING the relative equanimity with which Chris had handled the fact that his boyfriend was a werewolf, perhaps it wasn't too surprising that he was calm about the presence of a ghost. Dylan, however, felt like freaking out.

"A ghost," he said, for maybe the hundredth time. "We just saw a goddamn *ghost.*"

Chris nodded and gave a jaw-cracking yawn. "I know, dude. I was there." They were huddled in Dylan's bed, the blankets pulled up tightly as if they were kids hiding from the monster under the bed.

"It was glowing and hovering and… and it looked really creepy."

"Yeah, it did. But I gotta tell you, Dyl. Given the choice between a ghost and a homicidal werewolf, I'd take the ghost. It didn't try to hurt us. Well, it interrupted some nice bonking on the kitchen floor, but that's still way better than being mauled."

Dylan's heart skipped a beat. Actually skipped a beat—he didn't know hearts really did that. "I know who it is," he said shakily.

"Yeah?"

"Andy. It has to be Andy."

Chris whistled. "Poor bastard. First he's a werewolf and now he's a ghost. Least he didn't have to be a zombie. Zombies are the most disgusting monsters."

"Chris!" Dylan restrained himself from strangling his oddly cheerful boyfriend. "This isn't a joke. I killed Andy and now he's haunting us. That smell I've been sensing—it's his grave." He glanced nervously at a section of wall which, if transparent, would have given him a view of the gone-to-wild forest of Christmas trees where Andy's corpse had been buried. Christ! He hadn't been able to get rid of Andy when the bastard had been alive, and now Dylan was really stuck with him.

Chris bumped his shoulder against Dylan's. "Fine. I'll be serious. But you need to chill. He's been around for a few days at least and he ain't done nothing dangerous."

"That doesn't mean he won't. Maybe he's just working his way up to it. You know, toying with us. I can fight people and wolves, Chris, but I don't know what to do against a ghost."

It occurred to Dylan that only a few years earlier, this entire conversation would have been unimaginable. The only supernatural creatures he'd encountered back then had been in horror movies, which he'd never been a big fan of anyway. And he hadn't been a violent person. Never even got into schoolyard fights. Yet here he was: a werewolf discussing what to do about the ghost of the man he'd murdered.

"Look," said Chris. "It's been a rough day. Deadbeat dads and dead exes should not just show up unannounced. But probably nothing's gonna slaughter us in our sleep. Let's get some rest and deal in the morning."

"Yeah. Okay." Dylan reached over and clicked off the light, and the men snuggled together comfortably. Within minutes, Chris was snoring softly. Dylan stayed awake for a long time afterward, though, worrying.

NEITHER of them mentioned Chris's father the next day. Just as Dylan had predicted, the fingerprints in the spare room showed through the paint. He swore and slapped on another coat. Then he and Chris ripped up the hideous shag carpet, revealing a hardwood floor that was scuffed and scratched but salvageable.

"We gonna rent a sander when we're in town tomorrow?" Chris asked.

Dylan had been so preoccupied with Chris's father and the ghost that he'd almost forgotten to worry about the upcoming meeting with his boss. "Yeah. We can work on it over the weekend if you want."

The previous night he'd been scared by the ghost, but today he was mostly just pissed off. Andy had come into his life unbidden. Yes, Dylan had been awed by the man's good looks and flattered that Andy wanted *him*, and Dylan had invited him to his house and had a few days of very willing sex. But of course Dylan hadn't suspected his new bed partner was a werewolf, and once he'd learned the truth—the hard way, with a nasty bite to his leg that changed his life forever—he'd kept himself distanced from Andy. When Andy kept showing up at his door, Dylan consistently told him to go the fuck away. But still Andy had persisted. He'd come very close to killing Chris, and Dylan had been forced to kill Andy to stop him. But even that wasn't enough to keep him away, it seemed, because here he was, haunting them.

"Dyl, you're brooding again."

"I can't help it."

Chris sidled over, displaying his most cheerful leer. "Betcha I can find a way to distract you."

But Dylan shook his head. "I don't…. What if he watches?" Even the thought of it made his skin crawl.

"Then the fucker's gonna get a really good show."

"I can't have sex with you with a ghost looking over my shoulder! Especially not him. And I don't want him to… to watch you." Dylan admitted to himself that he felt pretty possessive about Chris. He would have liked to blame the wolf, but if he was honest, he'd have to admit the emotion originated from Dylan the man. He'd never before had a relationship like the one he now had with Chris, and he didn't want anything intruding on them.

"So we can't fuck until we get rid of him?" Chris demanded.

"I… no."

Chris scowled. "What if we go over to my place?"

"Chris, Andy's grave is just as close to your house as it is to mine. And he died on your living room floor. What's to stop him from haunting your house too?"

"I dunno! Ain't nobody filled me in on the laws of ghosting."

"And I seem to have misplaced my supernatural handbook." Both of their voices had begun to rise, and Dylan made an effort to calm down. None of this was Chris's fault, and there was no point in yelling at him over it.

Chris still looked angry. "You're the college boy. You're the one who's supposed to know shit."

"Somehow in architecture school I missed the days we discussed phantoms."

Now a small smile flickered at the corner of Chris's mouth. "Maybe you should've had classes on designing paranormal-friendly homes. I bet you could make a good livin' off that. You know, sunproof rooms for vampires, great big bathtub for the monster from the Black Lagoon, really tall doors for Frankenstein."

"It's Frankenstein's *monster*."

Chris rolled his eyes, then bent like a hunchback and drawled, "It's Franken*steen*, not Franken*stine*." They'd been watching a fair amount of Mel Brooks on Chris's DVD player. Chris shuffled around in his best Igor impression for a moment or two longer, which made Dylan laugh, and the tension between them evaporated.

"There's gotta be books on this shit, right?" Chris asked. "Exorcisms, things like that. Is there an occult bookstore in town? I know there's plenty of them spirit-aura-healing-Wicca-goddess-herbal places, and probably a lot of Jesus-loves-you stores too. Maybe they got some helpful books."

"Maybe," Dylan said doubtfully. He'd actually thought about this issue before, back when he first realized what he'd become. But he'd resisted trying to find werewolf literature, partly because then he'd be truly admitting—in black-and-white print—what he was, and partly because he was afraid to find out more of the truth. What if being a werewolf was even worse than he knew already? Usually, he liked to have a pretty good handle on things, but in this case ignorance and avoidance felt best. Rick had called him chickenshit over it, but Rick wasn't the one sprouting fur every twenty-eight days.

Chris gestured toward the doorway. "So you wanna go downstairs and Google bookstores?"

"Not really. I guess we could probably find something, but then we'd have the same problem we'd have if we just looked up ghosts online: how do we know the writers aren't full of crap? I'm not in any position to evaluate an author's expertise on ghosts, and I sure as hell don't want to screw this up. What if I make things worse?" He wasn't sure what worse would even mean, even—a bigger ghost, a scarier ghost, *more* ghosts? None of those would be good.

"So then, what? We need to talk to someone, right? In person. Then we can ask a shitload of questions and figure out if they know what the fuck they're talkin' about. Where do we find a ghost pro? Yellow pages? Maybe they're under pest control."

"This isn't *Ghostbusters*, Chris." As soon as the words were out of Dylan's mouth, though, a flash of memory hit him.

He was a sophomore in college. He'd escaped the dorms for the evening and was hanging out in the slightly moldy apartment inhabited by his friend Ery Phillips. The two of them had been spending the night smoking joints and watching Bill Murray comedies from the eighties. They'd just finished *Tootsie* and Ery was about to put *Stripes* into his old VHS machine.

"I like *Ghostbusters* better," Dylan had complained. "Why can't we watch that?"

"I don't own that one."

"Why not? It's funny." Dylan began humming the theme song.

Ery shook his head. "Because my grandma is a spiritualist and she says the movie is offensive and because I've already had my fill of hearing about ghosts, thanks very much."

Now, eleven years later, Dylan sighed. "I think maybe I have an idea."

CHRIS narrowed his eyes slightly as Dylan booted up his laptop. "So you and this Ery dude were college pals."

"Yeah. We met in freshman English."

"Was he your boyfriend?"

"Not really."

"What the fuck does that mean?"

"We fooled around a couple of times. Didn't really work out. We're not each other's type."

Chris still looked slightly put out, and Dylan had to work hard to suppress a smile. He liked the fact that Chris was so transparently jealous. Just as Dylan felt possessive of Chris, it was nice to know that Chris was possessive of him.

"What the hell kind of name is Ery anyway?" demanded Chris.

"I don't know. That's just what his parents called him, I guess."

"Stupid-ass name."

"Maybe. But he's a nice guy and maybe he can help us."

But Chris wasn't ready to be mollified. "If he's so great, how come you ain't friends with him no more?"

"I don't know. We just grew apart after school." That wasn't quite true. Yes, they'd seen less of each other after graduation, when both of them were busy starting their careers. But they'd kept in touch pretty frequently, went out to movies or had dinner together now and then. Sometimes Ery dragged Dylan to a trendy gay bar, where Dylan always felt nerdy and unattractive and out of place. Then the whole werewolf thing happened and Dylan, horrified and afraid, had cut off contact with everyone except immediate family and coworkers. He still felt bad about it. He didn't even have Ery's phone number anymore—he'd lost it when he broke his phone a few months earlier. He had to hope that Ery had the same old e-mail address and would be willing to contact him.

He opened his e-mail program and typed a quick message: *Hey, Ery. I'm sorry it's been so long. I'm a shithead and it's a really long story. But I could use your help. Could you give me a call—please?* He added his own number, just in case Ery had lost it or deleted it from his contacts. After sending the message, he clicked the laptop closed.

Chris was standing at the study window, arms folded on his chest. Dylan walked over and embraced him from behind, digging his chin into Chris's shoulder. "I do not now, nor have I ever, felt about Ery Phillips the way I feel about you," Dylan said.

"Sorry. I'm being a dick."

Dylan knew it was really difficult for Chris to apologize. And he was aware by now that when Chris felt vulnerable or uncertain, he responded by lashing out. Defense mechanisms. God knew Dylan had plenty of his own. Man, the two of them could make a shrink very, very rich.

"Let's go have some lunch," suggested Dylan. "I'll make it."

As Dylan had known it would, the offer made Chris pull away and shake his head determinedly. "Not a chance in hell. C'mon. You can uncap the beers."

After they ate, Chris and Dylan sat in the living room to discuss plans for the mudroom they intended to add outside the kitchen. That was the entry they used most often, and Dylan was tired of tracking debris into the house. He wanted a space big enough to store boots and coats, with a door large enough for bulky furniture and the other crap he sometimes needed to move in or out. But he didn't want the addition to be too large or take too much time to complete.

As they talked, Dylan sometimes caught a whiff of the ghost's grave scent, and a few times he sensed movement from the corner of his eye, but the phantom didn't make a full showing all afternoon.

Chris made pizza for dinner. They carried the hot pie over to his house and ate in front of the TV. But just as Jon Stewart was starting up, Dylan's phone rang. He glanced at caller ID—not a number his phone recognized.

"Hello?" he said.

"Dylan? Ery."

"Hey! Uh, hang on just a sec." Dylan put the phone down and looked at Chris. "It's Ery."

"I can leave if you want privacy."

"Stay right here," Dylan replied, earning a small smile. He put the phone to his ear again. "Thanks for calling me, Ery. I know I've been a total asshole."

"Yeah, pretty much. I wondered what happened to you, but when you stopped answering my e-mails and voicemails…."

"I know. There's a reason for it. A really… really fucked-up reason, actually, and one you'd probably never believe anyway."

"Now you've piqued my curiosity for sure." Ery didn't sound especially angry, but then he was an easygoing guy. "Is your fucked-up reason related to why you need my help?"

"Pretty much."

After a very brief pause, Ery asked, "What can I do for you?"

"I think this is the kind of thing that's better to explain in person. Do you still live in the area? Could we meet?"

"Sure. I live off Belmont."

Dylan glanced over at Chris, who was doing a bad job of pretending to watch *The Daily Show*. "Are you free tomorrow afternoon?"

"Yeah, I can blow off work. Want to meet at that café on Thirty-Fourth? At, say, three?"

"Perfect. Thanks for calling me, Ery."

After they said their good-byes, Dylan returned the phone to his shirt pocket. "So you're gonna see him tomorrow," Chris said, eyes still on the screen.

"*We're* going to see him tomorrow. And don't forget you're meeting Matty too. So if you want to grill my friends for all the dirt on me, you have until then to make your list of questions."

Chris finally turned to look at him. He was grinning widely.

CHAPTER 7

CHRIS was nervous as hell as they drove to Portland on Friday morning, but he didn't want to show it. He was glad, however, that Dylan was the one handling the morning traffic, because Chris might have rear-ended someone or just run the damn truck off the road. Instead, he complained about Dylan's choice in radio programming— really, *Morning Edition?*—jittered his legs, and wished he was back on Dylan's haunted farm.

They crossed to the east side of the river, the skyline of downtown Portland behind them. Dylan's office was located in a former industrial building that had been converted a few years back. It was all smooth concrete and glittery metal with exterior ductwork fashionably exposed, and its windows glinted brightly in the morning sun. Dylan brought the Silverado to a halt in front. "If you want, I can park and we can go in together."

"What's there to see?"

"Nothing exciting. Office stuff. Desks, computers, papers. We have models of some of our projects, though, and those are pretty neat."

Chris shook his head. "Sounds thrilling. I'll pass, thanks." Actually, he might have been interested to see the models, but he knew he'd feel uncomfortable in that shiny building, with everyone staring at him and wondering if today was Take Your Hick Boyfriend to Work Day.

Leaving the engine idling, Dylan climbed out of the driver's seat so Chris could scoot over. Chris handed him the messenger bag that contained Dylan's laptop, notes, and—as far as Chris knew—keys to the universe. But before he left, Dylan leaned over and gave Chris a firm kiss on the lips. "Have a nice day, dear," he said with a grin.

"Knock 'em dead."

Dylan waved as he strode toward the building.

Now Chris had nearly three hours to kill. He began not far from Dylan's office, at a place that sold antique and reproduction hardware and plumbing. He didn't buy anything. But it had occurred to him that it would be relatively easy to add a big sink to Dylan's planned mudroom—the kitchen plumbing was in the wall close by—and it might be convenient to be able to wash hands or rinse off dirt before entering the house proper. He used his phone to take a few pictures of potential sinks and then, just because he could, sent Dylan a quick text: *XOXOX.* The minute he hit Send, he decided he was being way too girly, but by then it was too late.

His next stop was a home improvement store, where he rented a sander. There weren't any tool rental options closer to home, so they'd have to drive back into the city to return it, but not for a week. While he was there, he stocked up on the other supplies they'd need to refinish the floor. Dylan had lent him his credit card, which felt a little strange, but lately their separate finances had been blurring anyway. He'd recently talked Dylan into buying and installing a truck bed cover, and now it came in handy because Chris could store all today's stuff back there and lock it up safely.

Plenty of time remained before he had to pick up Dylan. Chris detoured to the donut place Dylan had introduced him to—the one that had pastries in weird but delicious flavors as well as pastries shaped like penises—and bought a boxful. He ate two of them as he drove across the river, his sights set on bookstore browsing.

After circling for a while, searching for a parking space, he gave up and parked in a paid lot. The bookstore was enormous, so many rooms full of books that they gave you a map when you went in. But among those hundreds of thousands of volumes, he couldn't find anything useful about ghosts or werewolves. He did pick up a couple of mysteries, a thick tome by Bill Bryson, and *The Gay Kama Sutra*. He might not get to use the last of those until they'd evicted the goddamn ghost, but he could at least plan ahead.

Once he checked out, it was time to retrieve Dylan. Before pulling out of his parking space, he cleared off the passenger seat by stowing the pastry box on the floor underneath.

Traffic was a little heavier than he expected—he was not used to driving in the city—and he ended up a few minutes late. Dylan was standing in front of his building looking impatient. "Thought you'd forgotten me," he said as he climbed into the passenger seat.

"And I thought I was the one with abandonment issues. So where's Matty?"

"She went on ahead in her car. She'll save us a table."

"'Kay. Where to?"

Dylan gave directions and Chris pulled out into traffic. "So how'd the meetin' go?" he asked.

"All right."

"You're bein' kinda quiet, but your head ain't exploded. What're the boss's big plans?"

"He wants me to work directly with him on this one. There's this building in Old Town. A really long time ago, the feds owned it, and lately it's been used for a lot of different things. It's in fairly rough shape. But it's been bought by one of those for-profit universities—you know, the ones that advertise on TV all the time—and they want it converted into classrooms and offices."

Chris pulled onto the bridge approach. "Sounds more straightforward than your futon queens. I bet these guys actually give you some clue ahead of time what they want."

"Yeah, they will." Dylan didn't sound especially optimistic. "Cryptic clients aren't the problem this time."

"Then what is?"

"I design houses, not commercial space. The considerations are completely different. Plus, this is a historic building and we have all sorts of codes and restrictions to deal with. Not to mention the scale of the thing. Over a hundred thousand square feet! We're talking a forty-million-dollar budget here, Chris." Dylan had been waving his hands around, but now he looked at Chris. "What are you grinning about?"

"It's a big fucking deal and *you*'re the one who got chosen for it."

Chris could hear Dylan swallow. "I... yeah. But what if—"

"Don't give me that bullshit. Your boss ain't gonna hand this to you unless he knows you can do it. *I* know you can do it. You're gonna fret and be all angsty and hard to live with, and you're gonna blow them all away. Again." Chris said these words with deep conviction, because he knew they were true.

Dylan squeezed Chris's leg. "Thanks."

A few minutes later, Chris parked the truck—this time on the street—and they walked half a block to the restaurant. Chris was relieved to see that the place wasn't too upscale. Dylan was wearing a sports jacket over a button-down and expensive jeans, but Chris looked like he'd just stepped off the farm.

The place was pretty packed, but a voice called almost as soon as they entered. "Hey! Dylan! Over here!"

Matty was waiting for them at a table near the back. She was short and round. Her straight black hair was cut into bangs, and she wore big circular glasses that made her look a little like an owl. She was wearing a brown skirt and some kind of peasant blouse, and when she waved at them, Chris saw she had a colorful parrot tattooed on the inside of her arm. "Hi!" she chirped as soon as Chris and Dylan drew near. She had dimples. "I'm Matty. Obviously."

Chris shook her hand. "Chris. Also obviously."

Everyone sat down, perused the menus, and ordered: fish and chips for Chris, steak sandwich for Dylan, some kind of fancy salad for Matty. She kept sneaking glances at Chris, clearly trying to get his measure.

For a while Dylan and Matty talked shop, which was probably necessary given the big new project, but Chris felt a little left out. But when Dylan started going on about structural beams, Matty suddenly hit him on the shoulder. "Enough! We can do this later. I want to hear all about the man who's finally stolen your heart." She looked at Chris expectantly, while Dylan squirmed and blushed.

"Not much to tell you," Chris said. "I'm just a hired hand."

"That's not what I hear. Dylan says you're really great at construction, and a whiz with engines, and that you cook better than any chef." She sighed theatrically. "God, if I find out you give good massages too, I'm going to jump off a cliff."

"Don't know about massages, but I'm not bad with my hands. Or other parts." He waggled his eyebrows suggestively, which made her cackle and made Dylan look like he wanted to melt under the table. Excellent.

"But how do you put up with Dylan's moods? I used to share an office with him, you know, and sometimes he is so negative about himself."

"I am not," Dylan protested weakly. They both ignored him.

Chris said, "I know. Been trying to teach him what a talented bastard he is. Someday maybe he'll listen."

"Yeah, and then he'll get a big head and we'll be all 'Well, we knew him when…'. And he'll forget all about us little people. Well, not you. I think you're pretty memorable."

He decided that he liked Matty a lot.

The three of them ate a pretty good lunch, and while they ate, Chris and Matty did their best to embarrass Dylan. Dylan piped up every now and then but mostly looked back and forth between them as if he might have regrets about letting them meet. But Chris was having fun. Matty wasn't intimidating at all. Turned out she liked a couple of the trashy cop shows Chris enjoyed but Dylan refused to watch, and she knew the words to every show tune Chris could think of. She laughed a lot and didn't seem to think Chris was beneath her. In fact, when the meal was over—Chris paid, for once—she insisted he stay in touch.

"Don't be a stranger," she said as they left the restaurant together. "I want to hear lots more good stories from you."

"We'll have you over for dinner as soon as we get a little more work done on Dylan's house," Chris said. *And after we get rid of the ghost.*

She clapped her hands. "I've been dying to see the farm. And eat your cooking!" She gave both Dylan and Chris squishy hugs when they parted.

"You two seemed to hit it off," Dylan remarked as he slid behind the steering wheel of the truck.

"She's adorable."

"Not so adorable at eight in the morning when you have a looming deadline," replied Dylan, but he was smiling.

"We didn't lay it on too thick for you, did we? Never seen your face turn all those shades of red before."

"I was completely mortified, but that's okay. I'm really glad you two get along. It's… I've never done a lot of socializing. It's nice."

"But she doesn't know about your monthly problem."

Dylan shook his head. "No. Just you, Rick, and Kay."

"She'd be cool with it. Hell. She'd probably build you a Dyl the Werewolf blog or Facebook fan page or somethin'."

"I don't know…."

"You shoulda learned already, dude. If you can't be honest with someone about such an important thing in your life, you ain't gonna have much of a relationship with them. Would you hide from her that you're queer?"

"Of course not. I think I told her I'm gay the first day I met her."

"Well, same thing."

They were stopped at a light, so Dylan turned to look at him. "Being a werewolf is *not* the same thing as being gay."

"Ain't so different. Deep, dark secret for some folks. Lotsa people judge you, misunderstand you. Think there's somethin' wrong with you. And it ain't somethin' you can change about yourself." He smiled. "Course, I think man-on-man sex is a whole lot more fun than getting furry, but you seem to like the wolf shit as long as you ain't killing nobody."

Dylan shook his head. "Maybe I'll tell her later. After we get rid of Andy. Want to go have some coffee or something?"

"While we wait to have more coffee with your old fuck buddy? Sure."

INSTEAD of drinking coffee, they ended up wandering around a little. The neighborhood had old houses, some small but some pretty big. Some were run-down and quite a few had been turned into apartments, but others were in great shape, all fancy gingerbread and fish-scale trim. As they walked, Dylan pointed out features he liked and modern additions he thought were misguided. He got really animated when he talked about things like that—it was fun to listen to him, to watch him wave his arms all over.

They went into a couple of shops too. One of them had a section of stuff for pregnant ladies, and Dylan held up what looked like a chunky pastel tube of toothpaste. "Kay's birthday's coming up. Do you think she'd like this?"

Chris took the tube and read the label. "Stretch mark remover? Dude, you give her this shit and it's you who's gonna be the next ghost."

Dylan ended up buying her a kit to make a casting of her belly— "She'll like it. It's a craft project."—and a CD of songs the saleslady said would aid relaxation during labor and delivery.

"God, you couldn't pay me to be in the room when she's having that baby," Dylan said as they left the shop. "I'm thinking of buying Rick a Kevlar vest. Maybe a suit of armor."

"I bet they're gonna make great parents." Chris didn't know either of them that well, really. But he'd seen them in a crisis, with Andy's corpse in a bloody puddle in his living room and Dylan half-dead in his bed. They'd stayed calm and helped him take care of things.

And he knew they loved and supported Dylan, which was good enough for him.

Dylan locked his purchases in the truck bed and the two of them walked to the coffee place. It was about ten minutes to three. The café had tempting but overpriced baked goods on display, and the sound system was playing something foreign. The place wasn't too crowded, just a handful of student-looking types bent over iPads and laptops, and two baristas with impressive collections of tattoos and piercings.

While Chris staked out a quiet table near the rear of the café, Dylan went to the counter and ordered coffees. He carried them over and sat down. "We used to come here a lot to study. The location wasn't all that convenient for me, but there weren't a lot of distractions and the coffee's good." He grinned. "Plus this really gorgeous guy used to work here. Ery and I spent hours drooling over him."

Chris knew his jealousy was stupid. Dylan had known this Ery guy—and the hot barista—long before he met Chris. Besides, Chris trusted him. A man who would endanger his own life and kill his ex-lover to protect you was not the type to go fooling around on you. Chris scowled at him anyway, and Dylan rolled his eyes. At least both of the employees currently behind the counter were female.

The coffee *was* good. Once upon a time, Chris used to drink the instant shit because it was cheap and easy. He was a cheap and easy kind of guy. But then Dylan had moved in next door and started brewing solid gold beans that had been fertilized by unicorns and picked by virgin nymphs, and Chris had to admit, Dylan's coffee tasted a whole lot better than freeze-dried crystals. Now he'd come to appreciate a decent cup, and this stuff qualified. He was just about to say so when the café door opened and a man walked in. The man took one look at Dylan and his whole face lit up. He came running over.

Ery Phillips was short and slender and *bright*. He sported a screaming purple tank top and canary-yellow jeans, with high-top sneakers in orange and red. His dyed-blond hair was gelled into impossibly tall spikes. He carried a messenger bag adorned with glittery pink skulls.

Dylan and Chris both stood. Dylan was smiling broadly, but Chris felt awkward as hell.

"Jesus, Dyl. What the hell happened to you and how can it happen to me? You look fantastic!"

Dylan gestured at Chris. "Chris happened. Chris, meet Ery Phillips. Ery, this is Chris Nock. My... my everything."

Ery's eyes went very wide, Dylan looked embarrassed by his own declaration, and Chris felt like a choir of heavenly angels was singing in his fucking heart. "Nice to meet you," Chris mumbled.

"Oh my God. You two are.... Oh my God. Hang on." Ery dumped his bag onto a chair and pulled a phone out of his back pocket. "Can I take a picture of you two? Jeez, you guys look like the cover of a romance novel. Only you're wearing shirts."

Of course Dylan blushed, but Chris laughed and pressed up against his side, snaking an arm around his waist. They didn't have any photos of the two of them together. Maybe Ery could e-mail them this one.

Ery snapped a few pictures, shoved the phone into his bag, and darted to the counter. He came hurrying back soon afterward with an enormous paper cup clutched in his hand. It occurred to Chris that this didn't seem like a person who really needed more caffeine.

"Is this who's been keeping you away from me?" Ery asked Dylan as they all sat down.

"No. Chris and I... we're still pretty new."

"Well, he's been doing something for you, because you never looked this good before." Ery tilted his head a little. "New workout regimen?" He turned a little to look at Chris. "I bet you're a personal trainer."

Chris almost snorted coffee through his nose. "I'm just a handyman."

"Okay. I want to be pissed off at you, Dyl, but I want to hear your story even more, so I'll be civilized. What's going on?"

Dylan looked at Chris, who shrugged and held his palms up. The way Chris figured it, this was pretty much Dylan's tale. Or tail, as the case might be.

After a very long slurp of coffee—which Dylan probably wished was something a whole lot stronger—he set down his cup and rubbed his face. "Okay. Look, don't interrupt, okay? Because what I'm about to tell you is impossible and can't possibly have happened, except it did. You can voice your disbelief when I'm finished."

"That's quite a lead-up. Shoot." Ery settled back in his chair expectantly. So did Chris, even though he knew what Dylan had to say.

Dylan looked around furtively, as if afraid someone might be listening in. Nobody was seated anywhere near them, and the music and the *zhoop* of the cappuccino machine drowned conversation pretty well.

"About two and a half years ago I went to that bar, Bleachers, and—"

"I believe so far," Ery interrupted, even though he wasn't supposed to. "You love that lame place."

"Not anymore I don't. But I was there that night, and I sort of hooked up with this guy. Andy." Dylan grimaced apologetically at Chris. "This was long before I met Chris. Andy came back to my place and we had sex, and then… and then he bit me."

While Dylan paused—not for dramatic effect, but thinking how to phrase the next part—Ery looked confused. "Bit? You mean, like, some sort of weird BDSM thing?" Then he paled. "Oh, God. He didn't give you HIV, did he?"

"No. He did infect me, though. Ery, Andy was a werewolf. And he bit me, so then I became one too. I'm not talking metaphorically here. I mean that every full moon I turn into a genuine wolf."

"That's not possible."

"I know. I told you that. But it's true. So I moved out to the middle of nowhere because I didn't…. I need to hunt once a month. I'm dangerous. That's why I pulled away from you, and away from almost everyone. I figured I'd be safer out in the boonies. I bought this great

70

old house on twenty acres, and it's so isolated I have only one neighbor." Dylan glanced to the side. "The ever-handy Chris Nock."

"And ever-sexy. Don't forget that part," Chris added.

"And ever-sexy," Dylan agreed. "I telecommute mostly. My boss loves my work. I love Chris. Things were going pretty well. But Andy wouldn't give up on me. I guess he wanted some kind of... pack thing. Someone to run with. Hunt with. He'd bitten other people before, but they... they died. I kept telling him to go away but he kept coming back. And then...." Dylan stopped to fortify himself with more coffee. "And then he tried to kill Chris. So I killed Andy instead."

It really was that simple, Chris thought. Weird but straightforward, and totally logical if you bought the initial premise. Based on Ery's facial expression, the initial premise was a long way from being bought.

"You *killed* someone?" Ery squeaked. The two women at the closest table turned to look at them, blinked, and then turned away.

"It was self-defense!" Chris said. "Or defense of me, anyway. I was usin' only a broken coffee table leg to hold off a hungry wolf. And Dyl almost got killed himself. He got... he got real torn up." He had a thought and nudged his companion. "Show him your scar."

Somewhat reluctantly, Dylan lifted his hair to reveal the mark high on his forehead. But it wasn't really that impressive a mark, and it was the kind of thing he could have gotten from walking into something sharp. So Chris poked him. "Show him the other ones."

"I'm not going to strip in the middle of a coffee shop, Chris."

"Don't be a goddamn baby. Just lift your shirt."

Dylan shot him an evil look but dutifully pulled his hem out of his jeans to reveal a good stretch of his torso. Ery leaned over the table for a closer look. "Oh my God, Dylan!"

Chris nodded. "You shoulda seen it when it happened. He heals real fast, but for a while there, he looked like somethin' from a Tarantino flick."

"Romero, more like it," muttered Dylan. He tucked his shirt back in and had another sip of coffee.

Ery had leaned back again and was slowly shaking his head. "This is… this is a lot to take in."

With a sympathetic nod, Chris said, "Yeah. Took me a while to deal, and I saw it with my own eyes."

"But you stuck with him even after you found out he's… he's…."

"Yeah."

"Wow." Ery pointed a finger at Dylan. "Either this is the biggest pile of steaming bullshit ever, or you landed yourself a hell of a boyfriend."

"I know," said Dylan and gave Chris's shoulder a squeeze. "So Andy's… Andy's dead. But the story's not over. A few days ago a ghost showed up at my house."

While Ery still hadn't bought the whole wolf thing—Chris could tell—he nodded knowledgeably about the spook. "What kind of ghost?"

"I didn't know there were kinds."

"Sure. They manifest in all kinds of ways. Some of them you can barely tell are there, and a few are right in your face. Some of them look pretty human and some of them totally don't. Some of them move stuff around, like poltergeists, and some—"

"This one has to go," Dylan interrupted.

"Ah." Ery spent a few moments pretending his coffee cup was fascinating, then squinting at the contents of the dessert case. "So *that's* why you've crawled out of the woodwork. Grandma."

The song on the sound system changed to something with sitars and drums, and all three men shifted in their seats. Chris was beginning to think that the banana bread looked pretty good. He'd bet that Dylan would eat some—his boy could really put it away. Wasn't worth three and a half bucks a slice, though.

"I'm sorry," Dylan said softly, looking down at the table. "I should've said something to you a long time ago. I've missed you, Ery. You're a good friend. Always have been." He lifted his gaze. "I really was afraid I'd do something terrible to you. Or that… I don't know. You'd be disgusted by what I've become."

After a long pause, Ery looked at Chris. "I'm not saying I believe this wolf stuff is for real. But if it is…. Chris, is Dylan out slaughtering people and terrorizing the countryside? 'Cause I can't really picture that from the guy who used to double-tie his shoelaces. The guy who spent freshman year nagging me about how I should buy health insurance. He used to find spiders in my shitty apartment, and he'd trap them in cups and take them outside."

"Dylan's the best man I've known," Chris replied simply.

"Okay, then," Ery said with a smile.

CHAPTER 8

ERY left them with a promise to set up a meeting with his grandmother that evening, and Dylan slumped over the table. It wasn't yet dinnertime, but he'd slept poorly the night before, and this had been a long and emotionally draining day. He was glad that Stender and Chris had confidence in his architectural skills, and—truth to tell—was a little bit jazzed over the new work challenge. He was enormously relieved that Chris and Matty had hit it off so well, if slightly horrified to think of the ways they might conspire against him. And he was glad Ery hadn't called him a psycho, didn't seem to hate him, and was even willing to try to help with the ghost situation.

But Christ, he needed a nap.

"Do you wanna head to that bookstore?" Chris asked. "Or maybe we can just hang out at a park or somethin'. It's nice out."

Dylan was suddenly struck with a much better idea. "Let's go get in the truck. My turn to pick the surprise destination."

"I bet it ain't gonna be a rodeo."

"Good guess."

They climbed into the truck and Dylan took them back over the river, into downtown. He stopped in front of a boutique hotel on Washington Street. He'd never stayed there, but Rick and Kay had—the night they got married—and they'd told him it was really nice.

"Stay here," Dylan ordered. "I'll go in and see if they have a room available."

"A hotel? Dyl, your house is only an hour away."

"But in this place, someone else is going to make the bed and clean up our wet towels. I bet they have room service. A big bed. And no ghosts." He tried to waggle his eyebrows the way Chris did, but he wasn't as good at it.

A slow smiled spread over his lover's face. "Sounds nice."

Before Chris could protest that maybe they could find a cheaper place, Dylan ran inside. He reemerged a few minutes later and hopped back into the truck.

"They don't want us?" Chris asked.

"We have a corner king deluxe room and we're all checked in." He shut off the engine just as the parking attendant came trotting over. "C'mon, Chris. Let's see what they have in the minibar."

But although Chris was trying his usual swagger as they entered the lobby, Dylan could tell he was a little intimidated. Fortunately, the free wine hour had just begun, and Chris seemed slightly more relaxed after a couple of glasses.

"We don't have no clean clothes," Chris said as they rode the elevator up. "Not even toothbrushes."

"We can go shopping."

Chris looked less than thrilled but didn't say anything as they walked down the hallway, their footsteps muffled by the thick carpeting. Dylan kept half an eye on the architectural fittings, because this building was roughly the same age as the one he'd soon be working on. Maybe he could write off their night's stay on his taxes as research.

When he unlocked their room, Chris walked in a few steps and then froze. "Nice."

"Yeah. It is." The décor was attractive—kind of hip but with some classic touches—and there were a bunch of throw pillows on the bed. Dylan had given up on his own throw pillow collection in the face of Chris's ridicule, but sometimes he still missed it. Dylan walked to the huge windows and admired the view, then spent a minute or two checking out the bathroom and the closet.

75

Chris was still rooted in place, rubbing the back of his neck, as if he were afraid he might break something. "Me and my mom, sometimes we stayed at a motel for a couple of days. When we got thrown out of our house or she broke up with her latest boyfriend. None of them places were anythin' like this. They were cheap. Could hear the people in the next room fucking."

"I can't guarantee how soundproof these walls are, but this time we'll be the ones making the noise."

Only slightly mollified, Chris shrugged. "This must be costin' a fortune."

"It's not that bad. I got a AAA discount. Anyway, I can afford it. I got that bonus and the big raise at work, remember? And I haven't spent it on anything except the house."

"Yeah. I know. You're rollin' in dough."

Dylan sighed as he realized what was really bothering his lover. Dylan stood close to Chris and lightly pushed his shoulder. "If I actually paid you for all the work you've done at my place, you'd be rolling in dough too."

"Don't want your money," Chris said with narrowed eyes.

"The way I see it, at this point it's pretty much *our* money." Dylan had been thinking about this for a while but knew it would be a sore subject for Chris. Dylan hoped that maybe they could sit down one of these days and have a big grown-up talk about wills, insurance, and similarly squirm-worthy topics. He didn't want to do it now, though, when he was tired and emotionally drained.

Chris snorted. "I didn't draw them houses."

"No, but you supported me when I did. I wouldn't have got through the last months without you, Chris. I mean it. You're... I've been thinking of you as my partner."

That earned him a smile. "Next thing you're gonna be tryin' to shove me into a fancy white dress."

"No, but I bet you'd look delicious in a tuxedo."

Dylan was just about to propose that they get naked, when his phone rang. "Hi, Ery." He tried not to sound disappointed; Ery was, after all, doing him a favor.

"Grandma says you can come over tonight. Is eight okay? She's playing cards until then."

"Sure, eight works."

Ery gave him the address and then rang off.

Dylan looked at Chris, who was leafing through the information binder. "We have about ninety minutes."

"Then let's get that shoppin' done. And grab some food."

"Really?"

"If you're gonna be payin' an arm and a leg for that bed, I don't wanna be hurried. I wanna take my time and have my way with you."

A pleasant frisson ran down Dylan's back. He liked it when Chris had his way with him. Chris's way was pretty much Dylan's way, actually. "Okay."

At Dylan's insistence, they headed over to Nordstrom. Chris had possibly never been in the place and looked around warily, like an explorer who'd just landed on an alien planet. Dylan steered him in the right direction, chose a pair of charcoal-gray pants and a really nice red shirt for him, and dragged him to the dressing room.

"Try them on," Dylan ordered.

Chris grimaced. "This is the gayest thing I've ever done."

"Gayer than sex with another man?"

"Yep. No contest." But he went into the little cubicle, and when he came out, he looked amazing.

Dylan wolf whistled. "We have a winner."

"I feel like I'm wearin' a goddamn costume."

"But will you concede the possibility that we might someday want to go somewhere fancier than a Home Depot and a brewpub, and that you might need to wear something a little nicer than overalls and a Metallica tee?"

"You wish I dressed like this all the time?"

"No, I wish you wore nothing at all, all the time. But every once in a while, clothing is called for."

Chris remained slightly sulky but waited as Dylan tried on some new clothes too. Chris perked up slightly as they chose underwear, mostly because he could make loud, lewd comments about which style would best show off his and Dylan's assets. The older lady who worked in that department was not amused.

They stopped for toiletries at a drugstore, then had a quick meal of upscale burritos. "It's kinda fun, bein' downtown," Chris admitted as they walked back to the hotel. "Everything's so convenient."

"I always thought that when I could afford it, I'd love to buy myself a swanky apartment here. It wouldn't work out well for me now, though."

"Does that piss you off?"

"No. I think I've got it pretty good, actually." He bumped his shoulder into Chris's.

They dumped their purchases in the room and called the desk to have the truck brought around. By the time they exited the lobby, the valet was ready to hand them the keys.

"So where does Grandma Phillips live?" asked Chris.

"Not too far. Ladd's Addition."

It was a pretty neighborhood but slightly obnoxious for navigation due to the weird street plan. "Did you know Ladd was inspired by L'Enfant's plan for Washington, DC? And L'Enfant was inspired by Versailles." Dylan realized he was lecturing. "Sorry."

"Thanks, professor." But Chris sounded upbeat, his mercurial mood having shifted toward the positive as they drove.

Ery Phillips's grandmother lived in a mushroom-colored Craftsman bungalow with enormous blue flowerpots on the front porch.

The front garden was a cacophony of color; apparently the lady was an avid gardener. The house looked to be in good shape too, which pleased Dylan. He was always happy when houses were well cared for, maybe because he imagined some architect—in this case, no doubt, long dead—laboring over the plans. Dylan parked in front of the house, and he and Chris marched to the door.

Even though Dylan knew very little about Ery's grandmother, he'd been entertaining a mental image of her. In his head, she had long gray hair, probably a little tangled, and a crooked nose. She wore baggy dresses with lots of layers of fabric and a lumpy shawl over her shoulders. That was not remotely who met them at the door.

This woman must have been close to eighty, but she stood very straight. She was elegantly thin, with perfectly coifed blonde hair and carefully applied makeup. She wore a beige suit, a silky red blouse, and a fair amount of gold jewelry. "Dylan Warner?" she asked in a cultured voice.

"Yes." Dylan gestured. "And Chris Nock."

"Of course. I'm Delores Phillips. Please, come in."

The interior of her house was as tasteful and sophisticated as she was, with Persian carpets over polished floors, shelves and cabinets displaying intricately painted Asian dishware, and walls hung with delicate floral paintings. Not a single cauldron or black cat in sight. Dylan didn't know what she called the room she guided them into, but he thought it ought to be called a parlor. It had a very parlory look to it. Chris appeared less than pleased about having to sit on a spindly gilded chair, but he managed a muttered hello to Ery, who was waiting with a china cup in his hand.

"May I get you some tea?" Mrs. Phillips asked.

Dylan wasn't a big fan of tea, and probably neither was Chris, but he didn't want to be rude. "Thank you. That would be nice."

As soon as Mrs. Phillips left the room, Dylan leaned close to Ery. "What have you told her?"

"Not much. Nothing about... you know." He made a pathetic impression of a howling wolf. "You don't need to tell her that if you don't want to. She'd be okay with it, though. I just said you have a haunting issue."

"Thanks. Seriously, Ery, I owe you big time."

"Good. Then you can tell me your boyfriend over there has a twin brother who's also gay. And single."

"Sorry," Chris said. "I'm one of a kind."

Mrs. Phillips returned with a lacquered tray on which she'd arranged tea things. She poured and sugared before taking a seat. Chris looked a little silly with the delicate teacup in his big hand. Maybe Dylan looked stupid too. There were cookies, the round buttery kind with the fruit dollop in the middle. Dylan ate three.

"My grandson tells me you are an architect, Dylan," said Mrs. Phillips, breaking a slightly awkward silence. "Do you work here in Portland?"

He swallowed some tea to wash down the cookie. "Yes, for Stender and Associates."

"I am sure it is very interesting. Are you an architect as well, Chris?"

Chris nearly choked. "No. I… I do odd jobs, mostly. Nothin' important."

Dylan felt the need to bolster Chris in Mrs. Phillips's eyes. "He's really talented with his hands. At construction, I mean!" he added hastily, his cheeks heating slightly. "And mechanical things. And he owns a lot of acres of farmland too."

"My grandparents were farmers. And my grandfather's parents were among the first white people to settle in the Willamette Valley. Has your family been farming for generations as well?"

Chris's jaw tightened a little, but probably only Dylan noticed. "I'm not sure. We're not… close. Think so, though. I know they lived in Dylan's house for years. Maybe even built the old place."

"I believe a sense of continuity such as that can be very soothing. It's good to be aware of one's roots."

"Some of them roots're rotten," Chris muttered.

Mrs. Phillips gave a small regal smile. "Even so." She gestured impatiently at Ery, who looked a little sheepish as he poured another round of tea. But there was warmth in her sharp eyes as she watched her grandson, a deep fondness that made Dylan feel unreasonably envious. His parents had been fairly old when Rick and Dylan were born, and all the grandparents had died by the time Dylan hit his teens.

"Now," Mrs. Phillips said, waving the plate of cookies until Dylan took another, "Ery informs me you have encountered a spirit."

"A ghost, yes."

"And both of you have witnessed this spirit?"

"Only I caught a glimpse of it one time, but the other time we both got a pretty good look. And I've been… sensing it too. I've been feeling like someone's there." He decided not to tell her about the graveyard smell, because he wasn't sure whether an ordinary human would have caught it. Chris didn't seem to notice, but then sometimes his sense of smell was poor due to his smoking.

"Please describe it."

"Well… it glowed. And it was—"

"Did it appear to be human?"

"Yes. A man." He frowned. "Are there other kinds of ghosts?"

She set down her teacup and laced her hands in her lap. "Of course. Every living thing has an inner energy, even the most basic organisms. That energy is created at the moment a living thing begins to be, and it is shaped by everything that affects the organism. Some energies are very simple, of course, like those of a blade of grass. And some, like those of a human being, are enormously complex. Our energy can be depleted, it can be twisted, it can be made to grow. Love, for example, does magnificent things to one's energy." She smiled at Dylan and Chris, giving them a sort of benediction. And even though her obvious approval of their relationship shouldn't have mattered to Dylan, it did. He smiled back.

"You're not minding my lecture, are you, boys?"

81

Dylan shook his head and Chris said, "No way. This shi—this stuff is interesting."

"I was a schoolteacher for many years. High school English. I suppose it gets in one's blood, being a teacher. It affects one's energy." She gave a small self-effacing smile.

And then her expression grew solemn. "When a being dies, the energy is freed from the physical strictures to which it was bound. I have read a great many debates about what happens to that energy. My husband was a physicist and liked to remind me that energy can be neither destroyed nor created. So perhaps it simply finds a home in a new body. A blade of grass dies and another lives. Or perhaps many blades of grass die and their energies combine to be reborn in, say, a honeybee."

"Wow," Chris said with a small grin. "I'm gonna feel creepy the next time I take the Bobcat to Dylan's brambles. All them dead blackberry energies floatin' around, lookin' for somewhere to land."

Ery had been silent the entire time, but now he leaned forward in his seat. "I always thought that maybe this process could be a good thing. You know, kind of a promotion. Used to be a dandelion but—poof!—now you get to be a redwood. And the variety would be good too. Try things out. Gee, being an amoeba was kinda fun, but I wonder what it's like to be a hummingbird or a rhino."

"I think *you* were a hummingbird," Chris said to him, which made Dylan snort an inelegant laugh.

Ery didn't take offense. His good nature was always one of his best qualities. "Hey, that's cool. I like to wonder sometimes what I was before. Grandma told me that some people believe some of those memories come to you in your dreams, but they're sort of coded, because a human might sorta freak if he dreamed of being a jellyfish or a cactus."

Mrs. Phillips had poured more tea while Ery was talking, and Dylan suddenly realized he had to pee. But he also felt like they were getting closer to some useful answers, so he took a polite sip. "So where do ghosts come in?" he asked. "Something to do with those released energies, right?"

She nodded as if he were a student who'd properly diagrammed a sentence. "I do not know how long it takes for energy to be reabsorbed into a new host. Perhaps it happens immediately, or perhaps the energy waits for a time. Maybe sometimes it even takes a break between bodies, a sort of vacation from mortality." She smiled again, and Dylan realized she must have been very beautiful when she was young. She still was, really. "In any case, generally these events happen peacefully, and those of us who are near barely notice. I was present when my husband died and I felt very clearly the moment his energy—his spirit, his soul, whatever you wish to call it—departed. But it was not a sad event or a traumatic event. It was like... slipping off a comfortable old jacket. One moment it's conforming to your shape, and the next it's a meaningless pile of fabric."

Dylan wasn't certain whether he believed what this woman was telling them, although he supposed it was at least as plausible as people turning into wolves on the full moon. Her ideas were comforting, at least. His relationship with his parents had been somewhat strained, especially after he accidentally outed himself, but he loved them. He wanted to believe that after the car accident took their lives, they'd found some kind of peace—or entirely new lives in new bodies. Maybe his mother was a cat now. She'd always loved cats.

"I'm sorry about your husband," Dylan said.

"Oh, it was many years ago, and he'd been ill for some time. He was ready to go. And I like to think that perhaps he's still around me somewhere—in the flowers in my garden, maybe."

Mrs. Phillips gave Dylan another cookie. "Occasionally, people do not pass so easily. When they're not ready to go yet, when their deaths were especially traumatic. When they feel as if they have unfinished business. And then the energy stays put. It may even retain some of the host's shape, although usually not well. And these are the spirits we call ghosts."

Chris cut his eyes toward Dylan for a second and then cleared his throat. "Could they be stickin' around 'cause they want revenge?"

Dylan felt his chest tighten, but Mrs. Phillips only gave a small shrug. "Perhaps."

83

"And can… can they *hurt* people?"

"They can certainly annoy people, or frighten them. Most spirits are more lost than malicious, I think. But… yes. Energy and mass are the same thing in the end. If the spirit is very strong and very motivated, it may be able to manifest physically. And then it could harm someone if it chose to do so. This might take practice, however. Time. And the physical effort probably cannot be sustained for very long."

It hadn't seemed to take Andy very much time or practice, Dylan reflected. He must have been really pissed off. And he was a stubborn bastard when he was alive, wasn't he, so why should he be any different dead? It was at least a little comforting to know that he probably wouldn't be a threat 24/7.

Chris jiggled his leg impatiently. Maybe he had to pee too. But he scratched the back of his head and asked, "How do you get rid of one of these pissed-off spirits?"

"You might try ignoring it. I rather feel that some of them are just looking for a reaction, like a spoiled child, and if they don't get one, they'll go away."

"Yeah, but this one likes to watch while we— Um, I don't think we can ignore him."

Dylan felt his face go scarlet as Ery sniggered into his teacup.

Mrs. Phillips pretended she didn't notice, bless her. "If you require a more preemptive approach, I recommend you try to discover what is motivating the spirit and then resolve its conflict."

Well, that wasn't good. Dylan and Chris exchanged glances, and it was Dylan who responded. "What if we're pretty sure what's motivating him, and it's, um—"

"Being royally pissed off at us," Chris finished for him.

She sat back a little in her chair. "Ah. I see." Then she frowned a little. "But it seems unlikely that a spirit that has been freed recently would be capable of physical manifestations."

"Unlikely or impossible?" Dylan asked.

Mrs. Phillips sighed quietly. "Not impossible."

"So whatta we do?" asked Chris. "This guy… he was bad news before he died. Really bad. I don't think dyin's gonna improve his temper none."

"I understand." She stood—a little slowly, as if her joints were stiff—walked over to Ery's chair, and ruffled his gelled hair. Ery ducked and made a complaining noise, but he clearly loved it. "My grandson tells me that you're a good young man, Dylan, and I trust his judgment. And if you're a good man, then Chris must be as well. So I will presume that this spirit's antipathy toward you is unjustified."

"Ain't exactly unjustified," said Chris. "I mean, I can see why he ain't happy with us. But he got exactly what he was askin' for, and that's the truth."

She nodded. "There are a few methods of ridding oneself of unwanted spirits. Most of them are quite drastic, I'm afraid, such as burning the affected dwelling to the ground. I suppose the fire itself disrupts the energy force."

Dylan thought of his beloved home in flames and shuddered. "Is… is there something else?"

"Yes. Do you recall what I said about love? Love can alter energies, change negative to positive. In the case of a restless spirit, love could help it gain comfort and finally release it from the bonds it has formed for itself."

Chris shook his head. "There's no way in hell I'm ever gonna love this son of a bitch. Can't, not after he—not after what he did. I don't think Dylan's gonna be up for it either."

Dylan never had loved Andy. He barely knew him, really. They'd connected well enough physically and had a few days of wild sex, but even before Andy turned into a wolf and bit him, Dylan had been fully aware that there was no future for the two of them. He hadn't even really *liked* Andy. Andy was arrogant, selfish. He hadn't wanted to talk much, just fuck, sleep, and eat. And then he'd made Dylan's world a nightmare. Dylan remembered watching Andy chase and murder a suburban jogger, remembered Andy's dark hints of many such killings. Remembered seeing Andy in Chris's living room, with Chris cornered and defenseless. "No. I can't."

Mrs. Phillips didn't seem all that surprised. "But perhaps this person had family. Good friends. Someone who might remind the spirit of the good times that preceded the bad. If you could find such a person and persuade him to visit your home, I think perhaps your spirit might be released."

Dylan stood, asked to use the washroom, and hurried away. A few minutes later, as he stood in the little space, washing his hands in a powder-blue sink and looking at his reflection in a gilded mirror, he felt more despair than relief. He didn't know anything about Andy, not even his last name. He certainly had no idea where to find someone who loved the asshole. And if he did find such a person, how on earth was the man who killed Andy going to persuade that person to come out to the farm and exorcise the ghost?

Maybe he ought to just start stocking up on fire accelerants.

CHAPTER 9

DYLAN was silent as he drove them back to their fancy hotel, and Chris could tell his thoughts were far away.

"Your buddy's grandma was interestin'," Chris ventured carefully. "Not what I expected."

"Me either."

"Inside of her house was like some kinda museum. Or, I dunno. Fancy gallery or somethin'."

"It was nice."

Chris tried a few more conversational gambits, but Dylan responded with distracted monosyllables, and finally Chris gave up. At least it was a short drive. After the valet took the truck away, they stood on the sidewalk for a few moments.

"Wanna go get a drink or somethin'? Bet we could find a bar where they won't lynch a pair of faggots if we do somethin' wild, like holdin' hands." Chris knew Dylan sometimes wished for places near home where they could go every once in a while, just to relax, have a couple of beers, and be themselves. The one and only time Chris had taken Dylan to the local roadhouse, Chris had been jumped in the men's room by a couple of guys who remembered him from when he used to suck cock in back rooms. Dylan had rescued him from those fucktards, and that was the first time Chris had sensed something dangerous in his new lover—although he'd been thinking more CIA or mobster than supernatural furry beast.

"There's some gay bars nearby," said Dylan. "But if you don't mind, I'd rather head upstairs. I'm dead on my feet."

It had been a long and eventful day, and Dylan looked pretty wiped.

"That's cool," said Chris. "We'll save the house music and the go-go boys for another time."

Dylan didn't even have it in him for a proper eye roll in response. He just turned and headed into the hotel, Chris at his side.

By the time they reached their room, however, Chris had realized several things. First, a good part of the reason Dylan had spent a small fortune on the room was so they could screw ghost-free. Second, in the morning they were going to head back to the haunted farm, and given the difficulties in implementing Mrs. Phillips's extermination plan, it might be a long time before they could fuck again. And third, Dylan was wound up tighter than a garage door spring and really needed something to help him relax.

Dylan unlocked the door and held it for Chris. Then he grabbed the white plastic bag of toiletries they'd picked up earlier in the day. "I'm gonna go wash up."

"Go 'head. Gonna check out this flat-screen TV."

But as soon as Dylan closed himself in the bathroom, Chris hastily stripped off all his clothes. He could hear the water running, all the little noises in what was now a familiar nighttime ritual. Dylan liked to gargle at bedtime and he always, always flossed. Which was good, because that gave Chris time to raid the minibar for two tiny bottles of whiskey, which probably were going to cost more than an entire fifth would at a liquor store. He untwisted the caps, drained one of the little bottles in a single fiery gulp, and set the other on the desk.

Then he began to rub his cock.

It didn't take him long to get rock hard. All he had to do was think about Dylan. About the way Dylan felt moving inside him; the sweet pain of Dylan's teeth on his shoulder, on his nipples; the drag of Dylan's calloused hands over his skin. The way Dylan looked at him sometimes when they were… well, making love: like someone who'd been given an amazing gift, like he couldn't quite believe his good luck. The not-entirely-human growls Dylan sometimes emitted in the throes of passion, and the soft way he sighed when they cuddled up after.

The toilet flushed, the sink ran again for a moment, and Chris dropped to all fours. The carpet was mercifully soft.

Dylan came out of the bathroom wearing only his boxer briefs, caught sight of Chris, and froze in his tracks. His mouth was stuck open, as if he'd meant to say something but forgot how.

Chris crawled over to him. Very slowly, and putting the maximum swing in his rear end. He grabbed the remaining whiskey bottle off the desk as he went—he had to carry it in his mouth—and Dylan just stood there. Stupefied, but breathing a little raggedly.

When he reached Dylan, Chris knelt up and held the bottle out. He had to press it into Dylan's hand, and even then, Dylan simply held it. He was too busy watching Chris stroke his hard-on.

"Oh God," Dylan whispered.

"No, but I can understand the mistaken identity." Chris put an extra little twist in his hips that time.

Without taking his eyes off Chris, Dylan brought the bottle to his mouth and upended it. He shuddered and then coughed a little. Chris took the empty bottle from him and tossed it gently aside. It rolled under a blue-and-gold-upholstered armchair.

"Chris…."

Chris didn't answer, at least not with words. What he did was knee-walk a little closer until he was almost touching the other man. He smiled. Then he leaned in a bit and placed his open mouth over the growing bulge in Dylan's underwear.

Cotton didn't taste all that good. But he didn't care, because he could actually feel Dylan's cock harden beneath his tongue, twitch as Chris very gingerly scraped his teeth along the shaft.

Chris kept his own hands busy as he fondled himself, but Dylan didn't seem to know quite what to do with his. After a bit of waving them about, he rested his hands on Chris's shoulders, tightening his grip a little every time Chris increased the pressure on Dylan's cock.

But when Dylan moved again and began to push down his underwear, Chris quickly grabbed his wrists. "Uh-uh."

"But—"

"Nope." With a warning glare, Chris let go of Dylan's arms and grabbed his hips instead, then pushed at him until Dylan was facing the other way. That left his backside inches from Chris's face.

Even covered by fabric, Dylan's ass was spectacular. Really, Chris thought, he should take the time to admire it more often. Dylan's shoulders were broad and his upper body very well toned, but his torso was lean, his waist trim, his hips narrow, and his butt perfectly muscled. Each cheek fit nicely in one of Chris's palms, so he squeezed them a bit while he licked the salty skin at the small of Dylan's back. He had to restrain himself from humping against Dylan's legs like a dog. "I ain't the canine," he mumbled to himself.

Dylan tried to twist around to look at him. "Huh?"

"Nothin'." And to change the subject in a satisfying way, Chris captured Dylan's elastic waistband in his teeth and tugged it downward.

Undressing a guy without using your hands was harder than it sounded. But it was enjoyable work, because he had a close-up view of Dylan's rounded flesh, of the dark cleft, of the soft and downy hairs. Still, he eventually did have to use his fingers to ease the briefs down past Dylan's jutting cock. He avoided touching the cock itself, even though he could tell Dylan badly wanted him to. He let go of the briefs when they were just beneath the swell of Dylan's ass, then wrapped his hands around Dylan's hips to ensure that he stayed still. Chris put his lips very, very close to one cheek—but not quite touching—and breathed.

Dylan moaned a little desperately. "You're killing me."

Chris didn't hurry one bit. He blew little puffs of air. He ran his tongue across those sexy dimples and then, extremely slowly, down the crack. He let go of one hip so he could wedge one hand between Dylan's thighs—Dylan spread his legs the small amount that the briefs permitted—and he teased at Dylan's perineum, at the tender skin of his balls.

"Chriiiis." It sounded suspiciously like a whine, and Chris answered with an evil chuckle.

"You worry too much, Dyl. Gotta learn to relax and take things as they come."

"They'd come a lot faster if you'd stop teasing."

Well, *that* earned Dylan a noisy smack on the ass, followed by several soothing kisses. But then Chris remembered how exhausted the other man had looked as they slogged their way to the hotel room, and he took pity on him. Chris stood and turned Dylan into his embrace. Chris was a little shorter than Dylan, so Dylan's dick poked into his belly, and the bunched-up boxer briefs pressed against Chris's sac.

"Whatta you want, baby?" Chris murmured into Dylan's ear. He didn't often use endearments like that, and Dylan never did, but this seemed like the right time for one.

Dylan had his face buried in Chris's shoulder, so his reply was a little indistinct. "Want you."

"Good. And how do you want me?"

There was a brief pause as Dylan considered the possibilities. He was allowing a good part of his weight to rest on Chris, which wasn't unpleasant. "I want you in me," Dylan finally said.

"Really?"

"Really."

Usually, Chris bottomed. Maybe it was a little selfish of Chris, but getting fucked into the mattress—or the floor, or the wall—really hard, getting his prostate massaged big-time by Dylan's generous dick, that was just the way he preferred it. Which was fine, because Dylan was usually more than content to top. But that didn't mean they didn't enjoy some variety. And Chris could understand that after a tough day like this one, Dylan might be eager to lie back and let someone else man the rudder. So to speak. Besides, after all the attention Chris had been paying to his lover's fine ass, both men were going to be disappointed if Chris and that ass didn't become better acquainted that evening.

"Sounds like a plan," Chris said.

He knelt long enough to slide the underwear down Dylan's legs, and Dylan used Chris's head to steady himself as he lifted first one foot, then the other, removing the last of his clothing completely. Then Chris stood, took Dylan by the hand as if Dylan were a blushing virgin on their wedding night, and towed him to the bed.

A brief pause followed, during which Dylan stood there and Chris swiped the zillion throw pillows off the bed. He hated the damn things and couldn't understand why someone, somewhere, had decided they were a desirable decorative element. He scrunched the fluffy duvet out of the way; then—finally!—he settled Dylan onto the bed.

Dylan lay on his back, his legs slightly spread, his arms sprawled carelessly, and smiled up at Chris. "I love you," he said.

They'd said that to each other a few times already, usually while Dylan was balls-deep in Chris, or else shortly after, when they lolled in a loose, sticky heap. But they didn't say it out of the blue like that, so plain and matter-of-fact.

Swooning was way too girly, so Chris grinned instead. "Ditto. Think that means our energies are... I dunno. Growing? Glowing? Whatever the hell it is they do."

"Definitely."

Chris had to run real quick to the bathroom to fetch the little bottle of K-Y from the drugstore bag. When Chris returned to the bed, Dylan rolled over onto his stomach.

Chris eyed his lover's ass for a moment before pouncing onto the bed beside him. He squirted a healthy stream of lube onto that inviting skin—making Dylan shiver slightly—and used one finger to gradually work it in.

"You're good at this," Dylan said. "Should have you do it more often."

"Wouldn't mind at all. 'Specially when I can make you do *this*." He put some pressure on the bumpy little gland and Dylan gasped and raised his butt a bit.

Very soon, Chris was on top of Dylan, trying to control his speed as he plunged in, then drew almost all the way out. Dylan grunted with every thrust, the bedsprings twanged, and Chris kept up a litany of half-swallowed blasphemies. Any guests in the next room were certainly getting an auditory show. Chris didn't care. Dylan was tight and hot around him, and so goddamn sweet.

Dylan came first, crying out and shuddering beneath Chris. Chris half expected to be evicted at that point. He knew Dylan had to be sore, and he must have been eager to roll over and go to sleep. But Dylan gamely kept going, still wiggling in tandem with Chris's movements, until Chris shouted too and collapsed on top of him.

"You're heavy."

"Some of us don't have the super-duper wolfman metabolism."

"Some of us have to breathe."

"If you couldn't breathe, you couldn't be bitchin'," said Chris. But he rolled to Dylan's side anyway.

Dylan immediately scooted closer and, as far as Chris could tell, fell asleep. Which meant Chris was the one who had to get up and find the right combination of switches to turn off the goddamn lights, and then try to stumble his way through an unfamiliar room in the dark. He tripped over one of the fucking throw pillows and almost fell. But when he climbed back onto the bed, Dylan stirred enough to tug the covers over them both.

"You win," Chris said.

"Win what?"

"Your surprise is better. I still like rodeos, but in fancy hotels, I get laid."

"Wish we could just stay here forever. Forget about ghosts and work…."

"And Jimmy Nock." Chris hadn't forgotten his father's surprise appearance, although he'd been trying to pretend the encounter hadn't happened and that a whole viper's nest of raw emotions hadn't been stirred up.

"Him too. Chris, I'm sorry I got you in the middle of this mess."

"My life was pretty boring before you moved in. Now it ain't." Chris ruffled Dylan's hair, which Dylan hated. "Definitely ain't boring."

"You can have interesting without mortal danger."

"Maybe. I'm still pretty thankful I didn't end up with a vegan B and B or an organic free-range tofu farm next door."

Yeah, he thought, pressing himself more tightly against Dylan. He'd take mortal danger any day if it meant he got Dylan too.

CHAPTER 10

DYLAN slept in wonderfully late, waking up with the arrival of the room service breakfast Chris had ordered. Chris brought the tray across the room and set it on the bed. "Better eat and shift your ass. They're gonna kick us outta here soon."

"Yesterday I asked for late checkout," Dylan said between yawns. "We have until one."

"So we have time to fuck again before we hit the road."

"I'm glad you have your priorities straight."

"Always."

Dylan sat on the mattress, cross-legged and nude, and ate sausage and eggs, a nice fruit salad, and a berry muffin. And there was coffee, good and hot. Chris had french toast but managed to get most of the syrup on Dylan—not by accident, of course, because after the food was gone, he licked it off.

Sticky and sated, they were pleased to discover they both fit in the shower.

Although Chris had complained yesterday about clothing shopping and the outfit Dylan chose for him, he again put on the charcoal trousers and red shirt. Dylan was tempted to rip them right off. "Wow. You do clean up nicely."

"This mean I can make you wear overalls?"

"Sure, but I won't look nearly as sexy in them as you do."

They packed up their few belongings and headed down to the lobby, where Dylan checked them out. Chris winced when he heard the total, but as far as Dylan was concerned, it had been worth every last penny.

Once the truck was fetched for them and Dylan started rolling down Washington Street, he asked, "Is there anywhere you want to go before we head home?"

"No. Just— Fuck! Forgot I bought these." Out of the corner of his eye, Dylan could see Chris rooting around under the seat. Chris sat up after a moment, a pink box clutched in his hands. "Still hungry?"

"Always. Did you get the kind with the Tang topping?"

Chris handed him an orange donut, and Dylan chewed happily as they inched through traffic.

IT WAS nice to get back home, ghost notwithstanding. Chris trotted next door to change into one of his grungier jeans and T-shirt combinations, while Dylan changed his clothes too. Then they lugged the floor sander and other supplies up the stairs.

"Dammit!" said Dylan when they entered the spare room.

"What?"

Dylan pointed to the wall beside the window, where the fingerprints were once again visible.

Chris walked over to squint at them. "Haven't you slapped, like, ten coats of paint over here?"

"I told you I couldn't just paint over them."

"Well, at this point I think your other option is ripping the damn wall out."

Dylan was too stubborn for that. He vowed to add a stain blocker and more layers of paint after the floor sanding was complete.

The room was already prepped for sanding: shoe moldings pried away, protruding nails set and puttied. Dylan had never used a drum sander before, so he watched Chris for a while before taking his turn. They had to go over the floor several times with various grades of sandpaper, sweeping and vacuuming between each round. When the main footage was done, they used Chris's edge sander and orbit sander to get the edges and corners.

"Looking good so far," Chris said, wiping the sweat from his forehead. "How 'bout some dinner? We can start the staining after."

"I should get started on the new project Stender dumped on me. I have a lot of research. How about we call it a day?"

Chris shrugged. "'Kay."

Dylan hadn't noticed the ghost all day, but as they walked down the hallway, he caught that earthy stink. "Wait!" he barked at Chris, holding up his hand. Chris froze in midstep.

The ghost appeared again, this time between them and the stairs. Even with late-evening sunlight forming pools on the hallway floor, the ghost glowed. It was hovering again, bobbing gently, and again the details of its face and shape were indistinct.

"Get the fuck out of here!" Chris yelled.

The ghost remained where it was. Dylan had the oddest impression it was trying to communicate something, although what dead Andy would have to say to him, he couldn't guess. Maybe it was just mustering up the power to vomit acidic ectoplasm onto them.

It inched a little closer, and Dylan and Chris backed up. There was nowhere for them to go, really. They could duck into one of the bedrooms, but then they'd still be cornered unless they wanted to leap out a window. Or they could pull down the ladder and climb up to the attic, but that would only put them higher off the ground.

As the haunt floated nearer, Dylan stepped in front of Chris. He let a little rage build inside him—not difficult under the circumstances. With his hands balled into fists and his eyes narrowed, he growled, "Stay the hell away from us. I didn't want you when you were alive and I don't want you now. Let your goddamn energy loose and go!"

The assholes who'd threatened Chris in the roadhouse bathroom had been scared enough by that look to take off, even though one of them had a knife. One had even pissed himself. But the ghost didn't appear intimidated. Which probably made sense. Dylan could rip a human to pieces, but he was distinctly limited with the spectral set.

Still, he was prepared to make his stand. No way would the bastard get to Chris. He hoped that if it came down to it, he would distract the ghost long enough for Chris to take off. Of course, Chris would undoubtedly be too damn stubborn to go anywhere.

Dylan decided to change tactics. "Look," he said to the ghost in as calm a voice as he could muster, "I'm sorry about how things turned out, I really am. I wouldn't have hurt you if you hadn't gone after Chris. I love him, Andy. Can't you respect that? Let your anger go and maybe you can find some peace." It was good advice.

But the ghost didn't disappear. Instead, it seemed to become very agitated. It sort of trembled in a way that made Dylan's head hurt, like strobe lights blinking too fast, and its margins grew hazy until it didn't resemble anything vaguely human. And then, to Dylan's relief, it disappeared.

"Shit," Chris said.

"Yeah."

"You were really scary, though."

"Thanks."

They didn't talk about the ghost while Chris fried up some burgers. As they ate, they discussed floor varnishes instead. Chris told Dylan about his idea to install a sink in the mudroom and showed him the photos he'd snapped of some possibilities. "I like this one," said Dylan as he looked at a farmhouse-style model. "It's a good size and the porcelain will look much better than stainless."

"Cool. The plumbing'll be a fairly easy job. I can handle it, if you trust me with your pipes."

Dylan purposely ignored the bad double entendre. "I trust you with everything."

After cleaning the kitchen, they retired to the living room and sat close to each other on the couch. Chris read a paperback while Dylan surfed a little, doing some preliminary research on the building he'd be working on and the applicable codes and restrictions. He wasn't in the mood to think about what kinds of considerations he'd have to keep in mind to make the space usable for a college; that could wait for another day.

It was, all in all, a tranquil evening. Not for the first time, Dylan was profoundly grateful for Chris's company. If Dylan had been stuck on his farm all alone, as he'd originally intended, he'd probably have gone nuts from loneliness by now. He wondered how Chris had endured so many days and nights by himself in his little shack, first with only his creepy great-uncle staring at him from next door, and then with not even that. Right now, Chris seemed as content as Dylan and as hungry for contact, leaning up against Dylan's side.

Dylan found a website that featured vintage photos of Portland. He clicked through the pictures, smiling as he recognized some familiar landmarks. But then he came to a view of Sandy Boulevard, circa late fifties or early sixties. There was a diner in the background and cars were lined up on the street, but what caught his eye was the young guy perched on a motorcycle, cigarette dangling between his lips, expression faintly mocking as he looked straight at the photographer.

"Oh!" Dylan exclaimed out loud as an idea hit him.

Chris sat up a little and looked at him. "What?"

"I think… I think I have an idea how to track Andy's roots."

THEY began the day a little grouchy because they couldn't have sex. Chris would have been willing, but Dylan had no desire to be caught in flagrante by the ghost again. It was bad enough to walk around the house feeling as if someone was watching him and half expecting something luminescent to appear at any moment.

Chris glowered as he made their breakfast, and they were curt with one another as they stained the newly sanded floor. It didn't help that the day was already very warm and stinging sweat dripped into their eyes as they worked. They were nearly done when Dylan leaned on the handle of the stain applicator and sighed. "You buried him, didn't you?"

Chris was on all fours in the final corner, applying stain with a brush. He glanced over his shoulder at Dylan. "Yeah. Not the most pleasant thing I've ever done. Why? You figure I did it wrong or something?"

"No. I'm not blaming you. I appreciate you cleaning up my mess. I was just wondering—what did you bury him in?"

"Bunch of dirt."

"No, I mean clothing."

"Wrapped him in a sheet, that's all. He wasn't wearin' nothing when he died."

Dylan nodded. He'd killed Andy while they were both in wolf form, and although Andy had morphed back to human at the very end, his clothing hadn't magically reappeared. "So you never found his clothes?"

"Nah. Maybe they were near his bike, but your brother took care of that. I didn't ask about it. Other things on my mind. Like nursin' you back to health so I could kill you myself."

"It was…. That was really a cool thing you did. Taking care of me even though you were really pissed off, I mean."

Chris sat up on his haunches and rubbed the back of his hand across his forehead. "You were a stupid dickwad for not trusting me with the truth. But I still loved you." Then he cocked his head. "Why are you all worked up over Andy's clothes all of a sudden?"

"I was hoping for maybe a wallet or something. I was also hoping I wasn't going to have to exhume the corpse to get to it."

"Well, you ain't gonna have to do no grave digging, but I dunno if Rick found a wallet or anything."

"I'll call him when we're done here."

As they finished the room, they both saw something flash past the doorway, as if someone were running very quickly down the hall. But of course when they checked, nobody was there. They each took a quick shower—separately, and in a businesslike manner, because of the damn haunt—and Chris said he wanted to nap for a while because the heat and stain had given him a headache. "Sleep here," Dylan ordered. "My place is cooler than yours." Neither of them had air-conditioning, but Dylan's house had higher ceilings, which helped a little. So Chris stripped off his clothing and lay starfished across Dylan's mattress, and he smiled when Dylan lugged a fan up from the basement, plugged it in, and pointed it in Chris's direction.

Not wanting to disturb Chris, Dylan took his phone down to the kitchen and sat at the table with a cold bottle of beer.

Rick picked up after two rings. "Hey, baby brother. What's up?"

"Floor refinishing. And how are you spending your Sunday?"

"We spent all morning discussing money shit as it relates to parenthood. The discussion only ended up in tears twice."

"Yeah, well I've heard women can get really emotional when they're pregnant. Hormones, I guess."

"Oh, they do. But I was the one crying." Rick sighed noisily and dropped his voice. "I'm scared as hell, Dyl. I know Kay's not due for another six months, but it's sinking in that this is for real. What if I'm a shitty dad?"

"You won't be. You'll be great."

"But how do I know that? Maybe Dad thought he'd be great too, and we both know he wasn't. I guess he tried, but he was always... I always felt like he was judging me. And the way he and Mom shut you out after they found out you were gay.... I'd never want to do that to my kid."

"You wouldn't." Dylan still felt a little bitter over his parents, even though they'd been dead for over a decade. He'd loved them and it had torn him apart that they couldn't accept who he was. He'd always wondered if they'd have come around eventually, given time. He wished he'd had a chance to settle things with them when they were alive. Yeah, maybe he could use a little counseling. He was, however, positive that his brother would be in a whole different league, paternally.

"You didn't call to hear me bitch, I bet," said Rick. "Sorry."

"Feel free to bitch any time, Ricky. But you're right, I did sort of have an agenda when I dialed."

There was a popping noise on the other end of the line, and Dylan smiled as he pictured his brother cradling a cold bottle in his hand, just the way Dylan was. "What's up?" Rick asked.

"I'm… kind of facing an issue."

"An issue that's not an existential crisis brought about by impending parenthood, I take it."

"Not unless there's something Chris isn't telling me." Dylan took a long swallow of his drink. "It's a long story, kind of, and I don't want you mixed up in it."

"Because that turned out so well last time you kept us in the dark," Rick responded sharply.

Dylan winced. "Yeah, I know. At least this time I'm not keeping anything from Chris. Look, nothing really ugly is happening yet, and if it does, I'll tell you, okay? Otherwise, you have worries of your own."

There was a long pause as Rick digested this. "So why call?"

"Um… when Andy… when you found Andy's bike, did you find his clothing too?"

"No. Not even a helmet."

Andy probably didn't use a helmet. "Where was the bike?"

"A couple miles down the county road, parked right on the side. Why?"

"It's that long story thing. What'd you do with it?"

Another pause, this time as Rick downed some of his beer. "I had to get rid of it."

"I know. I'm sorry you had to."

"Dylan, I'm a database administrator. I don't exactly have a lot of experience in getting rid of the evidence of... of supernatural homicides. I did the best I could."

Dylan was beginning to get worried. "What'd you do with it, Rick?"

"I... I dumped it in your pond."

It took a moment for the words to sink in. "You put a motorcycle in my *pond*?"

"Yeah. Felt kind of bad about it too. It was a sweet bike. But I couldn't think of anywhere better for it. So I rode it to your farm, drained the gas and oil, wheeled the thing over, and pushed it in. You told me the water was pretty deep, and it's too muddy and green and stuff to see the bottom, so I figured it'd be hidden. Is it a problem? Are the cops after you?"

Dylan shuddered. "No, nobody's after me. Not exactly. I just—I need to find some info on Andy. I thought the bike might have had registration or insurance papers or something."

"There was a saddlebag. I didn't look inside. It's still attached to the bike, I guess."

And the saddlebag had been under several feet of water for a month. Great. Dylan rolled the cold glass across his sweaty forehead.

"Dylan—"

"It's fine, Rick. I'm sorry I had to bug you about it."

"But what the hell's going on?"

"How about if we all get together next weekend and I'll fill you in, okay?" If Dylan was lucky, his problem would be solved by then.

"I hate it when you're cryptic, Dyldo. But fine, next week."

After the call ended, Dylan drained the rest of his beer, then tossed the bottle into the plastic bin he kept outside the back door. The bin was getting pretty full; he'd have to make a trip to the recycling center soon. Maybe he could even convince Chris to clean the mess off his back porch. It shouldn't bother Dylan if Chris wanted to decorate his own backyard in Twentieth Century Redneck, but it sort of did.

Dylan stood in the shade behind his house for a while, looking toward the slope that led down to the pond. "Fuck," he finally said before turning to go inside.

He decided to make sandwiches. Maybe he'd even bring lunch up to Chris. Chris would complain because he liked to think that Dylan couldn't even make toast properly on his own, but Dylan had been managing to feed himself for over ten years and hadn't died from it yet. Chris could survive one ham sandwich.

Dylan was just pulling the meat out of the fridge when someone knocked on the front door.

His first thought was that maybe there was some mail he had to sign for, but then he remembered it was Sunday. Nobody else ever visited unannounced. Nobody except Andy, but a ghost probably wouldn't bother to knock. Shrugging slightly, Dylan closed the fridge again and padded down the hall.

Jimmy Nock was standing on the front porch.

He'd obviously made an effort to clean himself up: his gray hair was combed and slicked back, and his pale blue button-down shirt looked stiff and new, as if he'd just taken it out of the package. He looked nervous as hell too, and surprised to see Dylan.

"Um… hi. Don't know if you remember me…." Jimmy patted his shirt pocket for cigarettes, didn't find any, and let his hands drop.

Dylan leaned in the doorway. "I remember you."

"I, uh, I was looking for Christian. Didn't know if he lived here but thought I'd give it a try. I was wondering if maybe you knew where he is."

"What do you want?" Dylan tried to keep his voice neutral but knew that a certain amount of hostility probably showed through. He'd seen the emotional state Chris was in after running into his father at the rodeo.

"I just want to talk to him. That's all, I swear." Jimmy looked down at his feet, then back up. "Just want to talk."

Despite himself, Dylan was moved. Maybe because Jimmy looked so much like his son, with those very same blue eyes that managed to show defiance, hope, and vulnerability all at the same time. "I don't think he wants to talk to you," Dylan said, but gently.

"Just give me—just ten minutes. Five. Jesus, it's been so long, and I got… I got things I need to say. Please. I'm his father."

"You ain't nothin' to me."

Dylan whirled around at the unexpected voice. Chris was walking quickly down the hallway toward the door. He was bare-chested, bedheaded, and his jeans were only half-buttoned.

Jimmy took a small step forward, then shuffled back a little. "Christian, please, I want—"

"It's Chris, asshole, and I don't care what the fuck you want. Go away."

"Okay. *Chris*. Can't we just talk? We can stand right out here. If you want, your… your boyfriend can stay too."

By now Chris was only a few inches behind Dylan. "That's real nice of you to give him permission to stick around on his own fuckin' property. I dunno if you were picturin' some kind of big ol' family reunion, but that ain't gonna happen 'cause you ain't my family. Dylan is my family. You're just a douche-bag stranger that's gonna get himself arrested if he don't leave."

Chris's voice had risen almost to a shout, and Jimmy looked more anguished than ever.

"You better go, Mr. Nock," Dylan said.

Jimmy wasn't as powerfully built as his son, and now he sort of shrank into himself and looked very small. He backed away a little. But he didn't step down off the porch. Instead, he dug into his back pocket. For a brief moment, Dylan thought the old man might be going for a weapon, so he planted himself more firmly in front of Chris.

But Jimmy only took out a battered old wallet. He unfolded it and, with slightly shaky hands, took out a business card. "This here's mine. I move around a lot, doing different fairs and shows and stuff. Don't have no cell phone. But the number on here, it belongs to a friend of mine. I check in with her almost every day, so if you leave me a message, I'll get it pretty quick."

Chris made a sort of growling noise and Dylan didn't move. So Jimmy shrugged one shoulder and then very carefully set the card on the little table near the door.

Jimmy looked past Dylan at Chris. "Please. Call me, son." Then he nodded briefly at Dylan, turned, and went down the steps. Dylan watched as he walked slowly down the gravel road; he limped a little. He got into an ancient pickup with a battered camper shell and drove away.

"You can burn the fucking card," Chris snarled before stomping off to the kitchen.

But Dylan slipped the card into his pocket instead.

CHAPTER 11

DEBATING how to get a motorcycle out of Dylan's pond so they could track down a dead werewolf's family—and, hopefully, get rid of a ghost—was crazy. It was also far preferable to discussing the fuckwad who called himself Chris's father.

"If you destroyed that earth dam, the pond'd drain," Chris pointed out. Then he took another bite of his sandwich. Dylan had insisted on making the thing, and it was too dry. Also the meat was piled on too thick and the sandwich really needed something with a bit of a kick to it, maybe a little pepperoncini. But Chris didn't complain.

"I have no idea how to wreck a dam, Chris. I'm an architect, not a civil engineer. And I certainly wouldn't know how to build up the dam again once the motorcycle was out. I don't want to lose my pond."

Chris nodded. He hadn't really liked that idea either. "You could hire someone. There's prob'ly companies that specialize in fishing vehicles out of water. You know, someone misses a curve and ends up in the Columbia or something."

"Then I might have to explain how a bike got in my pond and why it's taken me weeks to get it out. I think no witnesses would be best."

"Could fish it out ourselves with a crane." Chris took another bite and washed it down with some milk.

"Can we get a crane down to the pond?"

"Not easily." The pathway was narrow and steep, and the edges of the water were mostly overgrown with trees and other vegetation.

Dylan put his own half-eaten sandwich down on the plate. "We don't really need the whole bike, I don't think. At least, I'm hoping I can get what I need out of that saddlebag. Assuming the water hasn't ruined everything."

"So?"

"So I'm going to dive down there and get it. It's not like the water's that deep. I can manage it."

"I could do it."

"You can stand on dry ground and perform CPR if I fuck up." Dylan gave him a small grin. "At least I have health insurance in case I get hurt and end up in the hospital."

"D'you suppose an ER could figure out you're a wolf? I know the blood tests came back normal, but what if the docs started diggin' around a little?" It was one of the reasons Chris hadn't taken Dylan to the hospital after the fight with Andy. Looking back on it, he'd taken a big gamble with Dylan's life, but Chris hadn't been thinking his most clearly at the moment. Nearly getting mauled in your own living room, then seeing a wolf turn into the man you'd fallen in love with and had been sharing a bed with—all that tended to make a guy a little muddle-headed.

"There's been enough digging in my insides, thanks very much," Dylan proclaimed. "Let's hope I manage to get out of this thing unscathed."

"Can you be scathed?" Chris asked thoughtfully.

"Huh?"

"If unscathed means unharmed, then does scathed mean you're all fucked up? 'Cause I've never heard nobody say that word."

Dylan took a bite of food and chewed for a moment. "Comments can be scathing. That's got to be from the same root. Why the detour into lexicography?"

"I'm tryin' to distract you from doing something stupid."

"Nice try, but your chief method of distracting me is a no-go until we get rid of Andy. And the sooner I get that saddlebag, the sooner the ghost is gone. I hope."

Chris knew Dylan was right, but that didn't mean he had to be happy about it. "So you gonna do it now?"

"In a while. You're not supposed to go swimming right after eating, right? That's what my mom always insisted. She'd take us to the community pool sometimes during the summer, but not until an hour after lunch. Do you suppose any kid anywhere ever really died because he tried to do a few laps twenty minutes after he ate?"

"Doubt it." Chris turned a little and looked out the window, even though all he could see from this angle was sky and trees. "When I lived here with Gramps, I used to come over all the time and swim in Uncle Frank's pond. Nobody cared if I'd just had lunch. Never died of it."

"Do you miss him? Your grandfather, I mean. I never knew mine."

Chris shrugged. "I guess. He wasn't a bad guy. Took me in when Mom was too strung out to handle me, and then when she died. That couldn't have been easy. I wasn't an easy kid. But he wasn't a happy man. Didn't talk much. Once he gave up farming and started renting the fields out, he mostly just sat and read. Did crossword puzzles." Chris smiled slightly at a good memory. "When I got older, sometimes he'd ask me to help him out when he got stuck on a word." It had always flattered Chris a little that his grandfather thought him smart enough to be useful for something like that.

Dylan nodded and pushed some crumbs around on his plate, forming neat little lines, messing them up, then forming them again.

"How 'bout you?" Chris asked after a while. "You miss your folks?"

"Sometimes. We weren't really… compatible. Not even when I was little. I used to think maybe I was adopted or a changeling or something. But it wasn't like I had an awful childhood. Not like—" He stopped abruptly.

"Not like mine," Chris finished for him.

Dylan looked pained. "I didn't mean—"

"'S okay. My childhood sucked balls most of the time, and that's a fact. No use tryin' to pretty it up. But I had some good times too."

"Yeah, so did I. One time—I was about eight, I think—we all went to the coast for a weekend. We hardly ever went on vacations. Dad said they were a waste of money. But for some reason, this time we all piled in the car and drove to Lincoln City. Mom and Dad had rented this condo thing, so Rick and I got a room to ourselves. We ate clam chowder and poked around in tide pools and filled our pockets with rocks and shells. And both nights we were there, Mom and Dad let us stay up really late, which they never did. We all sat on the beach on driftwood and shivered a little and listened to the waves, and I remember my parents actually laughing together while Rick and I tried to find the constellations. It was really nice."

Dylan's voice had gone soft while he spoke, and his gaze was far away. He looked very young. Then he shook himself a little. "Sorry. Got carried away there. Let's go check the floor, okay?"

For a change, Chris cleaned up the dishes—there weren't many—while Dylan waited. Then they went upstairs, where the smell of wood stain was really strong despite open windows. They looked down at the refinished floor critically. "It's dry," Chris said. "Good thing about this heat."

"Yeah. Do you think we should do another coat? The can said it was optional, but we have plenty." They'd bought quite a bit because Dylan figured he'd need it for the other upstairs rooms eventually.

"Your floor, dude."

Dylan gave him an odd look, one Chris couldn't interpret, before nodding slightly. "I want another coat. Are you up to it? I can do it myself if your head still aches."

"Nah, I'm good." Actually, Chris was slightly hoping he'd get a headache, because then he could beg for another nap and Dylan's tender care—cool washcloths on his forehead, maybe—instead of thinking about fathers or ghosts.

But as soon as Chris was trapped in the corner with his can of stain and his brush, Dylan made a tentative throat-clearing noise Chris knew meant trouble. "What?" Chris demanded.

"I was just thinking."

"And?" Chris knew he was being belligerent, but he had a pretty good guess what was coming next.

"Your fath—Jimmy came here to see you. I think he kind of dressed up for it, even. I think he has something to say to you. Maybe it wouldn't hurt if you listened."

"I don't have to listen to a word that bastard says. Don't owe him a fucking thing."

"I know. That's not what I meant. I meant maybe you'd be better off if you talked to him for a little while."

Chris snorted derisively. "Yeah, right."

Dylan was pushing the pole of the lamb's wool applicator across the floor and carefully not looking at Chris. "Really. It might give you some closure at least. Maybe you'd stop blaming yourself so much."

"What?" Chris knelt up to blink at Dylan. "I don't blame myself for nothin'. He left 'cause he's a fuckhead, not because of me. I was just a little kid."

"Bullshit, Chris. You may be telling yourself that, but there's a part of you—way deep inside—that thinks he left because there was something wrong with you. That thinks your mother died because there's something wrong with you."

Now Chris felt slightly ill. "Wasn't aware you'd picked up a degree in psychology, college boy," he snarled.

"I didn't have to. It's how *I* felt. How I sometimes still feel. When my parents pretty much ignored me once they found out I was gay, a part of me felt like I deserved that kind of thing because there was something wrong with me."

"Ain't nothin' wrong with being queer. You're the one with the No H8 T-shirt. You know that."

111

Dylan's chuckle was more wry than amused. "Yeah. And I also know that my parents' car accident had nothing to do with me. Except I don't always know it *here*." He paused long enough to thud his palm against his chest. "And maybe I don't know everything there is to know about you, Chris Nock, but I'm pretty sure you're at least as good at self-blame as I am."

Not answering right away, Chris instead spread stain along the edge of the wall under the window. When he glanced up, he could still see those fingerprints, which reminded him how stubborn his lover could be about certain things. But Chris was stubborn too, and he didn't want to talk to Jimmy. Even thinking about doing so stirred up his emotions in unpleasant ways and made him want to retch. "Ain't gonna," he finally muttered, aware that he sounded like a truculent preschooler.

The response was gentle. "Fine. But maybe think about it just a little, okay? Please?"

Chris was going to answer—saying exactly what, he wasn't sure—but a huge crash came from downstairs. He and Dylan looked at one another in alarm, dropped their staining tools, and ran for the stairs.

"Holy shit!" Chris exclaimed when they got to the kitchen.

When Dylan cleaned up after meals, he always put away the pots, utensils, and dishes immediately, as though some fancy magazine was ready to shoot a photo spread. Chris, on the other hand, had left the sandwich plates and his rinsed milk glass on the counter, intending to put them away at some time in the future. Or maybe just saving himself a little work by reusing them for dinner. But now the dishes and the glass were in the middle of the kitchen floor, shattered into jagged pieces.

"There's no way those things just fell like that," he said. Which was true, because they'd obviously impacted a couple of yards from the edge of the cabinet.

"Has to be the ghost."

"Maybe he don't like your china pattern."

Chris expected Dylan to glare at him, but instead Dylan looked slightly terrified. Which wasn't good, because Chris had already learned that his werewolf lover didn't scare easily. "It means the ghost has learned to be solid," Dylan said, shaking his head. "That means he could hurt... hurt one of us."

Chris kicked at a piece of broken ceramic. "Why didn't he, then? Instead of tossin' around your kitchenware, he could've... I dunno. Sent that putty knife flyin' or beaned one of us with a can of wood stain."

"I don't know."

"You're the one was being the expert shrink a few minutes ago, Dyl."

That brought a glare, which was way better than Dylan looking scared. "I am not a ghost psychologist."

"Could be. In fact, if you get tired of drawin' pictures of houses, supernatural counselor would be the perfect career for you. Deal with vamps' addiction issues, prescribe Paxil for werewolves to take once a month, tell zombies their craving for brains is all in their heads."

Dylan pushed Chris almost hard enough to make him fall. "Jerk," Dylan said, and he couldn't stop his mouth from quirking upward.

Chris headed for the broom closet Dylan had included in his remodeled kitchen. "Let's get this mess cleaned up and go swimming."

CHAPTER 12

DYLAN could tell Chris was doing his best to chase away their unease over the ghost, and he appreciated the effort, even if he still wanted to run and hide under the covers like a small child. What kind of werewolf was he, spooked by a stupid... spook? A werewolf who knew the ghost had fairly good reason to be angry, and a werewolf who had someone to protect, that's who.

Under other circumstances, the excursion might have been fun. Dylan had cooled himself off in the pond a couple of times already—and the wolf liked to swim in it too—but he and Chris had never gone together. Under other circumstances, they could have skinny-dipped, could have splashed one another playfully and raced each other. Might even have found a suitable spot near the edge of the water for some damp, muddy, leafy sex.

They walked down the slope, Chris commenting on how much blackberry bramble still remained even after he'd attacked it with the Cat not long ago, then speculating again on how many pies they could cajole Kay into baking them. Yellow jackets buzzed and hummed around a tree stump, and Dylan reminded himself to consult Chris later as to the wisdom of and procedures for evicting the insects. A pair of crows called to each other from the tops of the feral Christmas trees. There were no signs of human activity within sight or hearing, but Dylan knew that tiny creatures skulked in the grasses and larger animals ran in the woods beyond.

The water of the pond was still, reflecting the trees that surrounded it. The resident family of ducks eyed the men from the far edge of the water. Only two of the babies had survived—Dylan wasn't to blame for the predation—and they looked fully grown now, so Dylan was optimistic about their future.

"You're sure about this?" Chris asked. "'Cause I'm still willing."

Without really planning to, Dylan grabbed him and pulled him into a fierce hug. "I know you're willing. But you stay here, okay?"

Chris grunted a reply and hugged him back.

Dylan stripped out of his clothing quickly, laid it on a downed tree trunk, and let Chris leer at him. He scanned the pond banks, looking for any sign of where Rick might have rolled the bike. But the plants grew quickly this time of year, and any marks Rick had made were gone. The dumping spot would have needed to be fairly near the pathway, because most of the rest of the pond edge was pretty much impassable to humans, let alone a man pushing a good-size vehicle. So probably the best strategy was to start nearby and work his way deeper.

He waded into the water. The mud squished between his toes; he wasn't sure whether he liked the sensation. The water was colder than he'd expected, but that was all right. He felt a little overheated anyway. The drop-off was steep—soon he was in up to his hips, and then his chest. With a quick glance back at Chris's anxious face, Dylan submerged.

As a kid, Dylan had been skinny and geeky and awkward, his nose always stuck in books. His father had signed him up for Little League one year, but that had been a disaster. Dylan had spent more time daydreaming about being an astronaut or examining the complex structure of dandelion flowers than paying attention to the ball. At school, Dylan was always one of the last kids picked for teams, along with pudgy Amanda Forswith and terminally nearsighted Billy Gonzalez. The only sport he'd managed at all well had been swimming, and even then he hadn't been good enough to make the high school team. But at least he knew the basic strokes and could get across the pool without drowning.

Now his body was more powerful than he'd ever dreamed and his movements surer, more coordinated. If he could try out for the team now, he'd make varsity for sure. He dived down and dragged his hands along the bottom of the pond, feeling blindly for the submerged bike. The water was completely opaque, so Dylan just closed his eyes.

His fingertips brushed against lots of things: tree branches, rocks, clumps of half-rotted leaves. Every time he emerged to gasp in a few lungfuls of air, he looked at Chris, who was watching him carefully. Sometimes Chris waved.

Dylan worked his way back and forth as methodically as possible. He was a little shocked by how deep the pond soon became; he had to go farther and farther on each breath. Then his hand brushed against something smooth and rubbery. His heart began to race with excitement, until he explored just a bit more and determined that the object couldn't possibly be a tire and wasn't connected to anything manmade. He dragged it to the surface anyway.

"Find something?" Chris called.

Dylan treaded water as he looked at the thing in his hands. "I think it's a dead pair of hip waders."

"Oh."

Dylan was tempted to swim to shore and dump the hip waders there. He didn't like the idea of garbage in his pond. But then he might lose track of where he'd been in the search, so he regretfully let his find sink back to the bottom.

He found more junk. Another boot, this one just ankle high. A tangle of some kind of synthetic fabric. Several rusted tools. A heavy chunk of yellowish plastic he couldn't identify. A metal bucket with a hole in the bottom. He even found a tire, but it was from a bicycle, not a motorcycle.

"Your relatives were slobs," he called breathlessly to Chris.

"So call the EPA on 'em. Dyl, you look exhausted. Take a break."

"No," Dylan said and dived again.

He felt fish brush against his legs a few times, and there were little snails of some kind on the pond bottom. He knew that otters and beavers ventured here sometimes, and he wondered if they were nearby, maybe wondering what the hell the crazy human was up to. His limbs grew heavy and he had an increasingly difficult time catching his breath. Chris swore at him pretty steadily every time Dylan surfaced, but Dylan had stopped trying to respond.

And then his fingers touched something hard and smooth. Fighting the instinct to push upwards, he felt around until he recognized what he was touching: a handlebar.

"Dammit, Dylan, this time I thought you'd drowned for sure. Get the fuck out of there before—"

"I found it!"

Chris blinked. "You found Andy's bike?"

"Yeah. Unless there are two motorcycles down there."

"Good. Then—"

But Dylan didn't hear the rest, because he was already underwater again. The bike was a long, long way down. Much deeper than a little farm pond ought to be, really. But he found it again, half-buried in muck. He traced along the body until he came to the rear of it, and to his immense relief, he found something that felt like a bag.

He tried to tug the bag free, but it was slippery and the strap was caught somehow. Buckled, maybe, or pinned under the bike. He couldn't find a way to work it free, and although he tugged as hard as he could, it remained stubbornly attached. He stayed under so long he felt dizzy by the time he broke the surface, and black spots danced before his eyes.

Chris had waded in as far as his knees and was pitching a fit. "Dylan! Goddammit, you asshole! Get the fuck—"

"Found the bag," Dylan gasped. "Can't... can't free it.... Need a knife." Oh, he was so *tired*. His muscles felt like loose rubber bands.

Chris cursed at him for a few moments more before tearing off his own clothes. Naked, he bent over his jeans—which was diverting even in Dylan's weakened state—rifled the pockets, then stood up with an object in his hand. Good old Chris, with his handy-dandy pocketknife. He should've been a Boy Scout.

As Dylan struggled to remain in place, Chris swam out to him with a few strong strokes. Chris had the handle of the open knife clenched in his teeth like someone from a Tarzan movie. Dylan took the knife from him as soon as Chris was within reach. Chris grabbed his arm before Dylan could dive again.

"Jesus, Dyl. You're barely stayin' afloat here. Let me—"

"No. I know where it is. I'll be right back." Before Chris could argue again, Dylan took a huge breath and ducked underwater.

The pond bottom seemed much farther away this time, as if it had somehow sunk in the past minute or two. The water was very cold. He couldn't hear much of anything—just his own muffled heartbeat and a few stray splashes. He dove and he dove, until he nearly expected to see the gates of hell open before his eyes. And when he was sure he couldn't go on any longer, he touched the bike.

It took a few more seconds to find the bag. Then he had to cut it free, which proved difficult. His feet kept floating upward, his leverage was poor, and the bag strap was thick and slippery. All his considerable strength had drained away. Yet he was convinced that if he didn't get the bag *now*, he'd never find it again.

By the time he finally cut the strap free, his lungs were burning and he was having a hard time distinguishing up from down. But he clutched the bag under one arm and kicked as well as he was able, hoping he was heading in the right direction. He was almost relieved when he saw light above him, except it seemed impossibly far away.

He couldn't move anymore.

This was a stupid way to die.

Something grabbed his free arm. Dylan tried to pull away but couldn't. All he could do was hang on to the damn saddlebag and try to stay conscious. And then somehow he was breathing again, sweet oxygen rushing in as Chris half cradled him, half dragged him to shore.

"You fucking idiot! You goddamn stubborn, stupid, fucking *moron*!"

Dylan lay limply in the mud of the pond shore, legs still in the water, too done in to laugh.

118

MOST people would have had difficulty being furious at someone while simultaneously giving the target of their fury a bath, but Chris managed to pull it off.

"—damn stubborn fool, always wantin' to be a fucking *hero*, not listening to anyone, pretendin' he's fucking immortal—" Chris had been going on like that for quite some time. Dylan's eyes were closed, his head pillowed by a folded towel Chris had placed on the bathtub rim. He couldn't possibly move a muscle, but fortunately he didn't have to. As harsh as Chris's words were, his movements were very gentle as he ran a washcloth over Dylan's sore chest.

Dylan was on his second round of bathwater, the first one having gone all brown and green from the pond muck that had accumulated on his hair and body. Chris had been a mess too, especially since he'd had to pretty much drag Dylan up the slope and into the house, but he'd taken a quick shower while Dylan began to soak. Now they were both naked and clean, and Dylan was mostly asleep.

"I want to look in the bag," he said. A huge yawn almost swallowed his words.

"Tomorrow."

"But—"

"If there's anything useful in that mess, it'll still be there tomorrow. You ain't doing nothin' today but eating some dinner and going to sleep."

"But what if the ghost—"

"If that ghost lays one spectral finger on the bag you almost died fetching, I'll tear the fucking haunt apart myself."

Dylan smiled lazily at the image Chris's words conjured. He didn't think Chris could actually do anything to the ghost, but Chris would sure as hell try. "Can I have dinner in bed?" Dylan asked. "Just cereal or something. Too tired to be hungry."

"Must be a sign of the apocalypse if you're not hungry."

"Hah."

Dylan didn't mind staying in the tub as the water cooled and he became all wrinkly, but eventually Chris fished him out. Dylan stumbled his way to the bed—which smelled deliciously like Chris—and collapsed onto the cool sheets.

"I'll be back soon," Chris said. He looked a little worried, as if Dylan might hop out of bed and disappear while he was gone.

But there was no chance of that. Dylan could barely hold his eyelids open. "'Kay."

He expected to fall asleep immediately, and in fact he did begin to drift. But he was still more or less conscious when he felt another presence in the room. He peeled his eyes open and wasn't especially surprised to find the ghost bobbing at the end of the bed like seaweed bobbing in gentle waves.

"Go away." Dylan didn't have the strength to make himself sound convincing, and of course the ghost ignored him. He still couldn't make out its features, which was a little frustrating. Especially since something about the ghost was niggling at him, like something he should be noticing but wasn't. It was a little like having a word on the tip of his tongue.

The ghost came a few inches closer, until it was right next to the footboard. Dylan wondered whether it could just sort of float through the wood and the mattress. Maybe it could just sort of float through *him*, which was an extremely unsettling thought.

"You're not going to accomplish anything like this," he told it. "You're already dead and I can't change that. Do you want me to apologize? Fine. I'm sorry I killed you. Now can you just *please* give up your energy to the great beyond? Maybe you'll come back as something really cool."

But instead of going away, the ghost became agitated. It shivered and flickered, and Dylan was almost positive that it made a sound like a word, but he couldn't understand it. With a bright flash that made him blink, it disappeared.

Chris entered the room a moment later carrying a tray laden with plates. The food smelled wonderful, even though Dylan wasn't hungry.

"Talkin' to yourself?" Chris asked, setting the tray on the dresser.

"No. Ghost."

"Ah. Had a nice chat, then?"

"I never did like having a roommate," Dylan said and caught Chris's flinch. "Except you," Dylan added softly.

Chris fussed with the food, pretending he hadn't heard. Of course, the truth was that Chris wasn't officially living with Dylan. He kept a toothbrush in Dylan's bathroom, and a comb, but not a razor; all of his clothing remained in his own house. He slept in Dylan's bed every night, cooked in Dylan's kitchen, but still referred to the big house as Dylan's. And although Chris sometimes made suggestions about renovations, Dylan made all the decisions.

It was stupid for Chris to keep his stuff in that crappy shack next door when Dylan had so much room. Hell, Dylan would be thrilled to build some shelves for Chris's books, and he'd happily help lug Chris's TV over. But actually and officially moving in together—that was a really big step. And even though Dylan knew in his heart that nothing could ever shake his love for this remarkable man and that he would never want any other partner, he hadn't yet asked Chris to move in. Chris had avoided the subject too. Quite possibly Chris wanted to keep his independence. After all, he'd been pretty much on his own for most of his life. Maybe he really wasn't ready to… merge.

Chris brought over a plate, some silverware, and a paper napkin. He plopped everything on Dylan's lap. "Ain't gonna spoon it in for you. You gotta do that yourself." He went back to fetch his own food before sitting beside Dylan.

"What is this?" Dylan asked, poking experimentally with his fork. He could identify potatoes and some kind of cheese, plus some green lumps he assumed were vegetables and some brown ones that were probably meat.

"Eat it 'n find out."

So Dylan took a big bite. He chewed a few times and then blinked at Chris. "Liver?"

Chris waved his fork in Dylan's direction. "Don't go tellin' me you hate the stuff. You eat raw bunnies. You can sure as hell choke down a little beef liver."

"The *wolf* eats raw bunnies."

"Ain't the wolf you? 'Cause I see you in his eyes. An' I see him in yours."

Dylan paused before replying. "I don't know. It's... hard to explain. It's kind of like when you get really, really drunk and you do all these things you'd never do when you're sober, and then later you can hardly remember them. Kind of." He took another bite. "Anyway, the food is really good. I was just surprised. Where'd you get beef liver, anyway?"

"Your freezer. Bought it a while ago. Figured all that iron and vitamins and shit might help you recover."

"Well, it's tasty."

"I used to make this all the time—fry up a bunch of potatoes and whatever else was handy. Even Gramps used to tell me it was good."

By the time Dylan cleared his plate and drank a glass of water, the last of his strength was gone. He barely noticed when Chris took the dishes away, and he was sound asleep long before Chris returned.

CHAPTER 13

A LOT of very strange and unbelievable things had happened to Dylan over the past few years. But sometimes he thought the most unbelievable of all was waking up next to a beautiful man—often hogging the covers—who then woke up too and gave him a broad, delighted smile. After years of loneliness, they were both still surprised to have found one another.

"Well rested?" asked Chris in a raspy early-morning voice.

"Yep."

"Sore?"

Dylan twitched a few muscles. "Nope." That was one of the perks of being a werewolf: superfast healing.

Chris's grin grew lecherous. "Good." And he reached over to stroke Dylan's morning wood.

Which felt really, really nice. But Dylan grabbed his wrist anyway. "The ghost," he stage-whispered.

"Fuck the ghost. No—fuck me instead." Chris slithered beneath the blankets and began to tease Dylan with his tongue and fingertips.

Dylan looked around furtively before pulling the covers over his head.

Unlike Dylan's first affair in college, he and Chris didn't have to leave their jeans on, scrunched down to their thighs, their shirts rucked up around their necks. They didn't have to muffle the sounds they made or seek out secluded locations. They wouldn't be interrupted by his mother. But it was still sort of exciting to hide under the blankets, to shush each other and then dissolve into laughter, to grope like a pair of desperate teenagers. Besides, with the absence of vision, other senses became more important: the heady odors of Chris and clean sweat and sex, the salty-slick taste of Chris on his tongue, the slightly rough drag of Chris's calloused fingertips along the insides of Dylan's thighs.

They didn't poke their heads out of the covers until they were both limp and breathless. Chris turned to look at Dylan. He licked his lips. "Werewolf. It's what's for breakfast."

Dylan poked him. Hard.

Chris laughed and scrambled out of bed, out of reach. He looked a little wild and thoroughly debauched. "What's the plan for today, boss?"

"Boss? Since when did you ever do what I told you?"

"Listened to you pretty good the other day when you ordered me to fuck you."

This time Dylan threw a pillow at him.

Chris hopped nimbly to the side and the pillow missed. "Wanna finish up the spare room?"

"No. I need to look at that damn saddlebag. But I think I should do some real work first. Stender's going to expect some progress soon." He didn't add that if the saddlebag was useful at all, the contents were probably going to distract him for a while.

"If you want, I can finish up the room while you work on your architect shit. There's not much to do—reinstall the molding, clean up a little...."

"Paint over those fingerprints again."

"I can manage that."

Dylan showered and dressed, then ate toast and the mostly raw bacon Chris had warmed in a pan. Chris went next door to change clothes, and Dylan booted up his laptop. While he worked, if he listened carefully, he could hear Chris moving around upstairs, pounding nails and generally sounding busy. Only recently had Dylan learned how pleasant that kind of companionship was.

Dylan was able to do quite a bit of research on the building he'd be helping with, and he made notes on ideas for converting it. A series of comfortable lounging areas would be useful—some as social areas, others more quiet. Students could plug in their computers, tablets, and phones and relax while they drank coffee and chatted or while they studied. In fact, he was going to suggest including space for a café on the ground floor. Some green space on the rooftop would be an asset. He would have to look into what kind of weight the roof could bear, but he was willing to bet they could plant some lush perennials and smaller trees up there. Rooftop plantings would help keep heating and cooling costs down and reduce water runoff, as well as provide a bit of an oasis. Maybe they could even stick a greenhouse up there for the botany classes or to grow some organic food for the café.

He was studying photos of the building's northern exposure, wondering whether the windows were big enough to convert part of the third floor into art studio space, when something upstairs crashed. It sounded suspiciously like broken glass.

"Chris?" Dylan shouted. "You all right?" He ran to the hallway.

Chris came trotting to the top of the stairs. "I'm fine. Window's toast, though."

"What happened?"

"Goddamn ghost tossed my hammer right through the glass. I like that hammer. It better not be wrecked."

"Was… was it aiming at you?"

Chris shook his head. "No. I was all the way across the room, peeling the painter's tape away from the doorframe."

Dylan wasn't sure whether to be frightened or reassured. "I think I better take a look in that bag."

It took him a few minutes to shut down the computer, and in the meantime Chris fetched his hammer from the soft ground beneath the broken window. "Hammer ain't broke," he announced when he returned indoors. "But you got a mess to clean up out there. Don't want you cutting a paw on all that glass."

"Wouldn't it be great if ghosts cleaned things up instead of spying on people and destroying things?"

Chris snorted. "Only you would want a housecleaner spook."

Apparently, Chris had left the saddlebag in the basement the previous night. Dylan decided he didn't want the slimy thing all over his kitchen or living room anyway, so he tromped down the slightly creaky steps with Chris right behind him. It was a pretty nice basement, actually, well waterproofed and with several small windows for natural light. The walls had been plastered at some point and were painted a soft gray. One small part of the basement had been partitioned off long ago for storage of canned goods, and a half bath was plumbed in but not finished. Most of the space was currently taken up by the furniture Dylan was storing for Kay and Rick, plus a few boxes of his own stuff that he'd never bothered to unpack. He also had a washer and a dryer down there, although he was thinking he might install small ones in his bedroom closet when he remodeled that room. A lot less stair navigation on laundry day.

A wooden table was shoved against one wall. It had been Dylan's kitchen table in the old house but didn't suit the current one. Nowadays, he and Chris ate off upscale reclaimed barn wood. Chris liked to tell Dylan what a dope he was for spending a small fortune on that artisanal table when he had a small barn of his own, just a few yards out the back door. In any case, the basement table made a good place to store tools and supplies for the current project in progress, and it was there that Chris had spread a plastic tarp and dumped the retrieved bag. A little muddy pond water pooled on the tarp.

"That prob'ly used to be some decent leather," Chris said, pointing at the still-damp mess.

"Oh, shit! I lost your knife, didn't I?"

"No big deal. I got another. I sure ain't gonna let you dive down in that pond to find it."

126

That was good, because Dylan didn't want a repeat of the previous day. "That water's really deep. It's kind of weird."

Chris grinned. "I'm learnin' that lots of things are weird when you're around."

Dylan poked hesitantly at the bag. It was black leather, with a row of decorative metal studs around the edges and a flap with two large buckles. He tried to unfasten them, but the leather was twisted and the metal warped, so he ended up using a pair of shears to cut the straps.

Most of what was inside the bag, exposed to pond water for a few weeks, was soggy and ruined. Dylan found some wadded fabric—it looked like maybe a long-sleeved shirt and jeans—slimy with mud, a silted-up and certainly nonfunctional MP3 player, and a pair of tennis shoes that had gone greenish. There was a hunting knife in a scabbard and a metal cookie tin that proved to contain a lighter and a little bit of pot.

"Andy was a stoner," Chris said. "Unless it was medicinal."

No wallet, to Dylan's disappointment. There was, however, a red vinyl bag. He unzipped it and whooped happily at what was inside: registration and license papers.

"I guess it makes sense," he said. "Even Andy was bright enough to have a waterproof container for the important stuff. We are in Oregon, after all."

"So what do they say?" Chris pushed close and tried to see around Dylan's shoulder.

The papers were well worn. Probably Andy hadn't bothered to update them in a long time. Dylan unfolded them very carefully.

The bike was registered to someone named Andrew T. Milligan. "Andrew," Dylan said softly. "It never even occurred to me that he was probably an Andrew. I wonder what the T stands for." There was an address too.

Chris snorted. "Your werewolf pal was from Sherwood? Did he hang out with Little Red Riding Hood and her brother Robin?"

Sometimes Chris's sense of humor was a little grating. Dylan decided to ignore the comment. "It's possible that it's been years since he lived there. When I met him, I kind of had the impression that he was...."

"Free as the wind?"

"Well, homeless. But yeah, in a carefree, rebellious sort of way."

They both stared at the papers as if the secrets of the universe—or at least the secrets of ghost exorcism—might be revealed if they looked hard enough. But the heavens didn't open up, and in the end, all Dylan gained from his aquatic adventure was Andy's full name and a location where he had possibly resided at some point in the past.

"Our private-eye skills suck," Chris concluded. "How come with all that fancy education, you never learned to hack into secret government databases or reprogram spy satellites?"

"I could probably track someone by smell, but only if the trail was recent."

Chris patted Dylan's butt. "Not real useful this time, but good to know, Fido."

Dylan copied the address from the paper into the notes app on his phone. Then he folded the papers and slid them back into the vinyl bag. He wasn't sure what to do with Andy's things. Just tossing them in the trash seemed wrong, somehow, but he sure as hell wasn't going to fling them back into the pond. After a few minutes of thought, he decided that for now, he'd just leave everything on the table in the basement. Maybe later he'd bury them beside Andy's grave.

"I'm going to go there today," he announced. "Now."

"Fine. Let's go."

"Chris, you don't have to—"

"If you think I'm gonna let you go alone, you're a lot stupider'n I thought." Chris had crossed his arms and set his mouth in a hard, stubborn line. It was very clear that arguing with him was only going to make him angry and delay Dylan's departure.

"Let's find something to patch the window and then we can go. We might as well return the sander and get some new glass while we're out. And we can stop for some lunch. We can make an excursion of it."

"I got a big plastic tarp we can use on the window if you want."

Dylan smiled at him. "Perfect."

They went back up the stairs. Chris trotted over to his house for the tarp, while Dylan went up to the spare room to fetch the sander. He was going to need it for the master bedroom too but wasn't planning to start that project for a while. Even if he could get the haunt problem settled, he was going to be busy for a while with the project for work.

The floor looked good, though. In fact, the entire room looked good. Chris had replaced the trim and cleaned up nearly all the tape and other debris. Aside from reglazing the window, all that was needed now was to install a new overhead light fixture—already purchased—and hang some kind of window covering. And find a way to cover those fucking fingerprints.

He walked to the gaping window and looked out at the poplar trees. He smiled as he caught a glimpse of Chris exiting the back of his house, walking across his crappy deck with a large sheet of folded blue plastic in his arms. Dylan remembered the very first time he had seen Chris while standing in this exact spot. Chris had wandered outside— wearing nothing but a T-shirt—to take a leak off the edge of his deck.

Now, Chris waved up at him after he passed through the gap in the line of trees. "Spyin' on me again?" he called.

"Just kind of hoping you might have your pants off again."

"Could be arranged. If you weren't insisting on going off and— Holy shit!" Chris came to an abrupt halt underneath the window and looked down at the grass.

Dylan craned out the window to try to see what Chris was looking at. "What? What is it?"

"The glass." Chris looked up at him, a bemused expression on his face. "All that broken glass has been gathered up in one big pile."

"But… how?"

"Had to be your ghost."

"But…." Dylan shook his head. He didn't understand this at all. Rather than continue speculating via a shouted conversation, he motioned Chris to hurry inside. A minute or so later, Chris jogged into the room.

Chris helped Dylan measure the window opening, and they taped the tarp in place. The light shining through the blue plastic gave the room a weird underwater look that reminded Dylan uncomfortably of his time in the pond. "Let's go before it gets too late," he said gruffly.

They were several miles away, rumbling down the state highway in Dylan's truck with Dylan behind the wheel, when Chris broke the silence. "You said you wanted your ghost to do maid service."

"It doesn't make any sense. Why would it clean up the glass? Do you think it's… I don't know… stockpiling it to use as a weapon?"

"That seems pretty advanced for a leftover spurt of energy. Not real smart, either. There's lots of shit much handier for it to use against us."

"I wonder if Mrs. Phillips would know what is going on."

"Wanna ask her? We could stop by her place."

Dylan shook his head. "Not today. Let's get this other stuff done."

"Starting with lunch."

CHAPTER 14

AT CHRIS'S insistence, they had burgers for lunch. Good ones, with decent meat and cheese, and with raspberry shakes to chase them down. Chris liked to watch Dylan eat because the guy did it with such enthusiasm, and also because the activity sent Chris's brain to pleasant memories of all the other things Dylan could do with that mouth. Maybe Dylan felt the same way, because when Chris licked the salt from the french fries off two of his fingers, Dylan groaned.

They returned the drum sander, which was way less fun, then picked up the new panes of glass and set them carefully in the truck bed. "Take the bumps easy," Chris warned.

"I will. I assume you know how to install these? I've never done that before."

"Yep. Even got the tools."

"You are a man of many skills."

Chris waggled his eyebrows happily. "Don't I know it."

Sherwood was a pretty long haul from the glass place, most of it along freeways where the traffic crawled. Chris hated being stuck among other vehicles like that—it made him feel claustrophobic. As Dylan liked to remind him, there were plenty of downsides to living in the boonies, but traffic wasn't one of them. Chris could stand smack dab in the middle of the county road that passed near his house, and not see a car go by for hours. The only time he had minded that was when he was a kid and trying to hitch a ride. Sometimes he ended up walking for miles or just standing there and waiting, usually getting soaked by rain in the process.

"God, I don't miss this," Dylan said, cutting into his thoughts.

"Don't wish you were still commutin'?"

"Nope. Drive-through was cool—but your breakfasts are much better than that anyway."

Chris turned his head away to hide a smile. Not just over the compliment, because he knew Dylan appreciated his cooking, but also over the reminder that Dylan wasn't miserable out in the sticks. Dylan had been saying for months that he intended to stay in his farmhouse and wasn't going to throw in the trowel and run back to the 'burbs. Chris was finally starting to believe him.

Chris used Dylan's phone to navigate them to the right address in Sherwood. The town had once been almost as rural as their own neighborhood, but over the years the suburbs had swallowed it. Nowadays most of the residents worked in the city or in some of the nearby high-tech companies. The street they were aiming for—Saturn Way—was in one of those subdivisions where all the houses looked the same and where the street names all followed an outer space theme.

"How do these folks find their way home every day?" he wondered out loud. "I'd prob'ly always be walkin' into the wrong house."

"The architecture doesn't show much imagination, does it? But most people can't afford to have a custom-built home."

"Most people prob'ly like a house just like everyone else's, and the same car, and the same Olive Garden or Applebee's for dinner. Then they watch the same stupid TV shows or, if they think they're smart, read the same books that someone told them were best sellers, and when they get up the next mornin', they all dress the same too."

Dylan stopped at an intersection and gave Chris a long look. "Not you. You are original. Unique."

"That good or bad?"

"Oh definitely good. Very, very good. I'd never go back to an off-the-rack lover again."

"Naw, you prob'ly ordered your lays from the Williams-Sonoma catalog."

"Well, I'm done shopping now."

Chris knew he shouldn't need all these small reassurances, and possibly Dylan was growing tired of giving them, but Chris liked hearing them anyway.

Dylan brought the truck to a stop in front of a beige two-story house with a double garage. A brown Chevy Malibu with a Jesus fish emblem was parked in the slightly weedy driveway, a stuffed animal of some kind perched in the rear window.

Dylan cut the engine but didn't get out of the truck. He sat there silently for several long minutes, staring at his lap, until Chris couldn't stand it any longer. "What're you gonna say?"

"I don't have the slightest idea." With a sigh, Dylan slipped the keys out of the ignition and opened his door.

Chris was right beside him as they walked up to the house and onto a small porch—a pathetic miniature of the broad porch that graced the front of Dylan's house. They passed a decorative flag—a drawing of a lighthouse and the words *God is our Light*—stuck in the ground beside the porch. An angel wind chime hung nearby, silent due to the lack of a breeze.

"Can you smell… anything?" Chris whispered.

"Somebody's cat's been pissing near the front door. That's all." Dylan rang the bell.

They didn't have to wait long before the door opened. The woman standing there was maybe sixty. She was on the tall side and fairly round, and she wore yellow sweatpants and a matching sweatshirt emblazoned with purplish flowers. Her gray hair was done up in careful curls.

"Yes?" she said, giving them both a cautious look.

Dylan took a tiny step forward. "Um, hi. I'm… my name's Dylan, and this is Chris."

"I give money to my *own* church and I don't want to buy any magazines or change to satellite TV." She looked as if she were about to slam the door in Dylan's face.

"Oh, we're not…. That's not why we're here. I'm, um, actually looking for someone. Sort of… an old acquaintance, I guess. I think he used to live here. Andy Milligan?"

Her expression went from distrustful to hostile all at once. "You're one of *them*, aren't you?" she spat.

Dylan blinked at her. "Them?"

"I can tell from the way you talk, the look on your face…. I won't have filth like you near my house!"

"But—"

"Go away or I'll call the police and they'll arrest you for trespassing. I will!" This time she did slam the door. Chris could hear the locks engage.

Dylan just stood there until Chris took his wrist and began to tow him away. "You're not gonna get any help from that old witch. C'mon."

Dylan put up enough resistance to make their trip back to the truck a slow one. They were almost there when someone called out "Hey! Wait!" and another woman came running around from the side of the house. She bore a considerable resemblance to the other woman and wore a similar outfit, but this lady was slightly thinner and at least twenty years younger. The daughter, no doubt.

Dylan and Chris paused alongside the truck and waited for her to catch up to them. "Are you friends of Andy's?" she asked breathlessly.

The men exchanged looks and Chris decided to let Dylan handle this one. "Uh, we… we knew him," Dylan said, then winced slightly at his use of the past tense.

Fortunately, the woman didn't seem to notice. "I'm Tammy. His sister. And I'm sorry Mom was kind of rude. She… feels pretty strongly about this stuff." She leaned in a little closer and dropped her voice. "Is Mom right? Are you guys... like him?"

After another quick glance at Chris, Dylan twitched his shoulder. "I'm not sure what you mean."

"Do you... you know." She flapped her hands and looked very uncomfortable. "Do you change?"

"I do," Dylan answered after a brief pause.

"Oh. You too?" She directed this question at Chris.

He shook his head, but not before Dylan moved slightly between them in an instinctive protective gesture that was probably unnecessary, but which made Chris's heart feel light anyway.

Tammy looked a little confused. "I thought you'd only hang out with your own kind. That's what Mom said. And she said what happened to Andy... being cursed like that... it was God punishing him for being... wrong."

"Wrong?" Dylan asked.

"You know. Homosexual."

"There's nothing wrong with being gay."

She took another good look at the two of them, and her face reflected comprehension. She took a step backward. "It's a sin. The Bible says so."

"Sure. The same part of the Bible that says eating bacon cheeseburgers is a sin. Am I going to hell for that too?" Although Dylan's words were confrontational, his tone was resigned, a little sad.

"That's not the same thing. It's not. Homosexuality is *wrong*. Mom told Andy none of us would have anything to do with him unless he asked Jesus for forgiveness. There are people you can talk to, did you know? Counselors and ministries. They can help you make the right choice. The godly choice."

Dylan put a strong arm around Chris's shoulders, drawing him close. "Being gay is not a choice. But even if it was, I'd choose Chris because *he*'s the right choice. *He* is my salvation."

Fuck. If there was one thing Chris was definitely not going to do, it was burst into tears in front of this woman. He hugged Dylan back though, very tightly.

Tammy was frowning. "It's not natural. It's why God cursed you too."

"I'm sorry you feel this way. It must have torn Andy apart to be rejected by his family."

True regret flashed across her face but was quickly replaced with a look of resolve. "We had to do it. We prayed over it for a long time. It's Andy's own fault for acting in… perverted ways. If he'd only asked the Lord for help instead, the Lord would have led him to the right path and that man wouldn't have bit him. Wouldn't have changed him into a beast."

"What man?" Dylan asked sharply.

For a minute Chris was certain she wasn't going to reply. But then her shoulders sagged a little. "Are you really his friend?"

"We're trying to help him," Dylan replied. Which wasn't a lie, really.

"He said the man who did it to him was dead. But there were, there were these people Andy was staying with. In Gresham. It was a long time ago. But he said maybe if we changed our mind someday…. We're not going to change our mind. He's not my brother anymore."

Dylan's voice was a little uneven when he responded. "Do you have the address in Gresham?"

She nodded and pulled a miniature address book from her pocket. The book had an image of a glowing cross on the cover. She opened the book, ripped out a page, and held it out to Dylan. "Here. If you see him, you tell him I'm trying real hard to forgive him. I'm still praying for him."

Dylan took the paper without saying a word. Then he turned, steering Chris to the truck. Tammy was still standing on the curb and watching as they pulled away.

DYLAN didn't drive them to Gresham.

In fact, for over an hour, he drove them nowhere in particular, just aimless twists and circles through the 'burbs. He didn't speak and Chris didn't say anything to him, but Chris kept his hand on Dylan's thigh and sometimes gave a little squeeze.

When Dylan pulled into a strip mall, Chris thought he intended to get gas. But instead Dylan pulled the truck into an empty spot in front of a nondescript bar called Bleachers. He cut the engine.

"You want a drink?" Chris asked, puzzled.

"It's not really a sports bar. I guess it used to be, but not now. Now it's a gay bar. A really boring one, for boring men. MSNBC on the TV. Married guys who want a quickie before they go home to their wives, or guys who pry themselves away from their computers just long enough for a bathroom blowjob."

"Don't really sound like my kinda place."

"Used to be mine, I guess. Ery teased me about it, but I felt comfortable here. Like I wasn't out of my league."

"Dyl, you—"

"It's where I met Andy."

"Oh."

Dylan's long fingers were wrapped tightly around the steering wheel; his knuckles were white. Chris was a little worried he might crack the plastic—Dylan was *strong* when he got caught up in emotions—but he didn't say anything. He also didn't remove his hand from Dylan's leg.

"He was just really hot and he picked me, and that's all I cared about. Nobody who looked as good as him had ever given me a second glance. So we went to my place and we fucked for a couple of days. And then he… well, you know what he did."

"Bastard!" Chris spat.

Dylan twisted around to look at him. "But maybe he wasn't, once upon a time. Then his family rejected him, and...." With a slight moaning sound, Dylan rubbed his face. Then he let his hands drop again. "I can't imagine what my life would have been like without Rick and Kay, without you. I'd be so.... I'm not a guy who needs a ton of friends, but I need someone. Everyone needs someone, or else you're just, just...."

"I *know*," said Chris, because he did. It wasn't a wish for self-destruction that had sent him to men's rooms at roadhouses and rest stops. As often as he'd told himself that he was strong, that he did just fine on his own, he'd still spent years feeling as if his soul was slowly crumbling. Until he met Dylan.

Dylan cradled a hand around Chris's cheek. "I had a little bit of family, a couple of friends. Even my parents, they weren't exactly thrilled when I came out, but they didn't disown me. They still let me stay in their house, and when they died, I still got their insurance money and stuff. And you and I found each other. Andy never had any of that. He almost ruined me and he murdered people, but maybe... maybe before that he was just lonely."

Embracing in the front seat of a pickup truck was awkward, but they managed it. Dylan felt warm and very solid in Chris's arms.

Eventually they pulled apart. "Do you want to go in?" Chris asked.

"No."

Dylan started the engine again. He got gas at the station near the corner and then pulled back out into traffic. But he didn't go far; after only a few blocks, he pulled into the parking lot of a larger shopping center, this one with an upscale grocery store, several boutiques, and some restaurants. There was also a big coffee place, and Dylan parked next to that. "Do you mind? I could go for some joe or something."

"No problem."

The coffee place was surprisingly crowded for a weekday afternoon. Dylan fit right in with the other customers, but Chris felt rustic and a little self-conscious. At least he managed to order a coffee without looking like an idiot. Dylan got something requiring use of a blender, plus a ridiculously oversized blueberry muffin.

One whole wall of the place consisted of glass doors that had been rolled up. Mothers sat at some of the tables outside, chatting with one another while their toddlers played in the fountain nearby. Dylan and Chris chose a table in a relatively quiet corner.

Chris didn't know what was going on in his boyfriend's head as he played with his phone, but he was sure it was a lot. Chris's phone was more bare-bones—that's all he needed—so instead he read a newspaper and people-watched. Everyone else seemed so content, so normal. He wondered what secrets they were hiding. Maybe some of them were werewolves too, or haunted by the ghosts of ex-lovers. Maybe some of them had been abandoned by their parents or raised by drug addicts. Certainly some of them must have done things they deeply regretted and must have had periods when they felt desperate and alone.

Dylan and Chris spent a long time at the coffee place. They didn't speak much, but sometimes Dylan would look over at Chris and give him a slow smile, and Chris would smile back.

The mothers and kids had all cleared out when Dylan stood and stretched. "Do you mind making another stop?"

"Gresham?"

"No. Not today."

"Okay. Sure."

They were nearly at their destination before Chris realized where they were going. "Rick and Kay's house?"

"Yeah. They should be home from work by now. Do you mind?"

"Nope."

Chris was dying to know Dylan's intentions but kept his gob shut. Clearly, Dylan was in a reticent mood, and Chris didn't want to nag him.

Kay looked shocked when she answered the door and found the two of them. "Is something wrong?" she asked anxiously, ushering them inside. Rick came trotting into the living room from the kitchen, still wearing his work shirt and tie.

"Nothing's wrong," Dylan said. "I just wanted— Is this a bad time?"

Kay answered. "No. We were just arguing about what to have for dinner. Everything Rick wants sounds gross to me. You guys want to join us?"

"I don't want to be a pain."

Rick grinned. "You, little brother, are always a pain. Now Chris, on the other hand—he's a delight."

Dylan flipped him the finger.

"Gonna have to watch that stuff pretty soon, Dyldo. Don't want to set a bad example for junior."

"I'm sure you'll set plenty of bad examples yourself, Dickhead."

Kay rolled her eyes. "Boys. Pregnant lady here and I'm starving. What's it going to be?"

After consulting with Chris, Dylan accepted the dinner invitation. They ended up ordering pizza—half meat-lover's and half chicken and diced tomato. The four of them chatted about babies and home improvement while they waited for the delivery, and then sat around the kitchen table to eat.

Chris hadn't spent a lot of time with Dylan's clan, but he liked them. He loved the way they supported Dylan, no matter his sexual orientation or species, and he appreciated the way they'd so easily accepted Chris into their lives. Neither Rick nor Kay had ever hinted that they disapproved of Chris in any way or thought him beneath Dylan. In fact, not long after Andy's death, when Chris was still nursing Dylan back to health and was still furious enough with Dylan that he wanted to tear him apart himself, Rick had called and thanked him for being there for his brother. And days after Dylan and Chris had reconciled, Kay had stopped by the farm—supposedly to drop off

140

another load of her grandmother's things for storage. She'd managed to pull Chris aside while Dylan was busy, and she let him know how happy she was to have him back in Dylan's life.

Now, they chewed on slices of pizza. Dylan and Rick drank beer, Chris designated himself driver and had water, and Kay downed a glass of some of some kind of horrible protein shake concoction that was supposed to be healthy. While they ate, they joked and teased easily. It was fun to watch Dylan regress a little as he interacted with his big brother, so that they were like a pair of overgrown teenagers. Then Kay got Chris talking about cars, because she was considering trading in her sporty little Toyota for a minivan or SUV, and Rick found out that Chris was a Seahawks fan and they began a long discussion of running backs and wide receivers, which left Dylan and Kay yawning and miming suicide.

After dinner they adjourned to the living room. Dylan sat next to Chris on the couch, fidgeting nervously.

"Is this about the motorcycle?" Rick asked. "You going to tell us why you needed it?"

"It's… it has to do with a ghost."

"A *ghost*?"

Dylan sighed and looked down at his lap. "Yeah. But that's actually not why we came by. Chris and I were just… well, it's a long story. I found out some stuff about Andy. I guess maybe I suspected some of it, but for some reason it really hit home today. Anyway, I really wanted to let you guys know how much I appreciate you. How glad I am that you're always there for me."

"Oh my God," Rick said, stricken. "You're dying."

Dylan looked up at him. "Not that I plan on."

"Then why are you telling us this?"

Despite the seriousness of the situation, Chris snickered. He loved Dylan with all his heart, but his boy wasn't exactly a world champion at sharing his feelings. Dylan elbowed him ungently.

"I just thought it was important to let you know. You guys are really great."

Chris decided he might as well chime in. "Yeah, you really are. Thanks for… bein' so welcoming. I know I prob'ly ain't your dream in-law."

Rick wasn't much better than his brother at expressing himself. He sat in his armchair, looking pleased and uncomfortable. But Kay leapt out of her seat and enveloped Dylan and Chris in a fierce pizza-scented hug. She was crying. "Stupid hormones," she sobbed when she pulled away, smiling and wiping her eyes.

CHAPTER 15

DYLAN had downed a few beers at Kay and Rick's, so when they left, Chris took the wheel. Darkness had fallen, and it was one of those lovely summer nights where the heat lingers enough to be comfortable and everyone wants to stay out late on porches and in sidewalk cafés. When Dylan was a kid, he'd loved nights like this—it had felt then as if the responsibilities of school were a million years away, and his parents would allow him and Rick to ride their bicycles around the neighborhood until very late, usually while wearing nothing but cutoffs and flip-flops. Dylan could remember clearly the way his chest would be sticky from drippy popsicles, and how his arms and legs would end up covered in mosquito bites. Hell, he could still remember exactly how calamine lotion smelled. He always had scabs on elbows and knees and one of the stupid haircuts his mother gave him at home. Rick would win all their bike races, but Dylan wouldn't care because he'd be imagining that his bicycle was flying, like the one Elliott rode in *E.T.*

"You okay?" Chris asked quietly.

"Yeah. It's been... there's been a lot going on these last few days."

"Least you can't complain you're bored."

Dylan chuckled. "I can't remember the last time I was bored."

A few miles rolled by. It was late enough that there wasn't much traffic, which was nice. Dylan was yearning a little for the peace and quiet of his farm. He watched Chris's strong hands as they turned the steering wheel. He liked those hands: the well-earned calluses, the fingernails that remained grubby no matter the amount of washing, the broad finger pads that could do delicate work or heavy construction with equal ease—and that could make Dylan shiver and moan.

"You know, Kay and Rick really like you. They're not pretending just to keep the peace."

Chris glanced quickly at him and then back at the road. "Yeah."

"Matty fell for you right away, I could tell, and I think Ery likes you too."

"Your point?"

"I'm not the only one who can see what a great guy you are. It's pretty clear to just about everyone, as soon as they get to know you."

Chris snorted derisively but couldn't hide the pleasure on his face. "You want to go to Gresham tomorrow?"

"No. I'm going to crack down and get a bunch of work done. I have another meeting with Stender on Friday. I want to have a lot of good ideas for him by then."

"You will," Chris said confidently. "But I'm gonna need some help if you want that window fixed tomorrow."

"Okay." That would be a nice excuse to take a break from his laptop. Dylan loved working with Chris, especially when Chris knew what he was doing and Dylan was a novice. Chris was a natural teacher—although he didn't seem to realize that—and was justifiably confident in his construction and repair skills. Which raised a question in Dylan's mind, all of a sudden. "Chris? How did you learn to do things like repair windows? Did someone teach you?"

"Gramps was good at fixin' things. When I was a kid, he didn't mind if I watched him. Sometimes he even let me help. Later on I had to learn things pretty quick if I wanted to keep food on the table. I'd see that someone's roof needed work, say, and I'd tell 'em I could fix it for 'em real cheap. And then I'd figure out what to do." He grinned. "I had this set of books on home construction and repair. Got 'em for a couple of bucks at a yard sale. They were old, but a lot of that stuff hasn't changed much over the years."

Dylan was impressed. It had taken him four years of college, months and months of internship, concerted study for the licensing exam, and a lot of on-the-job training before he was capable of doing his work. And even now, even after his recent success, he was still somewhat insecure about his skills.

He was so lost in thought that it took him a while to notice that Chris had turned off the highway. They were now bumping slowly and carefully down a dark and unfamiliar road, where trees loomed closely on either side and no other vehicles were visible. "Where are we going?" Dylan asked.

Chris just gave him an enigmatic smile. Dylan probably deserved it, after the way he'd dragged Chris around the suburbs earlier in the day.

They drove farther into the forest. A part of Dylan's mind—currently a deeply buried part, but it was still aware—noted that this would be a good place to run, and that there was likely ample game in the area. That probably was not why Chris was bringing them here, and it was the wrong time of the month to be thinking those thoughts, but still he couldn't help but file the information away for use later on.

The truck slowed and then came to a halt. Dylan couldn't tell whether Chris had chosen this spot for some specific reason or simply picked it at random. In any case, Chris turned off the engine and hopped out of the truck. Dylan followed him to the back, where Chris spent a few minutes digging around in the bed—carefully, due to the glass, and with some difficulty due to the lack of light. But eventually he found what he was looking for: an old blanket Dylan kept in the truck, mainly to use as extra padding for furniture and other things that might scratch or dent.

With the blanket tucked under his arm, Chris walked along the edge of the road. The scents of growing things were very strong, and Dylan could hear small creatures rustling through the leaves. Somewhere far away, an owl called.

145

"Can you see this path pretty good?" Chris asked, pointing.

It wasn't much of a path, just a narrow trail that had been cleared between the trees. Young plants grew in the middle of the trail and tree roots made it uneven. "Yes," replied Dylan. He had to admit he did enjoy his enhanced night vision.

"Then you better lead the way, 'cause I can't see a fucking thing."

"How can I lead the way if I don't know where we're going?"

"Just follow the path, genius."

The trail was only wide enough for one person, so Dylan went first, with Chris holding tightly to his shoulder. Dylan warned Chris of obstacles and held tree branches out of the way so they wouldn't whip back into Chris's face. Although Dylan still didn't know their destination, his heart was racing from excitement over the wildness of the place, over the intimacy of being alone with his lover so far from civilization.

He inhaled deeply. "A cougar has been nearby," he said in a near whisper. The smell of the big cat made his neck prickle and his jaw ache.

Chris's voice was hushed too. "Is it gonna eat us?"

"No. The scent's a couple days old."

"You are as good as a bloodhound, ain't you?"

"My senses are even sharper when I'm a wolf. You can't— I can't explain what it's like."

"Like when Dorothy lands in Oz and everything's in Technicolor?"

Dylan snorted. "Something like that."

After about a hundred yards, the trail took a fairly sharp turn to the right and began to rise up a steep hill, where dried pine needles shifted under their feet. Only a short time later, the trees abruptly stopped and the ground turned to soft, sweet-scented grass. As they reached the top of the rise, Dylan saw that they were above a rounded meadow. He could hear and smell water burbling nearby—a small spring-fed stream, probably—but he couldn't see it.

146

Chris dragged him to a stop, then stooped to spread the blanket across the grass. "Like it?"

"How'd you know about this place?"

"We're only about ten miles from home. I camped out here a few times when I was a kid. When I needed... when I wanted to get away from... whatever. Don't remember how I found it the first time."

As Dylan rotated slowly in place, taking in the surroundings, Chris kicked off his shoes and began to strip off the rest of his clothing.

"What are you doing?" Dylan asked, slightly aghast.

"Think that's pretty obvious." Now fully naked, Chris collapsed onto the blanket. He lay on his back with his hands pillowing his head, and with his legs comfortably sprawled. "Wanna join me?"

"But we're in public."

"Dude. Take a good look. You really think anyone else is gonna come strolling through?"

Dylan did take a good look, as well as a good sniff and a good listen. He didn't sense anyone human at all—except for Chris, of course. Chris, who was naked and grinning and—oh, fuck!—stroking his cock to hardness.

Suddenly, Dylan didn't really care whether anyone else was nearby. He slipped out of his sandals and peeled his own clothing away, then lay down beside Chris.

"Look up," Chris said.

"I'd rather look at you."

"Good. But look up anyway."

Dylan obediently turned his head to stare up at the sky. The moon was waning, which left the stars free to reign over the sky. They glittered like carelessly strewn jewels and made Dylan feel slightly dizzy. They were the same stars that shone over his own house, of course, but it wasn't often he bothered to notice them, even on those rare nights when the sky was clear.

"Nice," he whispered.

"That's energy too, right? Maybe some guys when they die, they get to be stars."

"You're being very poetic tonight."

"Was hoping that might get me into your pants."

Dylan turned on his side and pressed up against Chris. "I'm not wearing any pants."

"All the better to fuck you, then."

"Hey. That's my line."

Chris opened his mouth to respond, so Dylan shut him up with a kiss. God, he loved kissing Chris. He'd made out with guys a few times before—with his college chem partner, with Ery Phillips before they decided they made better friends than lovers, with a few of the men he'd hooked up with—but most of his sex partners wanted to fuck, not suck face. And even when he had kissed before, it had never been this satisfying. Chris tasted good. Always, no matter what he'd been eating, and even when he first woke up in the morning. He never grew much of a beard, so his face was never overly stubbly. He liked to take charge of kisses, thrusting his tongue into Dylan's mouth much the same way Dylan thrust his dick into Chris's body. And he made these tiny noises, little desperate whimpers that possibly nobody but a werewolf would hear, and he grabbed at Dylan's hair as if he never intended to let go.

Dylan could possibly have kissed Chris all night. But somehow Chris had managed to roll on top of him, and now, while the kissing continued, most of the activity moved southward, where hips rocked and where hands groped and stroked and squeezed.

"This was... a really... good idea," Dylan panted. And it was. Not just because it meant they could escape their ghostly voyeur, but also because something about being naked and having sex out in the middle of nowhere, out in the wild, was an enormous turn-on. He'd been learning lately to let his more feral instincts take over now and then, and not just on the night of the full moon. It felt *good*. Felt a little intoxicating, actually, but Chris's presence was just enough to remind him not to let loose too far. It was ironic, really—Dylan being tamed by someone like Chris. But then Dylan was pretty fond of irony.

Chris growled—more irony!—and slithered downward. As Dylan writhed, Chris mouthed at him, licking and nipping. When the wet trails he left evaporated, Dylan shivered. He closed his eyes and concentrated entirely on his other senses: hearing and scent and, oh God, touch. The blanket was a little scratchy, the grass beneath it springy. He gave himself up entirely to Chris and didn't try to muffle his own moans and grunts and cries.

When it all became too much, Dylan grabbed Chris's arms and rolled them over. Chris's eyes were wide open, glittering in the starlight, and his face was slightly flushed. The way his heart beat rapidly underneath Dylan made Dylan think of prey, made him want to devour Chris. And so he did: he bent so he could swallow Chris's heavy cock to the root.

"Fuck, yeah!" Chris yelled hoarsely. He clutched convulsively at Dylan's hair, tugging hard enough for a little good pain. Dylan had the feeling his partner wouldn't last long, and honestly, Dylan was very near the edge himself. Everything about the moment spoke of urgency—not out of fear or desperation, but simply out of the animal need to feel good and make the other man feel good too.

Chris bucked beneath him like a rodeo bronco. Dylan stroked himself fast and hard. His nose filled with the scent of Chris; his tongue registered Chris's salty-sweet taste.

"Gonna— Fuck, Dyl, can't— Gonna—"

Dylan only bobbed his head faster.

Chris spasmed and shouted something unintelligible; Dylan came the moment Chris shot down his throat.

And then Dylan knelt upright, threw back his head, and howled.

THEY dozed for a while, there under the stars. And then there was a good kind of silence between them as they dressed, and as Dylan led them back down the trail to the truck, and as Chris drove them the few miles home.

The porch light was on at Dylan's house and they'd left on the lights in the living room, so the house presented a warm and welcoming sight even if a ghost lurked somewhere nearby. They lingered together on the porch while Chris smoked a cigarette. He'd cut way back lately but hadn't quit altogether. Now they leaned against the railing—which needed painting—and watched the tendrils of smoke rise into the air.

"You had another long day," Chris said. "I can sleep over at my place."

"I wish you wouldn't."

Chris ducked his head but didn't quite hide his grin. "'Kay." He stepped off the porch to stub his cigarette out in the dirt, and then tossed the butt into the can he kept near the steps for that purpose. He looked a little tired as he climbed up again. It had been a long day for him too.

"Chris," Dylan began.

"Yeah?"

"I…. Nothing." It wasn't nothing. He'd almost asked Chris to just move in with him. But the words wouldn't quite come. Not because Dylan didn't want it, but because he wasn't sure how Chris would respond.

They watched moths whirl and dart around the porch light. Dylan supposed that little bulb called them the way the moon called him. He wondered whether there were other sorts of werecreatures besides wolves, and concluded that he was pretty lucky, comparatively speaking. What if he'd been turned into a wereslug instead?

"D'you still have that card?" Chris asked after a while.

"Which card?"

"The one he left here. Jimmy."

Oh. "Yes. It's in the junk drawer in the kitchen. I know you told me to get rid of it, but—"

"I'm gonna call him."

Dylan tried to keep his voice neutral. "Oh?"

"Yeah. Gonna let the fucker say his piece, I guess. Just this once."

"Why the change of heart?" Dylan asked, although he had an inkling of the answer.

"Maybe… maybe someday that Tammy chick is gonna be sorry she cut Andy off. Maybe even her mother will be. Doubt it, but you never know. But it's too late for them. They ain't never gonna be able to see him again. Never gonna be able to tell him they're sorry for treating him like shit."

Dylan settled a hand on Chris's shoulder. "You're not them. You have every right to be mad at your father and to refuse to let him back into your life."

"Yeah, I know. But I don't wanna have regrets someday. And I'm thinkin' I might regret it more if I never talked to him than if I did."

"Okay. Whatever you feel is best. And if you want—"

Crash!

The noise came from upstairs, at the back of the house. Dylan and Chris rushed through the front door, down the hall, up the stairs. The window was already broken, so Dylan wondered what the hell the ghost could have wrecked this time. The question was answered as soon as he flicked on the light: his laptop was shattered on the floor, plastic and glass and bits of metal scattered widely, as if the device had been hurled from a great height. But that wasn't what took his breath away or made Chris swear. Scrawled on the wall next to the window, written in thick black Sharpie, were two letters: F A.

CHAPTER 16

DYLAN was a lot less hysterical than Chris would have predicted. Maybe he'd overdosed on weirdness and was simply numb, or maybe he still had a few good endorphins running through his system after their al fresco fuck. Of course Dylan backed up his computer daily—he'd set it up to happen automatically, with all his files getting sent to something called a cloud—so he hadn't lost any of his work. Hell, Dylan was Mr. Safety. He probably backed everything up twice.

"Any idea what F A stands for?" Chris asked as he helped Dylan sweep up the mess.

"Not a clue. I think there was supposed to be more, though. Look." He stopped moving the broom across the floor and pointed the bristles at the wall. "There's a dot there, like maybe the ghost started writing a third letter."

"Maybe he meant to write *fuck you* but forgot how to spell."

Dylan shot him an annoyed look and returned to sweeping. "Aside from the fact that the ghost seems to be getting more demonstrative, I want to know what it has against this room. It had to carry my computer all the way up the stairs. Why not just wreck the thing downstairs?"

"And the pen. That wasn't in here either."

"And why my laptop?"

"Maybe the ghost wanted to update its Facebook status."

That time Dylan didn't even bother to glare.

After clearing away the debris, they turned off all the lights in the house and got ready for bed. By the time they hit the mattress, they were too weary to do anything but scrunch together and pull up the sheet.

"I guess I have to go computer shopping tomorrow," Dylan said, then yawned hugely. "I'll probably try to get an early start. Will you come with?"

"What about the window?"

"Let's just store the glass in the basement for now. I'm afraid if we install it, the ghost will only break it again."

Chris gave him a noisy kiss on the cheek. "'Kay. Computer shopping it is."

CHRIS dreamed of mountain lions that ate laptops and wore plastic crosses on chains around their necks. He might have been restless in his sleep, because when he woke up, Dylan had him pinned between his arms, as if he'd been trying to hold Chris still. Chris didn't really mind. He liked being held. In fact, he stayed in bed as long as he could stand it, but eventually his arms felt cramped. He managed to slither out of Dylan's grip without waking him.

Morning mist clung to the hills on the other side of the wheat field. He stood on Dylan's porch for a while, smoking and admiring the view. He loved those hills. Ever since he was a kid, he'd missed them whenever he was away for long, and his eyes seemed to feel less strained as soon as he caught sight of them again. There were times over the past years when his finances had been stretched so tight that losing the farm had been a real possibility. But he'd always found a way to squeeze himself out of debt, because losing the view of those hills would be like losing his soul. He wasn't sure he'd survive.

But he didn't feel that way about his house. As he walked over his deck and through the back door, he acknowledged that his house felt increasingly cramped and ugly. And lonely. Dylan might have a real ghost at his place, but Chris's house was haunted too, by memories. And many of them not especially good ones.

He took a shower in his mildewed plastic stall, shaved and brushed, and changed to clean clothes. More or less presentable clothes, since it seemed that another outing was in order. He'd been wanting to bring more of his stuff over to Dylan's for a while now, but he didn't want to impose. Yeah, he was pretty sure this thing he had with Dylan was for real, maybe even forever, but the possibility that it wasn't scared him half to death. Maybe he was afraid that if he carried over a couple of T-shirts and a pair or two of jeans, he'd jinx the whole thing.

He stood in his tiny living room, smiling as he remembered the first time he and Dylan had fucked. Right there, up against the ugly couch. But then his memories went farther back—much farther—and he recalled sitting on that couch when he was very small, listening to his father and his grandfather yell at one another. Either he hadn't followed the argument then or he didn't remember now what it was about, but he did know he'd been scared and he'd wanted someone to hold him and tell him everything would be all right. Nobody had.

"Don't be such a pussy," Chris muttered to himself.

He headed out of the house, and as he crossed under the poplar trees, he looked up at the square of blue plastic where a window should be. It was weird, but he wasn't exactly scared of the ghost; more like pissed off. The damn thing had gotten Dylan all worked up and was causing him to go poking his nose into Andy's past. Chris didn't care how fucked up Andy's family was—Chris was never going to forgive him for what he'd done to Dylan.

He knew Dylan wouldn't wake up for a little while yet, so he took the time to make a slightly elaborate breakfast: a concoction he'd invented himself, which was sort of a giant yeasty roll filled with crumbled sausage and caramelized chopped onion. It smelled really fucking good.

As he'd known would happen, the smell woke Dylan up, and Dylan followed his nose into the kitchen. He wore nothing but a pair of

Scooby-Doo boxers that were dorkily adorable, his morning stubble was thick, and his hair stuck up in all directions.

Without saying a word, Chris handed him the smoothie he'd just whipped up in the blender: raspberries, banana, yogurt, and a splash of OJ.

Dylan ended up with a pinkish mustache after taking his first sip. "How the hell did I ever start my mornings without you?"

"Gotta earn my keep, don't I?" Chris was only half joking. He'd been refusing pay from Dylan for quite some time now, but Dylan was paying for all their groceries, all the gas. He'd even insisted on paying Chris's electric bill, claiming that since he watched Chris's TV, he was using a good share of the power too. And yes, Dylan could afford it, with his big fat bonus and generous raise, while the only income Chris was getting was Bill Gorman's rent payments for the fields. But that didn't mean he was some kind of mooch—Chris was going to contribute whatever he could.

Dylan slurped more of his smoothie before giving Chris a fierce one-armed hug.

Chris slid a hand under Dylan's waistband for a palmful of muscular ass, and for a moment they leaned against one another, drawing a little comfort and strength. God, it felt good.

Dylan devoured breakfast while Chris ate more moderately. Then they moved the panes of glass out of the truck and carried them to the basement. Hopefully, the ghost wouldn't decide the glass was fair game. Dylan insisted on washing up the breakfast dishes, because heaven forbid there be a dirty pan on the stove for a couple of hours. Chris kept him company while he showered, shaved, and dressed.

They were almost out the back door when Chris stopped. He took a deep breath, then detoured to the one place in Dylan's kitchen where chaos reigned: the junk drawer. That was where Dylan kept papers waiting to be filed—receipts, warranties, and instruction manuals. The drawer also held bits and pieces of things that had broken and might someday be fixed, like the fancy weather gauge that was supposed to tell you the outside temperature, wind speed, and humidity. A dozen or so pens, half of which didn't work, and a couple of pencils with broken lead sat among the mess. And there was a business card.

Dylan waited silently while Chris picked up the card. It sported a tattoo-like design of a fire-breathing dragon. *Wyvern Hand-Forged Jewelry*, the card said in swirly letters. And under that, in a smaller font, *Tasha Fredericks*. There was also an e-mail address, a web page URL, and a phone number.

Before he could lose his courage, Chris marched over to Dylan and grabbed the phone from his shirt pocket. He'd left his own phone lying around somewhere, as he often did. He punched in the number from the card.

Someone picked up after only one ring, which startled him a little. "Hello?" The woman's voice was deep and scratchy, as if she'd been smoking heavily for years.

"Uh, is this Tasha?"

Big dogs were barking in the background on her end. "Yep. What can I do for you?"

"I'm, um… is Jimmy Nock there?" He wished he sounded assertive instead of scared to death.

There was a long pause, and then she said, very carefully, "Is this Chris?"

Chris had no idea who this woman was or what she was to Jimmy. It shouldn't have mattered to him at all whether she'd heard of him. But son of a bitch, it did matter. "Yeah," he answered gruffly.

"He's not here, honey. He's doing a fair for me down in Chico. But he's gonna be real glad to hear that you called. What do you want me to tell him?"

"Tell him… tell him I'm willing to listen."

"Oh, honey! I can't tell you how good that is to hear. Jimmy's gonna…." She sniffed loudly, then coughed. "Thank you so much. This is gonna mean the world to him."

They said their good-byes, and he shoved the phone into Dylan's pocket. "Let's go," Chris said, brushing past Dylan and out the door.

THEY had to go to a mall to look at computers. It was one of those huge suburban malls, full of packs of teenagers, screaming kids in strollers, and an inexplicable number of shoe stores. How many fucking shoes did people need? Chris owned three pairs—ratty old sneakers, good heavy work boots, and ancient but still pretty pristine dress shoes he'd bought for his grandfather's funeral—and that was plenty for him. Dylan, of course, had a closet full, with shiny work shoes, trendy boots, and vegan fair-trade sustainable hemp loafers and sandals—the latter group ugly as hell.

They spent a long time in the computer store, first with Dylan carefully narrowing his choices and then with him dithering over the final two options. When he started to become cranky, Chris dragged him to the food court and made him drink a really big coffee. "It's just a laptop, man." Chris said when they sat down. "You can afford a new one."

"I know. It's just… I don't know. More decisions." He laid his head down, burying his face in his crossed arms so that the rest of what he had to say was muffled. "Why can't all my problems just go away?"

"Now, where would be the fun in that?"

Dylan lifted his head a few moments later so he could sip more coffee. Chris grinned. "Kay looks great, don't she?" She wasn't showing yet, but evidently that crap about pregnant women glowing had some truth to it, because she had looked radiant. Maybe she was just thrilled to finally be expecting a kid.

"She does."

"You think she's gonna turn into one of them earth-mother types, with the organic carob everything and the Sanskrit chanting and Waldorf schools?"

"I don't know. I'm picturing her more as a soccer mom, myself. But I bet she starts wanting to redo the baby's room really soon. Don't be surprised if we get drafted into painting and building shelves. And assembling cribs. Rick sucks at anything remotely mechanical."

157

Chris nodded. He'd be happy to help. He liked feeling included.

Dylan's mood seemed to lighten as the caffeine took effect. "Rick told me they had a big fight over the baby's middle name the other day. They don't even know yet whether it's a girl or a boy, and here they are, arguing over names. Who uses middle names anyway, except parents when they're pissed off at you and newspapers when you get arrested for murder?"

"Always hated mine," Chris said.

"What is it? God, I should know your middle name by now, shouldn't I?"

"Don't know yours either."

Dylan made a face. "Buckley," he muttered.

"Buckley?"

"After William F. I told you they were really conservative. Rick's middle name is Reagan."

That made Chris laugh out loud. "No ideology for me. I'm Francis. And don't think Chrissy Francis didn't get teased for years over his girls' names."

The corners of Dylan's eyes crinkled when he smiled. "Nothing girly about you." Then he cocked his head thoughtfully. "Francis. Like Uncle Frank?"

"Dunno." Actually, Chris had never thought much about how his parents chose his name. He'd always figured it was something pretty random—a rousing game of baby-name beer pong, maybe, or the names of his mother's favorite drug suppliers.

"Huh." Dylan had long, clever fingers—artist's fingers—which right now were making neat little tears in the edges of his napkin. "You know, we've been spending all this time together, but there's lots of stuff we don't know about each other. I don't know when your birthday is, for instance."

Chris grinned at him. "September fifteenth, and I'm expectin' a really nice present. Like that router I've had my eye on for a while,

158

maybe. My favorite color's blue, I'm allergic to penicillin, I like chocolate better'n vanilla and hate lima beans, I'd rather bottom than top but don't mind switchin' now and then, I popped my cherry—with a girl—when I was fourteen years old, I ain't never been farther east than the Idaho border, and I've fallen for a goddamn werewolf who owns a haunted house." He sat back in his seat, arms crossed. "There. Now you know everythin'."

Dylan blinked a few times before a slow smile spread across his face. "November third, and for my present I want you to make that roast beef thing you did that one time, and your homemade onion bread, and that spice cake with the cream cheese frosting. And *I* seem to have fallen for a really smart guy disguised as a redneck hick." He stood. "Also, *fourteen*?"

Chris rose to his feet too. "Precocious. Her name was Crystal and she was three years older. I already knew I was a homo, but what fourteen-year-old boy's gonna pass up the chance to get laid?"

Once they returned to the computer store, it didn't take Dylan much longer to make his decision. The new laptop was thinner than the old one but had a bigger screen. He bought a new messenger bag to go with it—tempted by one that looked like an old-school Nintendo console, but instead choosing one in a more businesslike distressed brown leather.

As they were leaving the store, a pair of teens stared at them: a girl with about a million ear piercings and dyed-red hair, and a boy with eyeliner, gelled hair, and blaringly bright clothing. He reminded Chris of a younger version of Dylan's friend Ery. And because Dylan's arms were too full for him to defend himself, Chris gave his ass a really good squeeze—then laughed at the teenagers' wide eyes.

CHAPTER 17

THE address Tammy had given them was well outside of Gresham proper. It belonged to a small tumbledown house that had even less charm than Chris's shack. The house's front yard was bare and weedy except where an assortment of ancient-looking vehicles were parked, and next door was a low metal building that might once have had some industrial use but now looked to be in worse shape than the house.

"I guess not all werewolves have your knack for fabulous design," Chris commented as Dylan parked the truck.

"Guess not," Dylan sighed. His stomach felt knotted with anxiety and he just wanted to go home, but the ghost had to be dealt with. "Maybe you should stay in the truck."

"No way, José. I'm going with."

Dylan tried to look confident as he marched up the cracked sidewalk to the front door. Chris managed a pretty good swagger, but he was good at that sort of thing. There was no porch here, just a door that needed paint and an adjacent cracked window covered inside by what appeared to be a bedsheet. Dylan prepared to knock, but the door swung open to reveal a man in his midforties or so. He was a few inches shorter than Dylan, all wiry muscle under a dirty white tank top and faded jeans. His hair and beard were long and grizzled, and his face was deeply tanned. He looked annoyed.

"Whatta ya—" he began, then stopped as his nostrils flared. His eyes narrowed and his jaw tightened. Andy had been the only werewolf

160

Dylan knew, but Dylan could immediately smell what this man was. There were human odors to him—sweat, sour beer, grime—but also something else, something purely animal. Dylan instinctively placed himself in front of Chris. He felt his pulse quicken, the hairs on the back of his neck rise.

Without turning his dark eyes away from Dylan, the man bellowed, "C'mere! All of you!" Answering shouts came from inside the house, and within seconds, three men and two women crowded behind him. Every one of them was a were. The combined reek of them was nearly overwhelming.

"Who the fuck are you?" the man growled.

"Dylan Warner. I'm... I knew Andy. Andy Milligan."

The man surged out the door, followed closely by his pack. Dylan backed up several steps, nearly tripping over Chris in the process.

"Son of a bitch," the man said and spat into the dirt. "Shoulda known that faggot wouldn't be able to keep his fangs to himself. Where the fuck is he?"

Coming here had clearly been a mistake. These people were no more likely to surround the ghost with love than Andy's mother and sister had been. But it was too late for Dylan to run away with his tail between his legs.

Hoping his fear didn't show, Dylan straightened his back. "He's dead."

The crowd murmured softly among themselves and the leader spat again. "Saves me the work, then."

"Who are you?"

"Name's Chester. I'm in charge around here. Tell me what the hell you're doing in my territory, dragging your cocksucker with you."

Dylan could hear Chris take a breath in preparation for saying something—probably something that would get them killed—so Dylan took another step back and elbowed him hard in the chest. Chris swore but then shut up.

"I'm not going to stay," Dylan said to Chester. "And I don't want to cause trouble. I was just hoping you'd have some information about Andy. About his past. Did he have any friends, any people he liked to hang out with?"

"Why?"

Probably the truth wouldn't hurt. "Because his ghost is haunting me and I want to get rid of it."

Chester barked out a surprised laugh and then so did the others. They relaxed a little too, which was a good thing. "I'll tell you what I knew about that fucker. He was a loser, a pathetic little fruit, selling his ass like any common whore. Caught the eye of my boy Mikey. Mikey usually chased after bitches, but I guess he had a taste for meat that month."

The pack laughed at the attempt at humor; Dylan did not.

Chester raised a dirty finger and pointed it at Dylan. "Now, I got some rules here. And one of 'em is don't nobody add to the pack without my say-so. That's one of the most important rules, right after *shut the fuck up and do as you're told*." He turned slightly to glare at the people behind him, as if they might be considering insurrection. They all lowered their gazes submissively and he faced Dylan again. "But Mikey just couldn't resist Andy's skinny ass, could he? Wasn't the first time Mikey disobeyed me, but it was the last." His smile revealed surprisingly white and sharp teeth.

Apparently, that was too much for Chris. "You killed one of your own people?" he asked.

"They're mine to do what I fucking want. And if any of 'em don't like it, they can fight me for the pack."

To Dylan's eyes, none of them seemed at all eager to fight Chester. While they managed to send glares at Dylan and Chris, their body language was all about deference to their leader.

Dylan took a breath. "Okay. So Mikey's... gone. What about Andy?"

Chester shrugged. "Figured it wasn't his fault he got hisself turned. Told him he could run with us long as he kept his dick to himself and obeyed orders. You shoulda seen him crawling on his belly to thank me."

God, Dylan thought. Rejected by his family, his lover murdered, Andy had abased himself to these monsters in the hope of finding companionship. "What happened?" Dylan said, surprised to find himself so angry on Andy's behalf.

"He was okay for a while. But then he got these ideas in his head and stopped listening so good. Gave him the choice between leaving or dying, which was more than he deserved." Another shrug. "He left. I told him I'd leave him alone if he stayed out of my way and didn't turn nobody else. I don't want no other packs running around here. I guess he was too stupid to listen."

"He was lonely," Dylan said quietly.

"He was a fool. And now he's a dead fool. And a fucking ghost." Chester chuckled unpleasantly, and then his face turned cold. "How long until you bite him?" he demanded, jerking his chin in Chris's direction.

"I won't."

"You say that now, but when the moon is full, you gonna be howling a different song."

Chris had to butt in again. "I've been near him when he's a wolf, asshole, and he didn't lay a tooth on me. He *saved* me. Just 'cause you can't control yourselves doesn't mean he can't. He's better than that."

Chester growled low in his throat.

Dylan curled his hands into fists and growled back, and for a moment he wanted nothing better than to sink his teeth into that bristly neck, to feel flesh give way and hot blood spurt. He knew he'd lose the battle—there were far too many people for him to fight alone—but he had the feeling he could at least defeat Chester before being killed himself.

Maybe Chester had the same feeling, because fear flashed very briefly across his face. He put his arms out at his sides as if to stop the rest of the pack from rushing forward. "I'm gonna let you walk away from here today, Dylan Warner. But if I see your sorry face again, or if I hear you're forming a pack of your own… well, then I ain't gonna be so nice about it."

"Not a problem," Dylan responded evenly. And as much as he didn't want to turn his back on Chester and the rest, he decided there was no dignity in trying to walk backward to his truck. He'd probably trip over something and land on his ass. So he spun around, grabbed Chris's arm, and returned to the truck with all deliberate speed. Chester and his pack were still in the front yard, watching, as Dylan pulled away.

"Well, that was fun," Chris said after a mile or so. He sounded oddly cheerful. "You were really fucking scary, Dyl. The way you stared down that motherfucker—I thought he was gonna shit his pants."

"They came very close to killing us both," Dylan replied wearily.

"But they didn't, 'cause you're more badass than all of 'em put together." Chris said these words with such conviction and satisfaction that Dylan only grinned at him instead of arguing.

But still, after a few minutes, Dylan felt obligated to warn him. "This isn't a Tarantino movie, Chris. This isn't a game."

"But it is a game, least for those guys. It's a game of charades, right? I dunno what they were like before they were wolves. But then someone bit them, and they'd watched a lot of dumbshit movies and TV shows about what werewolves are supposed to be like, so that's how they play. Not like you. You're still a little bit of a geek and a neat freak, and you still listen to bands nobody's ever heard of and eat weird foods 'cause they're the latest thing, and you do your job and love your family. They're just posers, Dyl. You're the real deal."

Dylan's smile widened, because it was a really nice speech and obviously heartfelt. But deep inside he was still worried—and no closer to solving the ghost problem.

THEY stopped for lunch, Mexican this time. Chris tried to talk Dylan into another sex detour, which was tempting, but Dylan really needed to get some work done. If he went to his meeting on Friday empty-handed, Stender wasn't likely to be too sympathetic to an excuse of laptops busted by werewolf ghosts.

Dylan tried to appease Chris with a counteroffer. "Come into the city with me on Friday, and we can stay at that hotel again. Or try a new one if you'd rather."

"No. I ain't gonna be satisfied with once-a-week scheduled nookie. Ain't like we're married or anythin'."

Dylan wasn't sure if that was a complaint. Did Chris want something more formal between them? Was he waiting for Dylan to pop the question? That seemed unlikely—Chris was perfectly capable of getting down on one knee and proposing to Dylan, if that's what he wanted. Unless Chris was feeling insecure and was afraid Dylan would turn him down, in which case maybe he really *was* waiting for Dylan to say something, and possibly getting more doubtful the longer Dylan waited. But maybe Chris thought marriage was for girls and would laugh in Dylan's face if asked for a civil commitment ceremony or something, in which case Dylan would be shattered.

Jesus, being in a relationship was *hard*.

They didn't speak much during the rest of the drive home. When they got to the farm, Chris disappeared into his own house without a word or a backward glance, while Dylan went into his office to set up the new laptop. It was a nice computer, faster than his old one and with much better screen resolution. He hoped the ghost didn't decide to go after this one too.

Installing the software took some time, and then he had to download his files from the cloud. He Skyped Matty, who was in the office, and bounced some ideas off her. She wasn't formally involved in this particular project, but he valued her input and knew she'd be flattered to be asked. She liked his concepts for the school, especially the rooftop garden. "You should talk to Stender about LEED certification," she said. "It might be hard with an old building like this, but the Empire State Building managed a gold rating recently, so I bet you could pull it off."

"Good plan, Matty. Thanks."

"You betcha. So when you going to bring the arm candy around to town again?"

"Arm candy? I'm not sure Chris would appreciate being called that."

"Well, I like him. And you two are so sweet together you make my teeth hurt. You're adorable."

The good thing about Skyping was that she could see his sour expression. "We're grown men, Matt. We are *not* adorable."

She flapped a hand dismissively. "Oh, you're *way* adorable. The way he knows exactly how to tease you so you get all blushy, and the way you go all googly eyes at each other…. Jeez, Dylan, I'm glad you held out until you found the real thing. Mr. Right."

He wasn't very comfortable discussing this. He barely discussed the relationship with Chris, let alone with Matty. On the other hand, her view was a lot more objective than his own, or even than Kay's or Rick's was likely to be. "How can you tell it's the real thing? We just had lunch together."

"I can tell. You guys have more chemistry than a Nobel laureate." She pointed her finger at the camera so that the tip was waggling on his screen. "You listen to me, Dylan, and don't mess this one up. I'm good at this. I set my friend Jessica up with this boy back in high school, and now they're old marrieds and still madly in love. You and Chris— Who's that?"

She was looking at the screen, but her gaze was directed over his shoulder. He turned around to look, but the office was empty. When he faced her again, her brows were drawn together in puzzlement. "I could've sworn I saw someone behind you."

"What kind of someone?" Dylan asked carefully.

"Some guy. Chris's dad, maybe? Does he hang out with you guys?"

Dylan hadn't shared Chris's family situation with her. "No. He doesn't."

"Weird. Well, maybe it was some kind of Internet glitch."

"Probably. And I think I better get back to work. Thanks for the help, Matt."

"And the relationship advice," she said, grinning widely.

He shook his head fondly. "See you Friday. Lunch?"

"Of course. Bye, Dylan!"

After disconnecting the call, Dylan got up from his chair and had a good prowl around the house. He couldn't see any signs of the ghost—no more damage, thank goodness—but he kept catching that grave scent. Finally, he decided he wasn't going to get much done in his distracted state, so he traipsed to the basement and retrieved Andy's saddlebag. He returned the bike papers to the bag, along with the damaged remains of the other contents. Then, saddlebag in hand, he headed back up the stairs and out the back door. He stopped to grab the shovel leaning against the house.

Chris had buried Andy in the middle of Dylan's land, among the growing wilderness that had once been a Christmas tree farm. It wasn't a bad burial place; Dylan wouldn't have minded it for himself. The location was very private, without even a glimpse of house or road, and the air was fresh and pine scented. There were always lots of birds in the area, including a family of quail, and various animals lived nearby or passed through. Dylan had seen a doe and her fawn among these trees just a few weeks ago. Wildflowers added splashes of color to the green and brown of the ferns and trees; butterflies and bees busied themselves with the blossoms. It was a place of life, a place where either man or wolf would be pleased to have a final rest.

Except Andy wasn't resting, was he?

New plants already covered the disturbed earth, but Dylan easily found the small stone cairn he'd built to mark Andy's grave. He dug a deep hole very close to the resting place, and he tossed the saddlebag inside before refilling the space with dirt. "Sorry I can't give you your bike too," he said as he worked. "But there's no way I'm diving for that."

When the ground was even again, Dylan leaned on the shovel handle and looked down at the little pile of stones. "I'm really sorry, Andy. You got a shitty deal. Your family, Mikey, Chester's pack… even me… everyone dumped you. I can't love you. Not after what you did to me, and not after you almost killed Chris. And all the others—how many people did you kill, Andy? I just can't love you. But I can… I can empathize with you. And I can wish you peace."

Dylan tilted his head back so he could look high into the blue sky. "I love Chris. I really do, with all my heart. He's—like Matty said. He's the one. Let go of the anger, okay? It didn't help you when you were alive and it's not doing you any good now. Let yourself *go*. And let me and Chris be. Please."

There was no answering flash of energy. Not even a rustling of leaves in the breeze.

Dylan sighed, picked up the shovel, and tromped back to the house.

He spent the next couple of hours working at the new computer. He drafted a few very rough plans as well as a list of suggestions. Movable walls in some of the classrooms might be a good idea, to accommodate classes of varying sizes. They'd have to find a way to make sure those walls were soundproof, however. He remembered back to when he was in college—it seemed like every time he had an exam, the class in the next room was watching a loud movie.

The entire time he was working, the smell of earth was thick in his nostrils, although that might have been because he'd been digging in the stuff. He didn't see any ghosts or hear anything but the click-clack of his keyboard, but he felt like someone was watching him the entire time.

Just as his stomach began to complain and he started to worry about Chris, the back door slammed. "Still workin'?" Chris asked a moment later from the doorway.

"Yeah. Got a lot done, though. What have you been up to all afternoon?"

"Buried myself in that Impala I got behind my house. I got it for free last year from a guy after I helped him hang new kitchen cabinets. It don't run no more and his wife wanted it out of the driveway. I think if I poured a little time and money into it, I'd get it goin' again."

"If anyone can, you can," Dylan said with a smile—a smile that grew larger when Chris came up behind him and began to knead the stiff muscles in his shoulders. "Matty's going to have a conniption when I tell her you really can give massages." He leaned his head back against Chris's belly.

Chris grinned down at him. "You know I got good hands."

"Good enough to make us some dinner? Or did you eat already?"

Chris looked a little startled. "Wasn't gonna eat without you, man. C'mon. I bet you could at least manage to throw a salad together. With close supervision."

"Okay. But I have more work to do tonight."

"Leave it for now."

Dylan nodded, stood, and stretched. He hoped that after dinner he could persuade Chris to stick around, maybe read a book while Dylan slaved away. He liked knowing Chris was there, even if they were occupied in separate tasks.

Chris made something with chicken breasts, noodles, and a really amazing sauce, the components of which he smugly refused to divulge. Dylan's salad was passable too. While they ate, Chris talked about the things he planned to do to the Impala, most of which were a mystery to Dylan. He knew how to drive, how to check the oil and tire pressure, and in a pinch, maybe change a flat. It was fun to see Chris so enthused and so confident as he described things that needed his expertise.

Dylan washed up, and they had bowls of mint chocolate chip ice cream. Not homemade, although Dylan wondered if he ought to mention to Chris that somewhere in the back of his cupboards was a fairly expensive ice cream maker. Dylan had seen it in a catalog and decided that making ice cream sounded like a good idea, but he'd never gotten around to it. Chris might use it. Or he might spend half an hour poking fun at Dylan for buying useless kitchen gadgets. Dylan decided he'd bring it up another time.

The spoons scraped noisily against the bowls.

"I was thinking," Dylan said, surprising even himself.

"Yeah?"

"If Stender's happy with what I have so far and I can get a lot done—I mean, really get ahead—what would you think about taking a vacation?"

Chris squinted at him. "Vacation?"

"Yes. People do that, you know. Especially in the summer. We could spend a few days at the coast, or maybe head up to Seattle. I like Seattle. There's the EMP Museum—have you been there?"

"No."

"It's— Frank Gehry designed the building, and it's this, this *thing* that looks like a space alien's guts, all these curves and—and the exhibits aren't bad. We could ride a ferry, watch them throw fish at Pike Place Market. We could stay at a nice hotel and spend all day and night in bed."

Chris was just looking at him. Dylan couldn't read his expression at all. So he decided on a slightly different tack. "You said you've never been very far east. If you wanted, we could go... I don't know. Anywhere. Chicago. New York." He tried to smile winningly. "We could visit our nation's capital. Or maybe you want nature? We could go see the Grand Canyon or Yellowstone or Yosemite or... will you *please* stop staring at me like that and say something?"

"Sorry." Chris ducked his head and stared at his empty ice cream bowl. "It's only... it kinda hit me just now."

"What hit you?"

"It's kinda... kinda a new world for me." He looked up again. His mouth was curled slightly upward, but there was a solemnity to his clear blue eyes. "I'm not the kinda guy who goes on vacation, Dyl. If I'm lucky, I find a secluded spot to camp out for a night or two. I don't go to Seattle to admire the architecture, and I sure as hell don't go waltzin' off to Washington, DC."

"We don't have to if you don't want to," Dylan said.

Chris shook his head. "'S not that. I don't know if I want to 'cause I never even thought about it before. It was like… I didn't think about growin' wings and flyin' to Mars. Wasn't on my radar screen. And now I got a… got someone." He took a deep breath and let it out. "Got you. And you're fuckin' so far out of my league, and you're a supernatural creature who saves me, and there's ghosts, and your people don't hate me, and we can just get on an airplane if we want to and go anywhere. It's a little overwhelming."

Dylan reached across the table and wrapped his hand around Chris's. "For me too, believe it or not. None of this"—he waved his free hand around vaguely—"none of this was really on my radar screen either. But God, I'm really thankful I lucked into you. We can talk vacations later, okay?"

A little of the tension eased from Chris's face. "Yeah. Hell, maybe I'll get myself a passport."

Chris went up to fetch a half-read book from his bedside while Dylan put away the dishes. They headed together into the office, where Chris settled down in the armchair and Dylan at his desk. He pressed the button to wake up the laptop, ready to add to his list of ideas for the school.

Only, the list was gone.

In its place, letters in huge bold font appeared over and over, covering the entire page: F&*ILY FAMI(UHY FAMILY NOCK FAMILY H8#AL FAMILY NOCK HEAL FAMILY FAMILY HEAL.

CHAPTER 18

"YOU didn't mess around with my Word files, did you?" Dylan's voice sounded odd.

"Course not. You know the deal: you stay out of my cookin' and I stay out of your files. Why?"

Dylan nodded, just once. "You'll want to see this."

The strangled tone of Dylan's voice had Chris immediately on his feet and rushing across the room. He stopped behind Dylan's chair and peered over his shoulder at the laptop screen. "What the *fuck*?"

"Computer programs, they're just electrons, right? More energy? I think the ghost has learned how to do word processing."

"But—"

"I've been wrong all along. Dammit, Chris, I jumped to conclusions and I didn't *think*—didn't see what was right before my eyes."

Chris shook his head. "Me neither. I was just as blind." And then, because he felt like someone ought to, he said the truth that had just become obvious to them both: "It ain't Andy. The ghost is Uncle Frank."

DYLAN was slumped in a kitchen chair but looked as if he'd rather be jumping off the nearest bridge. He was halfway through his third beer and neck-deep in self-blame. "I should have known. It was so damn *obvious.*"

"Not really. Frank's been dead for years and Andy's the one who just kicked it. Plus Andy's buried right here and I think Frank's planted in some graveyard out near Hillsboro."

"I made a huge assumption and never questioned it, not even with all the clues the ghost left. God, Chris! The fingerprints, all the activity in the spare room, the way the ghost never tried to hurt us...." He gulped his bottle dry and set it on the table, then made a grab for Chris's, which was still mostly full.

Chris pulled his beer out of reach. "Yeah, we can see all the clues now, but they weren't all that clear until just a bit ago. Not like either of us owns the Guide to Ghostly Behavior."

"I should have *known!*"

Chris bristled. "Why? 'Cause you're such a smart guy and I'm a dummy can't be expected to figure anything out on his own?"

"That's not what I meant."

"Look here. It ain't all about you all the time. The ghost may be haunting your house, but it turns out he ain't even your ghost. He's my responsibility least as much as he's yours. And so you made a fuckin' mistake. Big deal! I make 'em all the time." Chris had allowed his voice to raise to a shout. He was tired of Dylan taking the blame for everything, as if he thought Chris was too weak to handle responsibility.

Dylan looked at him. "Am I one of your mistakes?" he asked quietly.

"Oh, for Christ's sake! Why the fuck would you think that? Because I've only told you a thousand goddamn times that you're the best thing that ever happened to me?"

"Because I did assume the ghost was all about me. Because I dragged you all over the state trying to look up Andy's people, and because I could have got you killed when I dragged you to Chester's pack." Most of the time, Dylan came across as a pretty confident guy. It

173

was only during moments like these that Chris was reminded of Dylan's own deep-seated insecurities.

Chris shook his head. "You really are a hopeless case." He stood, walked his beer bottle to the counter, and set it beside the sink. Then he returned to the table but didn't sit. "You didn't drag me anywhere—I wanted to go. And nobody got killed, not even talking to them bigots in Sherwood. And you're a big fuckin' idiot and I love you, asshole." He swallowed. "I love you."

Gazing up at Chris from the chair, Dylan appeared very lost and young-looking. So Chris came around behind him, grabbed the chair, and scooted it back from the table. Before Dylan could protest or get up, Chris moved in front of him and straddled his lap. He closed his fists around handfuls of Dylan's shirt and held on tight.

Dylan choked back a sob and wrapped his arms around Chris's body. "I love you too, Chris." It was hard for Chris to hear the words because they were muffled by his chest, but he knew what Dylan had said.

They stayed together like that for a little while. It was nice. It felt safe and comfortable and *right*, like there was nowhere better in the world to be.

Eventually, Dylan leaned back a little so he could look up at Chris. "This is serious," Dylan said.

"Just a ghost. Looking back at it, he's mostly more Casper than—"

"I'm not talking about the ghost. I mean us. We're serious. We're...." He laughed softly. "We're the real thing."

"Coulda told you that weeks ago. If we weren't the real thing, I woulda dumped you after I found out you'd been hiding your wolf."

"I know."

Chris could feel the movement of Dylan's body as Dylan took a few deep breaths. Then Dylan moved his hands to Chris shoulders. "If it's the real thing, can we stop doing it halfway?"

"Don't know what you mean."

"Be my... I'm not sure what the best word is. My partner. Yeah. And we can stop all this my house, your house stuff, and stop arguing over who's paying for things. Let everything just be ours. Even the ghost." Dylan managed a tiny smile.

Chris was finding it slightly difficult to make his lungs work, and his tongue was stuck way back in his throat. He felt a little lightheaded even though he'd only had a few sips of beer. When he didn't answer right away, though, panic began to fill Dylan's eyes. Chris chewed his lip. "So you mean not just for real, but for good."

"We already agreed, Chris—our foundation is solid. When I design a house, I design it to last well over a lifetime. And you build a house good and sturdy, don't you?"

"I do," Chris said, and then laughed when he realized exactly what he'd said. "You gonna want some sort of ceremony now? With organic cocktails served in mason jars and girls in thrift store dresses with floral tiaras. And a photographer with ironic tattoos, eyelet earrings, and a beard down to his chest."

"Yep. And he Instagrams all the photos." Dylan leaned in close again. "We can do a formal thing if you want, but I don't care about all that stuff. I just want you."

Chris didn't care about formalities either. It wasn't like he had anyone to invite. But man, he liked the sound of something permanent.

He ducked his head a little and began to lick and suck at Dylan's earlobe. Dylan groaned almost immediately and moved his hands down to Chris's ass. Nice. "Hair's gettin' kinda long," Chris rumbled, running his fingers through Dylan's strands.

"Want me to cut it?"

"No. I can hang on better this way." He shifted his hips slightly forward so that his groin was very firmly against Dylan's, and then traced a fingertip over Dylan's lips and under, where his soul patch used to be. He went back to nibbling on that earlobe, which suddenly seemed very tasty.

"Chris!" Dylan made a not-very-concerted attempt to push him away. "The ghost!"

"Here? Now?" Chris looked around the kitchen and saw nothing spectral. "Listen here, Uncle Frank!" he said loudly. "Me and my partner are about to get up close and real personal. If you don't want an eyeful, go float somewhere else for a while." Hell, maybe the old guy *wanted* to watch. He spent a lot of time spying through that window when he was alive.

When Dylan still looked doubtful, Chris clinched the deal by wiggling his hips a little and sucking on the spot under Dylan's ear that always drove him wild.

"Oh, God," Dylan said, clutching harder at Chris's ass, all possible objections pushed out of his head.

The kitchen chair wasn't very comfortable, but they never made it all the way to Dylan's bed—no, *their* bed. They got as far as the living room. They peeled away their clothing; then Dylan bent Chris forward over the back of the Pottery Barn sofa and began to lick maddeningly slowly down the knobs of his spine.

Chris loved the shape of Dylan, the way his body fitted to Chris's. He loved Dylan's cock sliding in the crack of his ass, and Dylan's hands holding his hips bruisingly tight, Dylan's breath hot against his skin. Dylan's fingers around his cock were so much cleverer than his own, Dylan's teeth just sharp enough at the nape of his neck, Dylan's too-long hair tickling at his cheeks. Unlike the men who'd fucked Chris before, Dylan was always tender, careful—but not *too* careful, thank God, because Chris craved a bit of roughness. And to be honest, knowing that the man behind him could kill him in an instant but hadn't, wouldn't—that knowledge made Chris's belly feel warm, made his balls tingle and his heart race. The irony wasn't lost on Chris. Dylan was the most dangerous person he had ever met, yet the only one with whom he could drop his guard completely.

But now he was dropping his head instead, arching his back and sticking his ass up higher, hoping Dylan would take the hint. And Dylan did: he grabbed the bottle of olive oil Chris had snagged as they kissed their way out of the kitchen, and drizzled it between Chris's cheeks, not even complaining about the mess it was going to make or the waste of an imported, extra virgin, three-dollar-an-ounce condiment.

In fact, the oil was apparently a plus to the ever-hungry Dylan, who dropped to his knees, spread Chris's cheeks, and dedicated himself to a rim job that soon had Chris swearing loudly and humping the goddamn couch.

When Chris almost couldn't stand it anymore, Dylan rose to his feet again. "Ready for me?" he asked hoarsely.

"I'm gonna impale myself on your dick if you don't hurry up."

But Dylan didn't really hurry. He applied more oil—lots of oil, so that Chris smelled like an Italian appetizer—and slipped slick fingers into Chris, thrusting and stretching and crooking just *so*.

"Dyl!" Chris was going to make good on his threat: he was going to throw Dylan to the floor and hop right on top of him.

"Mmm," Dylan hummed against his shoulder, distracting Chris from his plan. And then, mercifully, Dylan lined his cock up and slid inside with one long, smooth stroke.

Dylan tended to start out quiet when they were having sex, but he got louder as he got more excited, and that in turn got Chris's engine revving. So now Dylan slammed Chris into the couch hard enough to move it, and the sounds of flesh slapping against flesh and harsh breathing were almost drowned out by Chris's litany of *Oh God, yeah, like that!* and Dylan's string of half-formed words and unintelligible growls. It was probably a really good thing they had no neighbors for miles.

Chris came hard, holding the edge of the couch for dear life and gasping for oxygen, every muscle in his body clenching at once and then letting go and letting go, until he barely noticed Dylan crying out and then collapsing against his back. They melted together to the floor in an oily, sweaty, sticky mess.

CHAPTER 19

SOME small noise woke Dylan in the middle of the night. He didn't move—couldn't easily, the way Chris was plastered half across him—but he opened his eyes and inhaled the scent of earth.

The ghost was floating at the end of the bed, its face still blurry but perhaps slightly less indistinct. Maybe it was only because Dylan now knew the ghost wasn't Andy, but he no longer sensed anything threatening. Instead, it seemed sad. Yearning for something.

"I'm sorry," Dylan whispered as quietly as he could.

Chris stirred a little and mumbled but didn't wake up.

Dylan tucked a lock of hair behind Chris's ear. "You finally got through to us," said Dylan to the ghost. "We know who you are. We'll try to help you, okay?"

The ghost glowed a tiny bit brighter.

"I'm not sure what you want, so if you can tell us, that'd be great. Just, please don't wreck things anymore, okay? And be careful around Chris. He's important."

It was possible that the ghost nodded a little, and then it disappeared.

THERE was a new message on the computer in the morning. Dylan didn't see it right away. First he and Chris made love again—slow and lazy this time—and then they showered. After making a bacon-and-eggs breakfast, Chris dithered about whether to fix the ghost's damage in the spare room or to carry some clothing and books from his house to Dylan's. He finally decided on the former.

"You're gonna need more shelves," he said. "And another dresser, if you don't want my crappy one here."

Dylan smiled. "*We're* going to need more shelves. I can pick up some decent wood when I'm in the city on Friday, and you can build them, Mr. Handyman. We can choose a new dresser together."

Chris rolled his eyes. "Couple of milk crates or some cinder blocks and plywood would do just fine, Martha Stewart." But Dylan could tell he was teasing, and good-naturedly flipped him off.

Chris went upstairs to put stain blocker over the Sharpie and prep the window for repair, and Dylan booted up the laptop. As soon as he opened his Word document, however, he saw words he hadn't typed: HEAL FAMILY HELP HELP HELP.

That sounded a little too desperate for Dylan's liking. He was, however, impressed that the ghost had figured out how to affect the program even while the computer was turned off. Unfortunately, while Uncle Frank was clearly making a hell of an effort, his needs weren't quite clear. *Heal family*. What did he mean by that?

By the time Chris came back downstairs, whistling cheerfully, Dylan had decided on a possible solution.

"You look like a guy with a plan," Chris said to him, maybe a little warily.

"I am. I'm going to call Ery. How would you feel about some visitors?"

ERY was more enthusiastic than Dylan had expected. Even better, when Ery called back a few minutes later, he reported that his grandmother really liked the idea of an outing to the countryside, that she was eager to meet the ghost, and that she'd be willing to head out that very minute if that worked for them.

Dylan glanced over at Chris. "Yeah, that'd be great. Come on over." Then he gave directions and hung up.

While Dylan snuck in a little more work, Chris used the next hour to make some kind of quick bread that smelled wonderful. He was very funny about his baking prowess—always a little embarrassed, as if being able to throw together delicious treats made him less a man—so Dylan made sure to give his partner's butt a few good manly gropes.

Ery's Mini Cooper came puttering down the road just minutes after the bread was out of the oven. Dylan and Chris went out on the porch to greet their guests. Ery was again dressed as colorfully as possible, resembling some sort of tropical flower with an affinity for hair product, and Mrs. Phillips wore another expensive suit and a strand of pearls. Ery helped her out of the car, but she made her own careful way to the house. She had a fancy cane of carved wood that she used only sparingly on the uneven ground.

Dylan thought that one of these days he ought to build a proper walkway from the road, something attractive and welcoming and not too formal. Slate paving stones, maybe. He'd ask Chris's opinion later.

Ery offered his grandmother an arm to help her up the steps to the porch. He did it automatically, as if out of long habit, and that made Dylan smile. Ery was a good guy, and it was nice to see him so obviously belonging to someone. Dylan knew Ery had always had a solid relationship with his parents, but they'd moved to Minneapolis several years ago.

"Thank you for coming, and so quickly," Dylan said when the guests stood in front of him.

"I'm retired," said Mrs. Phillips with a smile. "I can do what I wish when I wish to, as long as my aged body cooperates."

Ery nodded. "And I skipped off work because there was no way I was going to miss seeing your house *and* a séance."

His grandmother gave him a slight glare. "It is *not* a séance. I will simply be having a conversation with the spirit."

"Yes, Grandma." When Ery grinned like that, he looked about twelve years old.

Chris held the door open as everyone trooped inside. The entry hall wasn't exactly spectacular—they hadn't yet gotten around to refurbishing it—but Mrs. Phillips nodded approvingly at the living room. "What a treat to see a grand old house like this one given its due! So many people would give up on it and build a new one instead."

"Well, I design new houses, so I think they're good too," said Dylan. "And this one still needs a lot of work. But I think when something has so much promise, it's worth keeping, even if it takes a lot of effort." Out of the corner of his eye, he could see Chris beaming brightly at his words. Good, because that's what Dylan had intended.

Chris offered to lead a tour, and their guests were eager to accept, although Mrs. Phillips said she'd stick to the ground floor. They oohed and aahed over the office, the kitchen, and the downstairs bath, and they approved of the plans to add a mudroom onto the back. Mrs. Phillips stared longingly out the kitchen window. "I do so wish I were able to tromp around the grounds a bit with you boys. Your property looks delightful."

Chris pointed at the blackberry bramble. "There's a pond down that way, with state forest on the other side. The rest of Dylan's land is mostly Christmas trees all grown up."

"It's not your land as well?"

He shrugged slightly. "I got that crappy little house next door and the fields. This all used to be one big parcel, but there was a family feud bunch of years back. It's probably what's got the ghost all worked up, actually."

"Ery tells me you feel you were originally mistaken about the spirit's intentions."

"It's my fault," Dylan said, ignoring Chris's eye roll. "I assumed it was… someone with a grudge. But now we're pretty positive it's someone else."

"This sounds like an intriguing story."

181

"I guess. Would you like to sit down and hear it?"

Everyone went back to the living room, where Mrs. Phillips and Ery found seats. Then Chris and Dylan retreated to the kitchen and had a hasty conference concerning refreshments. "We don't have any tea," Dylan said unhappily.

"Chill. Make some coffee, and if she don't like that, we got water and milk."

As it turned out, Mrs. Phillips didn't care for coffee, but she was content with water and thrilled with Chris's spice bread. "You must give me the recipe!" she enthused. "I bake very rarely nowadays, but I'd make an exception for this."

For once Chris was the one to blush and look slightly embarrassed—which was adorable, and Dylan was going to be very sure to tell him so later.

Soon, however, the conversation turned from cookery to hauntings. "Tell me about this spirit," she said.

Dylan and Chris looked at each other, and it was Chris who began to explain. "It's my uncle Frank. Great-uncle Frank, really. He lived in this house, died seven or eight years ago. Don't know why he's all of a sudden got his panties in a bunch, though. Neither of us seen any ghosts until just now."

"Is he one of the relatives who had the falling-out you mentioned earlier?"

"Yeah. Frank went off to be a soldier and his brother—my gramps—stole Frank's girl. Gramps had that shack next door built, the land got split up, and they never said another word to each other. Funny, though—they died only a few months apart. Gramps went first."

Mrs. Phillips was tapping her chin thoughtfully with one elegant finger. "Do you believe this rift is what is causing the spirit unrest?"

"Yeah, probably. He wrote stuff—tried to on the wall, and then he figured out how to use Dylan's laptop."

She looked surprised by this, and also a little amused. "Well, I suppose even spirits must change with the times. What did the spirit write?"

"Bunch of stuff about family—heal family, stuff like that. Wasn't exactly Tolstoy."

Mrs. Phillips gave Chris the same scolding schoolteacher look she sent in Ery's direction every now and then. Dylan was relieved to have avoided that look, and yet he thought that maybe it meant their guest was developing a certain fondness for Chris. Well, who could blame her? Chris was… endearing, once you looked past his hillbilly façade.

"Spirits have a great deal of trouble articulating themselves verbally. Perhaps that is one reason why this one took so long to manifest—it was gathering the means to communicate." She gave both Chris and Dylan a warm smile. "I do not believe that was the only reason it recently manifested, however."

Ery stood and walked to her side, then put his arm around his grandmother's shoulders. "I bet I know what you're thinking, Grandma. Dyl, Chris, how long have you guys been together?"

Well, that was kind of a hard question to answer, so neither of them did so right away. It depended on how you defined *together*. They'd started working together right after Dylan moved in, back in March, and they had sex not too long after that, but emotional closeness had taken even longer. And it wasn't until Chris discovered Dylan's werewolf identity—causing a rift and then a reconciliation—that they'd made a true commitment to one another. "A few weeks, sort of," Dylan finally said.

"Right. So you two make the love connection and that's when Uncle Frank makes an appearance. It's what Grandma said the other day—when love is in the air, the spirits get frisky."

"So me and Dyl are a spectral battery?" asked Chris.

"Totally. Jeez, I'm no ghost but I can feel the spark between you. I am so insanely jealous, you guys."

Mrs. Phillips patted her grandson's hand. "You'll find your own spark, dear. It's better to wait for the right one than to jump into something foolishly and out of desperation."

Ery made a face that suggested the two of them had had this conversation many times already.

But Dylan wanted to get back to the main point. "Okay, so Uncle Frank probably regretted the thing with his brother and that regret kept him from moving on. And now he's finally gathered himself together enough to complain about it. But what does he want us to do? Doesn't he realize that his brother's been dead longer than he has? I don't see how we can reconcile anyone now."

Mrs. Phillips turned to Chris. "Does the rest of your family get along?"

"There is no rest of the family. Just me." After a brief pause, he added, "And my father, who took off when I was in kindergarten." He didn't say anything about Jimmy's recent reappearance.

"Do you believe that perhaps he wishes you to contact your father?" asked Mrs. Phillips.

"Dunno why he'd care. As far as I know, they didn't have anythin' to do with one another when Frank was alive. And I never said a word to the old man. Hardly saw him either, except when he was watchin' us through that upstairs window."

She handed her empty bread plate to Ery, who in turn gave it to Dylan. She smoothed the skirt over her legs and adjusted her pearls slightly. "If you'll pardon me, I am going to attempt to contact this spirit. Why don't you boys continue your tour of the house in the meantime?"

Both Chris and Ery looked disappointed to miss out on whatever she was going to do, but Dylan was a little relieved. He'd had enough supernatural dealings already. After ascertaining that Mrs. Phillips didn't want any more food or water, they left her alone. As they walked out of the room, she wasn't doing anything more exciting than closing her eyes.

The spare room still smelled of fresh paint, and neither the fingerprints nor the Sharpie letters were visible any longer. Chris had removed the tarp from the window in preparation for repairs. The forecast didn't call for rain, so they were probably safe in leaving the opening uncovered, as long as none of the local wildlife decided to pay a visit.

"What are you going to do with this room?" Ery asked.

Dylan answered. "Just a spare bedroom. Except we'll sleep in here for a while when we're redoing the master."

"A lot of projects, huh?"

"Always. But Chris is really great at this stuff. I'm learning a lot from him."

Chris nudged Dylan with an elbow. "He already knows we're in loooove, Dyl. You don't gotta lay it on so thick."

Dylan poked him back. Hard. "But it's the truth."

After peeking at the view out the window, Ery turned back to them. He looked slightly nervous. "You know, if you guys ever need an extra set of hands, you could call me. I'm free most weekends. I'm not an expert or anything, but I'm usually not a total klutz."

Chris and Dylan exchanged looks and then Dylan replied. "We'd love to have you help out, Ery. Thanks for the offer."

"I don't want to be a third wheel or anything…."

"You wouldn't. I miss hanging out with you." Dylan winced a little. "I'm really sorry I cut you out of my life like that. It was a shitty thing to do. You're a good friend."

He glanced over at Chris, slightly afraid his partner would be seething with jealousy. But Chris wasn't. In fact, he smiled broadly before patting Ery on the arm. "We could always use some slave labor, dude. Come anytime." He waggled his eyebrows. "Just knock before you come in, okay?"

True relief washed across Ery's features, followed quickly by a smile. "I will. But if I forget to knock, I'll make sure to have my phone camera set to video, 'cause I bet you guys are smoking hot together."

Great. Dylan's turn to blush again.

THEY did a quick tour of the farm. Ery liked the pond, but he was especially enamored of the small barn. It was currently empty, but

Dylan had been thinking it might make a good garage someday. Ery had his own vision. "This would make such an excellent studio! You'd maybe want to put in some skylights, but there's so much space."

Dylan remembered that although Ery made a living as a commercial artist, he'd always loved to paint for fun. He preferred big canvases on which he could swipe and splatter like a reincarnation of Jackson Pollock. It wasn't Dylan's kind of art, but he'd watched Ery paint a few times and he'd looked as if he was having fun.

"Tell you what," Dylan said. "You lend a helping hand now and then and one of these days we will convert this to a studio, and you can use it whenever you want."

"Really?"

"Sure," said Chris, allaying Dylan's belated fear that he might object. Jesus, if Dylan was going to offer to be Chris's partner, he was going to have to remember to consult with him ahead of time on decisions like this. In an attempt to communicate all of this silently, Dylan gave Chris a sheepish little grin. Chris cheerfully flipped him off in return.

Mrs. Phillips was waiting serenely for them, her cane resting on her lap. "Did you have a nice time, boys?"

"They're going give me studio space in exchange for the sweat of my brow," Ery replied. "And the pond's really cute. They have ducks. Also lots and lots of blackberries. Are you going to get some animals too, guys? Goats maybe. I've always thought goats were cool."

Dylan cleared his throat. "Probably not the best idea."

"Why not?" Then Ery's eyes widened. "Oh! Ohhh. Yeah, okay."

Mrs. Phillips looked puzzled. "Have you something against animals?"

What the hell, Dylan thought. This lady was being nice enough to help him out, and on short notice too. He owed her some honesty. "I'm a werewolf," he sighed.

She blinked at him, then looked at Chris and Ery, as if expecting one of them to let her in on the punch line. But they only nodded at her.

"My hearing is occasionally poor, dear. Did you say that you are a *werewolf?*"

"Yes."

"Ah. Is this… a condition to which one is born?"

"No. I caught it. From the guy I originally thought was the ghost, actually."

"I see." And unexpectedly, her face broadened into a smile. "Isn't it wonderful? I will be eighty-four years old in September, and yet life still holds surprises for me. There is always something new under the sun, it seems. Or under the moon, in this case."

Chris snorted a laugh and Ery joined in. Dylan was just so relieved that he'd outed himself again without anyone taking up torches and pitchforks that all he could do was smile weakly.

She beamed indulgently at them before she became more serious. "I would very much enjoy discussing this with you at some point in the future, but I am an old woman, we have a long drive home, and it's nearly dinnertime. Let me tell you about your spirit."

Dylan decided he wanted to sit down. Chris came to stand behind him, hands on Dylan's shoulders. "Go ahead," they said in unison, which made everyone chuckle.

"I cannot actually speak with spirits in words, but I can receive images from them. It reminds me of the early days of television—well before your time, boys—when my husband would move the antenna around endlessly and only obtain a very fuzzy, grainy view. It made my head ache and I never did get in the habit of watching the machine." She shook her head slightly. "The spirit sent me images of you, Chris, and also of Dylan. And there was an older man whom I presume is Chris's father—you two look very much alike—and very fast glimpses of other people as well. A young married couple, I believe, and a few other men and women about your age. And there were a great many views of what I expect was your farm. Or perhaps I would be more accurate in saying *farms*."

"Okay," said Chris. "So what does it mean?"

"Just what the spirit wrote, actually. Family. He wishes you to reunite what remains of your family. I had the distinct feeling that he wants this not so much for himself as for you, Chris. For all of you. He realized belatedly how precious family is, and he wants to help you realize the same thing."

Chris's fingers dug into Dylan's shoulders. "What if… what if I don't make up with Jimmy? What if I can't?" He sounded lost, and Dylan wanted to fold him in his arms and hold him tight. Instead, Dylan settled a hand over one of Chris's.

"This spirit means you no harm," Mrs. Phillips said. "It certainly won't punish you if you cannot comply."

"But he won't rest either, will he? Uncle Frank will be stuck as a ghost."

"That's not your responsibility, dear. You must do what you think is best for you and those you love."

She looked tired. Ery must have noticed too, because he hurried to help her to her feet. As she slowly made her way to the car, Ery at her side and Dylan very close by, Chris disappeared into the kitchen. He reappeared when they were standing near Ery's car; he had a foil-wrapped package in his hand. "The rest of the bread," he said.

She took it with a smile. "Thank you. I will enjoy this for breakfast tomorrow. You won't forget to send me the recipe?"

"I'll have Dyl e-mail it to Ery."

Mrs. Phillips shook her head slightly. "The wonders of the modern age!"

Dylan opened the car door for her. "Thanks so much for doing this for us."

"It has been my pleasure. I do hope we can meet again soon so I can hear more about this werewolf business."

"Sure."

With Dylan's help, she managed to lower herself into the seat. Ery put her cane in the backseat but she held on to the bread. She smiled up at Chris. "You're good boys. I am positive that you will make the right decision and everything will work out for the best. My husband liked to tease me about my optimism—he called me Pangloss, you know. But I do tend to expect the best of people, and in all my long years, I've not often been disappointed."

Chris and Dylan waved as the car drove back toward the county road. Then they just stood there.

"Dyl, I—" Chris began.

And Dylan gave in to the impulse he'd been resisting for so long: he folded his arms around Chris and drew him close. "I love you," Dylan murmured. "I love you and we'll work this all out. No decisions today. No hurry."

After a brief silence, during which he allowed his weight to rest fully against Dylan, Chris pulled back a little. "I'm hungry. Let's go find something to eat."

"Isn't that supposed to be my line?"

They held hands as they walked back into the house.

CHAPTER 20

THE ghost watched Chris while he worked on Thursday. Chris couldn't see the ghost, but he could feel its gaze. Sometimes he even talked to it, chatting about what he was doing—"Warmin' up the putty"—or reminiscing about the times when he was a kid and he'd sneak onto Frank's property to swim or climb trees. He had the sense that the ghost was listening closely, although Chris didn't know if it really understood what he was saying. Maybe it just liked having a little company after all these years.

Dylan helped him for a short while, holding the glass steady while Chris installed the glazier's points. But then Dylan disappeared back to the office to work on his plans, leaving Chris and the ghost to themselves.

When the window was set, Chris headed out back of his house to tinker with the Impala. It was a glorious thing, really, to be outside shirtless on a beautiful day, half-buried in an old car and with a cooler full of beer near at hand—knowing that a good shower and a good man were waiting for him inside. Dylan even carried out a couple of sandwiches at lunchtime and sat beside him on the hood of an ancient brown Pontiac, eating and listening to Chris go on about car repair. And the sandwiches were fairly decent.

Shortly before dinnertime, Chris took that shower. Got himself good and randy too, thinking about his guy, so that he ended up going downstairs naked and erect, dragging Dylan away from the laptop, and riding him hard as any rodeo cowboy.

Dinner was scrambled eggs with chorizo and queso fresco, with tortillas and fruit on the side.

"Will you come into the city with me tomorrow?" Dylan asked. "We could have lunch with Matty again."

"Nah. I'm pretty close to getting that car runnin'. And we need a grocery run too."

Dylan looked a little disappointed, which Chris thought was nice, but he shrugged and shoveled another forkful into his mouth. "Okay. Want me to bring you anything back?"

"Hmm." A thought occurred that made him grin wickedly. "You remember that shop near the bookstore? You know, the one with the toys? Could pick up something there."

Dylan's eyes went a little glassy as he considered the possibilities. "Did you, um, have anything specific in mind?"

Chris considered. Butt plug? Cuffs? Maybe a nice leather blindfold or a silk G-string? "Surprise me," he said.

They watched a little TV over at Chris's place that night, and afterward lugged the set over to the big house and set it up in the living room on top of a table. Dylan frowned critically. "Should we get a decent stand for it or hang it on the wall?"

"Whatever you want, man."

"But you live here too."

Chris set his hands on Dylan's shoulders. "Look, Dyl. I'm never gonna particularly care what color you paint a wall or whether the armoire you buy is oak or walnut. You take care of that shit, and I'll make sure our cars stay runnin' and we don't eat crap, okay?"

"A partnership," Dylan answered with a smile.

"Yeah. So you decide where you wanna stick the TV and I'll take care of movin' the satellite service to this house."

"Do we have to have a dish on the roof?"

Chris patted him. "I'll put it somewhere where it won't look too redneck, okay?"

Dylan sighed. "Fine. Just don't fall off the roof and crack your skull. You don't have insurance."

Chris rolled his eyes, but in truth he liked the idea of someone fussing over him a little. Nobody on the face of the earth had ever cared before whether he was insured.

CHRIS looked up from making breakfast, and the sight of Dylan coming down the stairs nearly took his breath away. Dylan wore a pair of expensive jeans, a green shirt that set off the color of his eyes, and a blue-and-gray tie. He'd tamed his hair, at least for the moment, and he was freshly shaved. He looked like someone important. "You clean up nice," Chris mumbled as he transferred bacon to a paper towel-covered plate.

"Technically today's casual Friday, but I don't think I qualify since I'm not there the rest of the week. Besides, I think my dressier clothes were feeling neglected."

"We can go out somewhere fancy for my birthday—somewhere with a really good steak—and I'll wear that stuff I bought last week."

"I know just the place. They have killer onion rings too."

After they finished eating, Dylan began to clear the plates, but Chris pushed him away. "I'll do it. Just this once. You go be the big manly breadwinner." And then he gave him the now traditional architectural-good-luck kiss.

Chris sort of puttered around after Dylan left. He was rarely by himself anymore, which was a good thing, but a few hours of solitude in anticipation of a happy reunion were survivable. Besides, this way he could listen to his own music instead of lame indie songs by art school dropouts who didn't have a clue what to do with a guitar.

He checked on the upstairs window. The putty wasn't quite dry enough to paint, but with the warm weather continuing, it should be ready by the next day. Then he and Dylan could hang the curtain Dylan had picked out and move Dylan's furniture in. By Monday, they should be ready to do some fun destruction in the master bedroom. Chris really enjoyed knocking down walls.

But now the great outdoors was calling him—the great outdoors and one nearly functional Impala. He stuck a couple of beers into a cooler and headed to the de facto junkyard behind his house.

He loved the way old cars had so much space under the hood and relatively few parts. The Impala was a simple, straightforward beast, one that would purr and roar if you treated it just right. But considering the fact that his boyfriend was a werewolf, maybe the cat analogy wasn't the best idea. He whistled softly to himself as he worked, stopping now and then for a sip of cold brew. He had a quick sandwich for lunch and went back to work.

Chris was headfirst in the Impala's innards when he heard a vehicle approaching. It wasn't the put-put of the mailman's old Jeep, and it wasn't the powerful rumble of Dylan's Silverado. This engine sort of rattled and wheezed, and as the vehicle came closer, he could make out the rattle-thump of bad springs. He cursorily wiped his hands on a rag, grabbed his open beer, and walked around the house—just in time to see Jimmy Nock dismounting from a battered old Ford pickup with a rusty camper shell.

Jimmy saw him too, and came to a halt. They stared at each other for a minute. "Tasha said you called," Jimmy finally said.

After a pause, Chris said, "Yeah."

"So can I…. I'd really like to talk to you, son."

Chris bristled at *son* but managed to hold his tongue. He took a long pull from his bottle. "Want one?" he asked.

"I don't drink no more. Been sober for almost five years."

"Bully for you."

Jimmy either didn't notice the sarcasm or chose to ignore it. He came a few steps closer, but warily, as if he wasn't sure what the reaction would be. Chris held his ground, standing knee-deep in the weeds that grew in front of his house.

"We can talk?" Jimmy asked.

"Guess so." Chris considered a better spot for their conversation to take place. He felt stupid just standing there but didn't especially want to invite Jimmy into either house. For the first time, he wished Dylan had bought those expensive chairs he'd been contemplating for the big house's front porch. "This way," he finally said, jerking his head toward the back of the small house.

Jimmy kept well behind as he followed Chris around. He glanced at Chris's back deck but didn't comment on the cans, bottles, and broken furniture scattered there. He smiled a little when he caught sight of Chris's collection of cars and trucks. "That Pontiac was my dad's, wasn't it? I remember when he got it. Bought it used off this guy in St. Helens. He was so proud of that car."

"It don't run. Hasn't for years."

"Yeah." Jimmy nodded. He watched as Chris leaned up against the Cat, set down the beer, and fished a pack of cigarettes out of his pocket. Chris lit one, not offering one to Jimmy. But Jimmy pulled out and lit his own.

They stood and smoked silently for a while, not looking one another in the eyes.

Jimmy ground out the butt with his heel and stuck his hands in his pockets. He was wearing faded jeans with a plaid shirt tucked into the waistband. His belt buckle was a fancy one—maybe made by this Tasha person—and he wore pointy-toed cowboy boots. He cleared his throat. "These last couple of decades, they ain't been easy for me."

Chris could have guessed that from the lines on the man's face and the wariness in his eyes, but all he said was, "So? You think they've been great for me? Now—*now* things are pretty damn good. But that's a recent thing."

"Do you want that other fella here while we talk?"

"My lover? He ain't here."

Jimmy frowned. "Did he leave you?"

"*Dylan* won't leave me," Chris spat. "Dylan's a decent human being."

"I was… was tryin' to be decent too. In a fucked-up way, maybe, but I tried."

Chris shook his head and flicked his own butt into the dirt. He didn't know how he was supposed to react. Did this guy want forgiveness? Because Chris didn't know if he had that in him, especially if Jimmy was going to make up excuses for what he did.

"There was nothin' decent about what you did. Do you have any idea what it was like to grow up with Mom as my only parent? Half the time she barely knew I was there, and the rest…. She had *boyfriends*. A lot of 'em. She wasn't usually in any shape to stand between them and me, and even when she could've done somethin', well, they were payin' the rent, weren't they. Couldn't afford to piss them off." His mouth tasted acrid and bitter after he said these things. He'd never talked much about them with anyone, not even Dylan—although Dylan was a smart guy, and Chris was pretty certain his partner had figured it out for himself.

Jimmy's jaw worked. "I'm sorry."

"Not sorry enough."

Chris spun around and stomped back toward his house. He intended to go inside, slam the door, and get really wasted. But when he stepped onto the deck, something made him glance up in the direction of the poplar trees. He could see the window he'd just installed and, on the other side of the new glass, a face that was blurry but still managed to look anxious.

"Fuck," Chris swore to himself. He sat on the edge of the splintery wood, his legs dangling over the edge, and waited for Jimmy to catch up. The very first time he'd seen Dylan was through that window. Chris had been a little drunk, and he'd wandered outside to take a leak. He'd looked up, and for just a second he'd thought the old man was back, staring over at him. A few minutes later, after going inside and putting on some jeans, Chris had gotten a better look at his new neighbor-to-be. The guy was hot as hell—sexy enough that Chris nearly popped a woody just looking at him. But the guy had one of those stupid-ass soul patches, hundred-dollar jeans, and a T-shirt screen-printed with the image of an old-style boom box. And he'd been standing there with his prissy little real estate agent, staring at Chris the way someone might look at a squashed possum on the side of the road.

But Dylan had bought the place and moved in, and equal parts loneliness and horniness had driven Chris to give him a shot. Dylan had given his hick neighbor a shot too.

And look where they were today.

Jimmy sat on the edge of the deck, several feet from Chris. They each lit another cigarette.

"What do you remember about me, Chris? From when you were a kid?"

"Not much."

To Chris's surprise, Jimmy looked more relieved than disappointed. "I was a shitty father. I want you to know, though—I wanted a son. Was thrilled as fuck when you were born, even if I was scared to death. I used to picture us...." He stopped to take a drag. "You know what my dad was like. Hardly got a word out of him. Felt like I never really knew him, even though he was always around. I used to promise myself that I'd do better by my own kid, that we'd... that we'd be close."

"That didn't work out," Chris said flatly.

"No. I had good intentions, Chris, I really did. And you—God, you were this amazing kid! So smart. I'm not a smart man, never was. But you'd pick up on things so quick, without anyone even teachin' you. You learned to read when you were three years old, and I still don't know how. *Sesame Street* maybe."

Chris blinked at him. Of all the things he might have guessed he'd hear, testimony of his own intelligence wasn't on the list. Nobody ever called him smart. Well, Dylan did sometimes, but Dylan had a big old blind spot when it came to Chris.

Maybe encouraged by Chris's silence, Jimmy continued. "When you were hardly more than a baby, you'd take shit apart, like my alarm clock. Used to make me so goddamn mad, until I saw that most of the time you put it together again—the right way. And when I came home…. Chris, I'd be off working some crap job, just supposed to be grateful I could get work at all, and when I came home you'd scream *Daddy!* and come runnin' at me with this big ol' smile on your face. Wasn't no one ever that glad to see me."

Chris had a flash of memory: rushing toward his father, who was huge and strong, and being lifted up in the air, tossed high, laughing and screaming with joy. His father had smelled like sweat and cow manure.

"If I was so fucking wonderful, why'd you leave me?" he asked. This time he stubbed out his cigarette in the dirt of a nearby flowerpot.

"I didn't leave 'cause there was anything wrong with you, Chris. That wasn't it at all."

"*It's not you, it's me,*" Chris said sarcastically. "That's an old line."

"But it *was* me. Your mom and me—we wasn't gettin' along. I was drinkin', she was, well, I don't know what all she was doing. Drugs, other men. If I tried to confront her about it, she blamed me, told me she was fucked up 'cause I made her miserable." He shrugged. "Maybe I did. Was pretty much a mutual thing at the end."

Jimmy was wearing a ring on the middle finger of his right hand. He began to play with it, twisting it nervously back and forth as if it were too tight. "I was gonna take you away. Was gonna leave her and take you with me. Don't know where I'd've taken you. Here, I guess. I figured my dad would take us in and I could get a fresh start."

Chris wasn't looking at him. He didn't want to see the man's expression. It was difficult enough to hear the anguish in his voice—especially difficult when Chris was trying to harden his heart. "But you didn't," Chris said hoarsely.

"I came home from work one day. I'd had a few at a bar already—was doin' that then, sort of fortifying me to face your mother. Had a few more right as soon as I walked in the door. Hell, you brought me those beers. You'd do that, fetch me cans and pop 'em open for me, smiling and proud to be helpin' out. I got good and wasted that night. I usually did. And me and your mom was arguin', and you said somethin' smartass. Don't remember what. But I remember pickin' you up and yellin' at you, and you were cryin' and I just yelled some more and...."

Jimmy stopped talking and twisted around to face Chris. Chris looked over at him. Looked right into those eyes that so closely resembled the ones staring back from his mirror every day. "And?" Chris prompted, almost gently.

"Busted your arm." Jimmy took a deep, whooping breath and let it out again. "*Heard* the damn thing snap like wet kindling. Do you remember?"

Chris had a vague memory of an irritating, itchy cast. It wasn't something he associated with his father, in part because the timing of it was pretty vague to him. A couple of his mother's boyfriends had sent him to the hospital too, and he'd fallen off his share of trees and roofs and bicycles when he was a kid. He shook his head.

Jimmy's expression was strange. "Figured you'd been rememberin' that all along," he mumbled. Then, more clearly, "I left after that. Your mom was gonna call the cops on me, and anyway, I thought.... Fuck, I was so *ashamed*. To hurt a little boy. To hurt the son I loved." This time his voice cracked and he looked away.

Chris, though... Chris felt an odd lightness in his heart. No matter what Dylan or anyone else had said to him, and despite common sense, he'd always blamed himself for his father's disappearance. At the very least, he'd assumed there was something fundamentally unlovable about him, something that led both his parents to reject him and caused his grandfather to remain distant and cold. But now, if Jimmy's story was true, it turned out that Jimmy had abandoned him out of a twisted sense of love.

"But why didn't you come back? Once I was older, I mean. You never even sent me a goddamn birthday card."

"My life didn't improve none once I'd gone," Jimmy said. "Still drank. Still fucked things up. Moved around a lot. Ended up in jail a few times. And then a few years ago I had a scare. I was drunk drivin' and crashed my car into someone else. There was a whole family in that SUV. Little kids. Thank God none of 'em got worse than a little banged up. I got hurt worse. Spent a long time in the hospital. But for once luck was on my side and I ended up in drug court instead of the regular kind. The judge, God bless her, she sentenced me to treatment instead of jail. Wasn't the first time I tried to dry out, but this time it stuck."

Jimmy's hand went to his shirt pocket, as if he were going after another cigarette, but then he let his hand drop. He started playing with his ring again. "It stuck and I stuck with it, and I ain't had a drink since. And I met Tasha. She's… she's pretty special. She makes jewelry—well, you knew that—and she gave me a break, lets me sell it for her at these fairs and rodeos and shit. I do okay at it." He smiled faintly. "Tasha puts up with me."

Chris hopped down from the deck into the weeds. He stood with his back to Jimmy. "But you still never tried to get in touch. I ain't that hard to find, been living here for years. But you never tried, not until we ran into you at the rodeo."

"I was afraid."

Chris spun around to look at him. "Afraid of what?"

"You. You… hatin' me. I knew you must, but as long as I didn't see you, I didn't have to face that. I know it was chickenshit of me. My AA sponsor and Tasha both gave me hell over it. But I ain't a strong man, Chris. Not like you. The way you looked at me when you saw me at the rodeo, and later over on that porch…." He waved in the general direction of Dylan's house. "I knew you'd look at me like that 'cause I fuckin' deserve it, and that scared me more than anythin' ever has."

Jimmy's voice had grown strained; he made a visible effort to get himself under control. Then he slid off the deck and stood near Chris, almost close enough to touch. Chris realized with a start that Jimmy was shorter than him by a good couple of inches.

"When I saw you at the rodeo," Jimmy said, "it was like my biggest fear and my biggest hope both came true at once. After that—well, that's the closest I've come in years to havin' a drink. But I didn't.

And I could tell… you got someone who loves you, don't you? That Dylan looks like he'd walk through the fires of hell for you."

"He would," Chris said confidently.

"Good. I figured you maybe needed to know the whole truth of things. It's been poisonin' me for years, son. If you can't forgive me, I understand. But you still need to know that I loved you, and you were a hell of a kid… and judgin' by the way Dylan stands by you, I bet you're a hell of a man."

There was a hard, mean part of Chris that wanted to hate this man. Wanted to tell him how much his decisions had fucked up Chris's life, and wanted to punch him in the gut and tell him to get the hell off Chris's property. That might even feel satisfying for a while.

But then he glanced up past the poplars again. The ghost was at the window, just watching. Uncle Frank had watched from up there for years when he was alive, his fingers gripping the walls, leaving dirty marks on the yellow paint. Maybe he'd been mostly angry, but maybe he'd felt loss and regret too. And then he'd apparently decided that holding on to that fury wasn't worth it anymore—that by keeping a grudge against the brother who'd wronged him, Frank had lost far too much. Unfortunately, he'd come by this realization too late, after his brother was dead and buried, when his own health was failing and he was living all alone in a big house badly in need of repair.

Chris didn't want to be Uncle Frank—so he let his anger go.

It was as easy as that, just like dropping a heavy weight. And as soon as he did, he felt this amazing lightness. Something had been weighing him down for so very long that now he felt as if he might float away like a toy balloon. His knees almost gave out with the relief of it, so he clutched the wooden planks for support.

And for the very first time in twenty-five years, Chris smiled at his father.

They didn't embrace, didn't break down in tears. But Jimmy smiled back, looking suddenly years younger. And when Chris held his hand out, Jimmy shook it. Firmly. His hands were as hard and calloused as Chris's own.

"Why don't you come on inside?" Chris offered. "I can get you some cold water to drink at least."

"I'd like that."

Chris led him to the big house, which seemed to surprise Jimmy a little but for some reason felt right to Chris. "You know, I've never been in here," Jimmy said, looking around as they entered. "Grew up right over there but never once set foot through this door. I used to be real jealous—I was crammed in that little house with Mom and Dad, and Uncle Frank got this big place all to himself."

"I don't think Frank enjoyed it all that much."

"Named you after him, you know."

Chris stopped to blink at him. "You did?"

"Middle name, yeah. Christian was your mom's idea. She found Jesus 'bout when she got pregnant. Lost him again not long after you were born."

Somehow, Chris wasn't surprised by that revelation. But it was the origin of his middle name that interested him more at the moment. "Why'd you name me after him? Were you guys friendly?"

"Nope. Never said a word. But my pops was so sad over losin' him and too damn stubborn to do anythin' about it. Frank—I'd see him watchin', and I bet he had regrets too. I thought if I gave you his name, that might help smooth things over. Sent him a birth announcement and everythin'." Jimmy laughed softly. "Ended up with this envelope under the door at Pops' house, but with your name on it. Had a hundred bucks cash inside. No note. Did you ever talk to him?"

"Not exactly. But he kinda talked to me."

"Whatta you mean?"

What the hell, Chris thought. This was Jimmy's family too. "Come sit down. I got a story for you."

They began to head toward the kitchen. But before they got there, Chris heard another vehicle. Not Dylan's—wrong sound and it was too early for him to be home—but it sounded big. "Hang on," he said to Jimmy.

Jimmy tagged along as Chris walked back down the hall, out the front door, and onto the porch. A Suburban pulled up right in front. It was an old one, its metal dented and its white paint scratched. It stopped, but the engine didn't turn off. All four doors opened and a bunch of people piled out.

Chris recognized the driver right away. "What are you doin' here?" Chris called out.

Chester took a few steps toward the house, his pack close behind. He gave a slow, evil smile. "Decided I didn't like the idea of a stray mutt and his bitch in my territory. We're cleaning house."

Chris grabbed Jimmy's arm, dragged him back into the house, and slammed the door shut. He locked it, then shoved his confused father hard down the hallway. "For fuck's sake, man. Run!"

CHAPTER 21

DYLAN shouldn't have been nervous about the meeting with Stender. His job wasn't on the line; neither was his permission to telecommute. The futon queens' castle in Beaverton wasn't even complete yet, but it was already drawing a lot of advance buzz. There had been an interview with an important magazine, and a couple of other architectural firms had called, feeling Dylan out about his willingness to jump ship. Whatever happened today, he was not going to end up jobless, homeless, and desperate.

He was nervous anyway.

He gave the receptionist a shaky smile when he arrived at the office, then headed down the hallway to the office he used to share with Matty. She now shared it with Brian—a fact she complained about often. Brian was a good architect, but he was also obsessed with the Trailblazers, brought smelly lunches, and tended to talk to himself as he worked.

Both Brian and Matty looked up when Dylan knocked on their open door. Brian made a face and bent back over his monitor, but Matty smiled. "Ready to impress?"

"I hope so."

"Lunch with you and Chris afterwards?"

"Chris stayed home. He has a to-do list. I'm free, though, if you can tolerate me solo."

"Yeah, I guess so." She gave him a wink. "Good luck. Not that you need it."

Stender had explained to him at the beginning of the project that he and Dylan would take the lead but other people would be working on it as well. Even though today's meeting would involve only the two of them, they were booked into the big conference room overlooking the river toward downtown. "Good energies in that room," Stender had explained over the phone.

Dylan was a little early and the room was empty when he arrived. He wavered for a few moments over where to sit before choosing a spot and booting up his computer. Having learned a lesson from one of his prior important meetings, he made a quick visit to the bathroom to empty his bladder—and to check his hair and tie. Seconds after he returned to his seat, Stender sailed into the room. As always, he wore designer jeans and a black long-sleeved tee, both of which had probably cost him a small fortune. He smiled at Dylan and surprised him by taking the chair next to him instead of across the table.

"I'm very excited to see your concepts, Dylan." He'd brought an iPad instead of a laptop, and now he used a stylus to open some image files and a note-taking app.

"Thanks. It's been kind of a challenge for me. In a good way, of course!"

Stender had a smile that said nothing in the entire universe was worth worrying about. Dylan wondered if he practiced that smile during meditation sessions. "I'm sure you're up to the task. This wasn't meant as a test of your abilities, Dylan. I'm just trying to get you out of your comfort zone a little so you can stretch your limits. That's where true creativity happens."

"I appreciate your confidence."

"Dylan, if you meet my expectations, you could be looking at a partnership in a year or two. That would be a tremendous accomplishment for a man as young as you, but I have the feeling that Stender & Warner, PLLC, would take the architectural world by storm."

Dylan gulped. Yeah, no pressure, no pressure at all. "Thanks," he squeaked.

His boss adjusted his glasses a little. "I have to admit, I was slightly skeptical about you telecommuting. Generally, I find that a synthesis occurs when designers spend time with one another and bounce ideas around. In that milieu, everyone's productivity and originality is improved. But you've overcome my skepticism. Whatever you've found out there in the hinterlands seems to be working very well for you."

"I like it out there. I love my home, my partner." *My freedom*, he could have added. "I get a lot of good ideas when I'm working on my own house."

Stender nodded. "Physical activity can free the mind to pursue new pathways." He always talked like that, as if he'd spent a lot of time mainlining self-help courses on creativity. Dylan wondered if he spoke like that in the bedroom too: *You see, my darling, if you position your legs just like that, we'll have better access to your wellspring of inspiration.*

Dylan had to bite his tongue hard to suppress an inappropriate snort of laughter.

With a deep breath to steady himself, Dylan opened the file with his list of ideas. "This is just sort of a brainstorming thing for now," he explained. "I'm not necessarily suggesting we do all of this."

"Excellent."

So Dylan went through his list, explaining each item in some detail. Stender didn't react much other than to nod now and then or ask for a few clarifications. It was hard to read him, but at least he didn't seem horrified. And Dylan was pretty sure he saw an enthusiastic twitch when he described the rooftop garden. As he finished up, Dylan added, "Matty had the great idea of considering LEED certification. I've done a little research and I think we could pull it off. It's something the school could advertise, and it would also be a good selling point for your firm's future commercial contracts."

"*Our* firm," Stender said.

"I've drafted a few rough plans incorporating these ideas, just to give you a notion what I was thinking. I'm going to have to do more work on the feasibility of some of the options, though, and the cost considerations."

"That's fine. At this point rough ideas are all I wanted."

Dylan showed him the plans. Again, Stender mostly let him talk, although he pointed at a few things and asked some questions. He had a few suggestions as well, which Dylan took as a good sign: if Stender hated his ideas, he wouldn't have offered improvements.

Finally, Dylan completed his presentation. He leaned back a little in his chair and looked at his boss, who was smiling his Buddha smile.

After an exquisitely painful pause, Stender nodded once. "*That* is exactly what I was hoping for from you, Dylan."

Dylan let out a long and probably noisy sigh of relief.

Stender continued. "Some of your suggestions will need alteration, and you will need to look up the costs on everything. I have some ideas of my own, which I'll send in a detailed e-mail on Monday or Tuesday. You can respond, and by next Friday we can meet with the entire team. I want us all on the same page before we bring in the clients."

Feeling slightly light-headed, Dylan only nodded. Perhaps he managed a few more words before Stender shook his hand and glided out of the conference room. Dylan put his head down on the table and waited for his heart to slow to its normal speed.

When he felt more or less coherent again, he took out his phone and dialed Chris, eager to share the good news. But there was no answer. That was nothing unusual—Chris hadn't yet gotten into the habit of keeping his phone nearby. He'd never before had the need to stay in contact with anyone. At least Dylan had bullied him into remembering to check the device periodically for messages. It wasn't that Dylan didn't trust him or that he had control issues, it was only that he missed him. And ever since the nearly fatal incident with Andy, Dylan worried about Chris as well.

Voice mail came on. "Hey, Chris. It's all good. I miss you. I'm going to have lunch and make a stop or two, but I'll be home well before dinner. Give me a ring when you get a chance, please."

He ended the connection and began to power down his computer.

HE AND Matty took separate cars to a restaurant she was especially fond of on Northwest Twenty-Third. The food there was good, but Dylan had always assumed it was their spectacular dessert case that had really won his friend's loyalty. As always, parking in the area was challenging, making him miss his old Prius and the way it fit neatly into tight spaces.

Matty knew already that the morning meeting had gone well, but she still gave him a big hug when he met her in front of the restaurant. "Is Chris going to congratulate you properly when you get home?" she asked.

He blushed, which had probably been her intent. "Why the interest in my sex life?"

"A lot of straight women think boy-sex is really, really hot. It's just like the straight guys who like to watch lesbians, I suppose, only I'm not sure the porn world has quite caught on yet to the potential market here."

He shook his head. "Maybe you should start a new business."

"Maybe I should. You and Chris can be my first stars."

Dylan imagined getting naked and having sex in front of cameras and an audience. His stomach lurched and his face burned hot. "I don't think so."

"Spoilsport."

They were shown to a table near the window. The waiter was a good-looking guy who did his best to crawl into Dylan's lap while still maintaining an air of professional decorum. Even after a couple of years, Dylan still wasn't used to the avid attention he received. Before

Andy had bitten him, most men barely spared him a second glance. For a while he'd sort of welcomed the admiration—at least it made quick hookups a pretty sure thing—but not anymore. His heart was taken. He tried to radiate an aura of unavailability that didn't quite work. He preferred going out with Chris because Chris gave a death glare to anyone who paid attention to Dylan, making his territorial claim very clear.

As soon as the waiter took their orders—pasta for each—Dylan checked his phone. No missed calls.

"Something wrong?" Matty asked.

"I'd hoped to hear from Chris by now. I thought he'd be checking up on me." He shrugged. Probably Chris had gotten deeply involved in car repair and had lost track of the time.

"You guys really are joined at the hip. Told you."

"Hmm."

He changed the subject to the school project, which she was excited to hear more about. She seemed pleased by Stender's enthusiasm over the LEED certification thing, and when Dylan told her what Stender had said about a possible partnership, she squealed loudly enough to make the people at the next table turn and stare. Veering away from shoptalk, she bemoaned her lack of dating prospects and sought his advice on a vacation to Hawaii she was considering for the fall. The pasta was good, and she persuaded him to share a piece of chocolate bombe cake for dessert.

Chris didn't call. Dylan and Matty split the bill, had another hug, and walked in separate directions to their cars. As he walked, Dylan again tried ringing home but got no answer.

He considered heading straight back to the farm but decided Chris might be disappointed if he didn't get an X-rated gift. Hell, Dylan might be disappointed if he didn't *give* an X-rated gift. So he got into his truck and drove to the toy store. It again took him a while to park, and he had to endure angry stares from pedestrians and bicyclists who were upset with his very ungreen form of transport.

The store was fun, though. He and Chris had driven by but never gone in. The salesclerks—a young man with a dyed Mohawk and a young woman with impressive biceps and a lot of tattoos—gave him cheery greetings. It wasn't one of those skeezy places where trench-coated customers skulked in corners and where he'd be afraid to touch anything without a liberal application of antibacterial gel. This store was large and well lit; the displays of leather and lace, plastic and faux fur, rubber and steel were all attractive and enticing.

It was hard to make a decision. He'd never really used toys before, and he was a little leery of the really kinky stuff. He didn't know exactly where Chris's tastes might lie and what might freak him out.

He ended up with a basketful of items: a paddle covered in black fake fur, a red blindfold, a black leather cock ring with an attached vibrator, and a surprisingly beautiful butt plug made of purple and clear glass. Just thinking of using these things with Chris made his pants feel too tight. He was going to check out, but along the way he passed a display of collars and ended up selecting a black leather one with shiny metal studs. Maybe he'd slip that on the next time Chris made a canine-themed joke at Dylan's expense.

The saleslady chatted about the weather while she rang everything up, and asked him whether he needed any batteries.

As he walked back to his truck, he realized he'd spent longer than he'd intended in the store. He'd have to come back again, next time with Chris. He fantasized briefly about Chris in black leather chaps and nothing else. Maybe that rodeo had caused a lasting effect on his psyche.

Chris hadn't returned his call, and there was still no answer.

The traffic seemed to crawl especially slowly, and he swore steadily as he drove—he swore at the other cars impeding his progress, and he swore at himself for what he was sure were needless worries. He even imagined he could smell the turned-earth scent of Uncle Frank's ghost, which was ridiculous. Still, he tailgated and lane switched and generally made a nuisance of himself, and when he finally hit an open stretch of highway, he drove as fast as he thought he could get away with.

Finally the truck bumped onto the gravel of his and Chris's road, dirt spraying out behind him. He came around the curve and saw two vehicles that didn't belong: an old Ford truck with a camper, which he remembered from Jimmy Nock's previous visit to the farm, and a battered Suburban he didn't recognize.

Calm down, he told himself as he brought his own truck to a screeching halt. Maybe Jimmy brought friends. But his heart was thud-thudding in his chest and a thin film of sweat had formed over his skin. He jerked the keys from the ignition and vaulted out of the cab.

"Chris!" he called, even as he ran. "Chris!"

There was no answer. But as he sprinted to his front porch he caught a strong scent. It was familiar—he'd experienced it a few days earlier in Gresham. Chester and his pack.

The front door was wide open, but not in a welcoming way. Someone had kicked a hole right through it and then most likely reached in to disengage the locks. He was still shouting as he entered. "Chris! Dammit, Chris, where are you?"

When there was no response, he paused and took a few deep breaths. He could smell his partner, of course. Also another man, one who smoked cheap cigarettes and spent time around hot metal, and whose scent was similar to Chris's. Jimmy. And there was the reek of werewolves. Five or six of them, he thought; it was hard to tell. The only comforting thing was that he didn't smell blood. The graveyard smell of the ghost was very strong, and Dylan didn't have the time to puzzle out the meaning of that.

Forcing himself to move slowly, he tracked the scents down the hallway and into the kitchen. The back door was open as well, this time without signs of damage. It was possible that Chris had doubled back and was now somewhere inside the house, but Dylan decided that was unlikely. He followed the trail outside.

He'd never really thought much about scent-tracking dogs, but he now had a new respect for them. True, his senses were somewhat dulled in his human form, but he had the impression that even as a wolf, he'd have had trouble finding the right path through the confusion of odors in the backyard. Chris had spent a lot of time there since the last good rain, so his scent was everywhere. So were Jimmy's and the pack's, but theirs crisscrossed with the dozens of trails left by a variety of mammals, snakes, birds, and even insects.

When Dylan had been very, very young, his mother occasionally let him amuse himself by looking through her box of costume jewelry. Maybe she should have suspected even back then that her younger son wasn't exactly gender compliant. But Dylan used to enjoy looking at the glittering earrings and shiny pins. And he'd spent long periods trying to tease apart the tangles that formed in her necklace chains.

That was what tracking was like right now—teasing apart a few desired scents from a tangle of others.

After what felt like hours, he found himself down at the edge of the pond. But there he lost Chris and Jimmy's scents altogether, and even after spending many increasingly frantic minutes casting around, he couldn't pick them up again. "Chris! Chris!" As before, his calling was fruitless.

What he could find, however, were the tracks of Chester and his pack—moving away from the pond, back up the slope. This slightly encouraged Dylan. Maybe they'd lost Chris and Jimmy too and had given up the chase. Or maybe, a darker voice whispered in his mind, his lover and Jimmy were carried away in the pack's arms. Or were lying dead at the bottom of the very deep pond.

He realized he was making a desperate sound, a sort of keening whine, and forced himself to be quiet.

He couldn't decide what to do: search longer around the pond—maybe even cross to the forest on the other side—or follow the intruders back up the hill. He finally decided the latter. As he went, he considered calling 911, but to what end? How was he going to explain werewolves to the sheriff's department? Besides, it would take the cops a good twenty minutes to arrive, and that might be far too late. Dylan didn't know how much time had already passed since Chester and the others arrived.

Dylan tracked Chester through the Christmas trees—right over Andy's grave, in fact—and then to the line of poplars. He broke into a run when he saw Chris's back door hanging open again. The last time that had happened, Dylan had discovered Chris cornered in his own living room by Andy in wolf form.

There were no wolves in Chris's house this time. Chris wasn't there either. But Chester was, along with four members of his pack: three males and one female. They were taking up all the space in Chris's small living room. Chris's books lay scattered everywhere, torn to pieces; the ugly old furniture had been slashed and broken; and for some reason most of the pack looked a little singed around the edges.

"Where is he?" Dylan yelled at Chester, who was holding a book in his hands.

Chester smirked and ripped the volume in two, then tossed the pieces aside. "Your bitch is quite a bookworm, isn't he?"

"Where is he? What the fuck do you want?"

As Dylan shouted, two of the men slunk into place behind him, cutting off his escape through the back door. Chester and the others fanned out to form a circle around Dylan, with Chester directly in front of him.

"We want you, of course. Don't mind taking out your bitch too, but it's you we're after."

Dylan's heart raced and his lunch was heavy in his stomach. He couldn't tell from Chester's words whether Chris had been harmed, and it was pretty clear that Dylan himself was in deep shit.

"You agreed to leave me alone if I stayed away. I stayed away. Why are you here?"

Maybe Chester practiced his smile as often as Stender did. But Chester's smile was pure malice. "Change of heart. Decided it was too dangerous, having a lone wolf running around. I got connections, so it wasn't too hard to track you from your plates."

Dylan didn't especially care *how* these assholes had found him. "I'm not a wolf, for Chrissake. I'm a man. And I don't give a shit—"

"You're a *beast*," Chester growled, prowling a step closer. "You're trying to convince yourself you're a regular guy with a little monthly problem, but that's bullshit. Box of Kotex ain't gonna solve what ails us. We may be walking on two legs right now, but deep down inside where it really matters, we're *animals*. And you're intruding on my territory."

"This is *my* land!" Dylan shouted. "You're the goddamn intruders."

Another evil grin. "Maybe I figured it's time to expand a little."

Dylan looked at Chester and realized his own fundamental mistake. When they'd confronted each other in Gresham, they'd both realized Dylan was probably stronger than Chester. Dylan had told himself that didn't matter because he had no desire to lead a pack or defend territory or any of that other crap. But Chester had exactly those desires. To him, Dylan was a threat that needed to be eliminated if Chester wanted to preserve his own skin.

Dylan was currently surrounded, but Chester clearly felt cornered too. That wasn't a good thing at all.

Forcing himself to breathe evenly, forcing his voice to remain quiet, Dylan tried again to defuse the situation. "We don't have to do this. I don't want to challenge you. I just want—"

"Don't fucking care what you want, boy!" Flecks of spittle flew from Chester's lips. He stepped closer and so did his companions.

Dylan reached for the phone in his pocket. The cops wouldn't get there in time, but he had to do *something*. But as soon as the device was in his hand, one of the men behind him jumped forward and grabbed his arm. Dylan managed to push the man away, but in the process he dropped the phone. It bounced away and the woman gleefully stomped it to pieces with her boot.

That was the second phone he'd lost in an attack this year.

Still, he tried one more time. "Let's settle this like reasonable people."

Chester shook his head. "No. We'll settle this like wolves."

And to Dylan's utter horror, Chester began to change.

Dylan had seen a man shift to wolf once before, but at the time he'd been undergoing his own agonizing first change and hadn't been in any shape to observe. Now, though, he had a very close-hand view as Chester's face elongated into a muzzle and his teeth became long and sharp, as his body twisted and bent—his clothing torn off in the process—and as gray fur grew through the skin like a time-lapse video of a wheat field sprouting. Chester moaned and growled as this happened. His brown eyes lightened to gold; his ears became pointed, tufted with fur; and a long tail unfurled from his ass.

"But it's not a full moon," Dylan whispered. It was, in fact, very near the new moon, and besides, sunset was still hours away. But there was no mistaking what he'd just witnessed, just as it was undeniable that the men and woman around him were undergoing their own snarling, screaming transformations.

He thought to run as they were changing. But they'd catch him as soon as they gave chase. And in any case, where would he run to? He still didn't know where Chris was and whether he was safe. As long as Dylan remained here, the intruders would remain distracted.

Within minutes Dylan stood in Chris's living room amongst the wreckage of Chris's belongings, surrounded by a pack of wolves.

A terrible certainty settled in his heart. There was nothing he could do to survive this encounter. And worse, there was nothing he could do to stop the pack from finding Chris once Dylan was dead, and ripping him to shreds too. Assuming they hadn't already done so.

Grief, regret, and self-loathing hit him so hard he could barely keep to his feet, and they left no room for fear. But there was another emotion there too, one that felt almost delicious as it pounded through his veins. Rage. Even the anger he'd felt when he saw Andy attacking Chris paled in comparison to the fury that filled him now. Andy, at least, had been his alpha, and Andy had been trying—albeit in a wholly twisted way—to build a family of his own. Chester just wanted to destroy.

And suddenly, so did Dylan.

There was a little door inside him, one he'd been guarding very carefully for over two years, even though he didn't consciously know it existed. It was made of thick, rough planks bound together by heavy iron. Now, Dylan yanked open that door.

The change rippled through him more viciously than ever. Bones and tendons reformed into new shapes as he fell to all fours. His back bent agonizingly, his jaw and skull pinched and twisted, the insides of his skin felt as if they were being scrubbed by steel wool. It was glorious. Usually he managed to get his clothing off before a transformation, but now his body tore it to shreds. He kicked it impatiently out of the way. He lowered his head and his ears, lifted his lips to bare his fangs, and growled very deep in his chest.

Dylan didn't wait for the others to attack. He could no longer think clearly about *why* he was maddened or what this intruder had done to him. All Dylan knew was that he needed to feel his teeth sinking into hot flesh.

He leapt.

Chester was taken by surprise. Maybe he'd never truly been challenged before. He yelped as Dylan's weight knocked him to the ground, then tried to scramble back to his feet. But Dylan already had his jaws clamped tightly in place around Chester's throat. The heady taste of fresh blood filled his mouth, and Chester's struggles beneath him felt weak and useless.

If it had been just the two of them, Dylan would have won easily. He was younger than Chester and stronger, and he'd gotten the upper hand immediately. Dylan had more to fight for. But it wasn't just the two of them.

Another wolf slammed into Dylan, mouth aimed at his throat. Because of the way Dylan was pressed against Chester, that wolf got only a poor toothhold, mostly just fur. But then another wolf thudded into him from the other side and the remaining two dug claws and teeth into his legs and belly.

He released his grip on Chester to snap at one of the others. His teeth grazed along a muzzle, causing the creature to yip and fall back, but now Chester was free and struggling to his feet. A heavy weight landed on Dylan's back and sharp teeth dug deeply into his back. He roared and fell to his side, knocking the assailant loose, and then backed up against the wall, already bleeding. Five pairs of unblinking yellow eyes looked at him, not a spark of human mercy in any of them. Still, Dylan wasn't afraid, at least not the way a man would be. He was going to die. But before he drew his last breath, he was going to do as much damage to these bastards as possible.

CHAPTER 22

CHRIS had to give it to the old man—when Chris told him to run, he did, and without stopping to ask questions. Ran pretty fast too, although by the time they made it down to the pond, he was wheezing loudly.

Chris didn't have an escape plan. He was pretty much acting on instinct. He knew from experience as well as common sense that Chester and his crew would have no trouble breaking into the house and then busting down any doors that got in their way, so hiding indoors wasn't going to work. Calling the cavalry—the cops, Dylan, the fucking National Guard—wasn't an option either, because Chris's phone was sitting on the kitchen counter in the big house. Wouldn't have helped him anyway; nobody was going to get out to the farm fast enough to do any good. Their isolation from neighbors was a grand thing when Chris wanted to wander outside bare-assed or when Dylan went all furry, but not so great when it meant help was a couple of long miles away. Even the county road was a good distance away, and it wasn't heavily traveled.

On a full-out sprint across the wheat fields, Chris might have gotten away. Not Jimmy, though. And although Jimmy still wasn't at the top of Chris's favorite-people list, there was no way Chris was going to leave him to the wolves.

So they ran past the blackberry bramble down to the pond. As they reached the water, he heard a series of muffled booms, followed by alarmed shouts. He didn't know what the hell that was, and he wasn't about to wait and find out. He splashed right into the water. "Know how to swim?" he called back over his shoulder.

"Used to" was the panting reply.

The pond wasn't especially wide, and after not too many strokes, Chris used branches to lever himself onto the opposite bank. He turned around to give Jimmy a hand up.

The slope here was really steep, and everything was thickly overgrown with ferns and brush and probably goddamn poison oak. Dylan might not have much trouble navigating when he was down on all fours, but it was a challenge for the two-legged. Chris tugged at Jimmy's arm until they were out of sight of the water, then pulled him down to the ground. "I hope they can't track us here," Chris said.

"Track?" Poor Jimmy was having a hell of a time catching his breath.

More banging came from up the hill, followed by more yelling. Then the voices grew nearer, so Chris held a finger to his lips and hoped like hell Jimmy could quiet his lungs. Jimmy was clearly trying to be as still and silent as possible, so more points for him.

Feet splashed into water and then stopped. "They must've gone into the woods," said an unfamiliar male voice. "Pete and I can go get them."

"No." That voice Chris recognized—Chester. "They're not the real threat. We can get them later. For now, we need to track down the wolf."

"Maybe he's not here. I didn't see his truck."

"Then we'll give him a nice little welcome home party."

Chris's hands curled into tight fists, and it took all his willpower not to burst out of the woods and go after that son of a bitch. But he knew what one werewolf was capable of, let alone a pack, so he tensed his muscles and remained in hiding.

A woman said, "What the *hell* was that in the house? I don't want to poke around if we're going to find more of that."

"Yeah," a man chimed in. "Those zaps fucking *hurt*."

Chris frowned. What were they talking about?

But Chester had an answer. "Must've been some kinda high-tech security system or something. We'll stay out of the big house. He's not in there anyway. Paula, you stay here and give us a shout if the bitch comes out of the woods. And keep your ears cocked in case I call you."

"Okay." Paula didn't seem particularly thrilled with her assignment. Chris wasn't thrilled either, because as long as a guard was posted, he and Jimmy were stuck in the woods. It wasn't very comfortable, but worse than that, he had no way to warn Dylan.

"You got a phone?" he whispered as quietly as possible.

Jimmy shook his head gravely.

Fuck. In front of them was a pack of hostile werewolves and in back were miles and miles of woods. Chris had a pocketknife in his jeans, and they could probably make some makeshift weapons out of tree branches, but that wasn't going to be enough. Besides, stakes were for vampires, weren't they?

Insects and leaves tickled at Chris's bare shoulders and back, and his wet jeans chafed.

Jimmy was on his belly and had finally caught his breath. He scooted a few inches closer so he could put his head very close to Chris's. "Who are they?" he asked, mouthing the words more than speaking them.

Well, that was kind of a long story, wasn't it? "Bad guys."

"Guns?"

Chris didn't know the answer to that. "Dunno. But really dangerous."

"How?" Jimmy was surprisingly calm, and it occurred to Chris that his father might have gotten himself into a few ugly scrapes over the years. Probably none exactly like this, however.

Well, they had time to kill anyway, and if Chris didn't distract himself, he was going to do something stupid. "They're werewolves."

"What?"

"Werewolves. Yeah, they're real. Dylan's one too. Changes at the full moon. Seen it myself, more'n once." He sighed. "There's ghosts too. Uncle Frank's haunting Dylan's house, in fact. That was the story I was gonna tell you."

Jimmy looked at him as if he was seriously questioning Chris's sanity. Chris couldn't blame him. Chris was a matter-of-fact kind of guy who wouldn't have believed a word of this shit if he hadn't witnessed it himself. Then Jimmy sort of shrugged, maybe deciding the immediate danger was a more pressing problem than his son's mental state. "Whatta we gonna do?"

"Wait," Chris replied unhappily. Wait until either Chester grew bored and went away, which seemed unlikely, or Dylan appeared—and had to face an angry pack by himself.

Fuck.

IT WAS a long, long wait. The more he lay there in the dirt and leaves, the more ways his stomach found to tie itself into knots. Jimmy asked a few questions about the werewolf thing, like maybe he was trying out believing, but mostly he lay silent too. Chris knew Dylan had pretty good hearing and Paula probably did too.

Every now and then a bit of a breeze would bring them wisps of voices from the farm, but not enough to make out the words.

Chris tried to work out a way to get to the road. Then he could wait for Dylan to arrive and tell him to turn the fuck around. But the topography of the place was too challenging. The pond was in the way, as was the truly impenetrable mess of blackberries that ran at the back of Chris's plot of land. He should have taken the Cat to that bramble long ago, but he'd never anticipated needing an escape route. Maybe he could find a way through the forest, but he'd never been back here, not even when he was a kid. He was as likely to get lost as anything else, plus he wouldn't be able to help making a ton of noise if he moved.

God, he'd never felt as helpless and useless as he did at the moment. Dylan could rush in and save him from a homicidal wolf, but all Chris could do was hide in the bushes like a goddamn coward.

He didn't wear a watch, so he didn't know how much time had passed when he heard his name called. "Dylan," he hissed and then bit his tongue to keep from shouting back. He began to shake with the tension, swearing softly when Dylan called him again.

"Can't just let him get killed," he moaned.

Jimmy grabbed his wrist. "Chris, what—"

"Gotta *try*," Chris said. And he began to work his way back to the pond. When he heard Jimmy following close behind him, Chris turned to glare. "Stay *here*."

Jimmy shook his head. "I just found you. Ain't gonna let you go without a fight."

Under other circumstances, Chris would have been impressed, maybe even a little touched. Now he was just scared to death.

He got within sight of the pond just in time to see Dylan's back as Dylan disappeared over the top of the hill. Chris would have called to him, but a woman was crouching down low behind some bushes. Paula, no doubt—she must have been trying to hide from Dylan. Too chickenshit to take him on herself. Or maybe she was going to wait until Dylan was distracted and sneak up behind him.

Chris pulled out his pocketknife, swung open the blade, and deliberately made enough noise to draw Paula's attention. She snapped her head in his direction, giving him a feral grimace, then looked back up the hill, as if she couldn't decide what to do. She must have made up her mind, because she kicked off her shoes, her eyes locked on Chris. He waited for her with his tiny little knife. There was a rustling and cracking beside him as Jimmy tore a branch from the nearest tree.

Before Paula jumped into the water, she changed.

Chris had seen Dylan's change as recently as the last full moon. But even when it was some chick who was trying to kill him, and even when she was across the pond instead of in the same room, the transformation was stunning. Her body stretched and twisted in inhuman ways; her clothes went to pieces and dropped away.

"Holy fucking mother of God," Jimmy breathed.

"Told you."

"Thought you said it took a full moon. There's no moon, Chris."

"I know. Guess there's some twists I didn't know. Dylan's missing the manual."

The wolf leapt smoothly into the water and began to swim across. She was dog paddling, but she was good at it and was making swift progress. Chris's bowels felt watery. He'd seen way up close what one of these beasts could do—and how much punishment they could take and still put up a deadly fight. His knife and Jimmy's stick weren't going to be worth shit. But they were all they had.

"C'mon, Fluffy," Chris called with way more bravado than he felt. "Come get me."

And then Paula disappeared beneath the water with a strangled yelp.

"What the fuck—" Chris and Jimmy said in unison.

The wolf's head and front paws reappeared again, but she was clearly struggling to remain above the surface and maintain forward momentum. She yipped and made a few desperate splashes—and then submerged completely, as if she'd been jerked hard.

She didn't reappear.

Chris turned to Jimmy and they blinked at each other. "Dylan says there's a lot of junk down there. She must've got caught up on somethin'," Chris said.

Jimmy gave a doubtful nod.

It was a troubling mystery, but Chris didn't have time to play Sherlock Holmes right now. He jumped into the pond.

"Chris! There might be somethin'—"

Chris ignored Jimmy's warning. Yeah, there might be something dangerous in the water, but there was certainly something deadly on the other side—and Dylan. Chris splashed across the pond as quickly as possible. He paused only for a moment when he reached the opposite bank. Just long enough to shake himself dry like a dog and to give a hand to Jimmy, who'd followed faithfully right behind him. Together they ran up the hill.

The big house looked empty, the back door hanging open. Then Chris caught a quick movement off to the side, just underneath the spare bedroom. The thing he saw was glowing brightly and sort of pulsing in an agitated way. Uncle Frank, no doubt. Uncle Frank was pointing a ghostly arm in the direction of the poplars.

"Jimmy, my phone's in the kitchen. Go call the cops."

"What're you gonna—"

Chris didn't wait for Jimmy to finish the question. Instead, he sprinted toward his house. As he got closer, he could hear snarling and growling from inside, as well as the crashing of something heavy. He put on more speed, but before he made it to the trees, something slammed into his back hard enough to knock him off his feet.

For a moment he couldn't move. All the breath had been knocked out of him, and it felt as if something was trying to rearrange his interior organs. It fucking *hurt*. He thought he'd been shot. But when he managed to rise to a seated position, there was no blood, no holes that didn't belong. There was, however, a very strange feeling under his skin and along his spine, a sort of tightness and a tickling buzz that reminded him of the time he stuck a knife in a toaster.

"What the fuck?" he murmured, not for the first time that day.

He was very thankful to be able to stand again. He felt a little bruised but not exactly in pain. None of which mattered, because the fight in his house was still going on.

Stupidly, and with no hope of doing anything but delaying the inevitable, he ran up onto his deck and into his house.

His house was full of wolves. They all looked very, very large, crammed into his little living room. Large and scary, with raised hackles and bloody teeth. He had no problem, however, identifying which wolf was his: the one in the corner, who had fur very much the same color as Dylan's hair, and who had several ugly wounds on his muzzle and body.

Dylan saw him first, his yellow eyes widening. He barked something that was unmistakably a warning. Chris didn't have to speak wolf to know he was being told to run the fuck away. A couple of the other wolves turned to snarl at him as well. Chris held up his dumb little pocketknife. "Make my day." He was very proud that his voice didn't waver.

And then several things happened at once—all so fast, in fact, that he couldn't really track them all. Dylan jumped forward, latching his teeth into the neck of one of the wolves that had been distracted by Chris. A few more of the wolves leapt at Dylan, and blood splattered against the wall.

A scrawny wolf with blackish fur spun around and came at Chris, who took a half step back into the doorway. He lifted the blade into position. And from deep within himself he felt a *surge*, a flow of power so strong it was like having a nuclear blast in his stomach. Energy crackled out of him and hit the attacking wolf with a nauseating sizzle. The wolf fell to the ground, twitching and foaming at the mouth.

But that wasn't all. The energy continued to pour from him, hitting all the wolves—Dylan included—so that they dropped at once, like puppets with cut strings. And the energy hit the destroyed books and the damaged furniture, it hit the walls, it slithered into the insulation and wires.

There was a *boom* loud enough to deafen him, and flames erupted everywhere at once.

Chris felt suddenly as weak as a day-old kitten. But he didn't think. He ran into the room as fast as his rubbery legs would take him, he skirted the still-twitching pack, and he grabbed Dylan by the bloody scruff of his neck. And then he pulled with all his might, dragging Dylan over the other wolves, out of the room and onto the deck, down into the weedy patch that passed for his backyard.

224

He collapsed to the ground. He could feel the heat of the burning house behind him, but all his attention was focused on Dylan, who lay very still. "Dyl? Jesus, Dylan?"

The injured wolf rippled like a reflection in a funhouse mirror— and then was a man again, naked and bleeding, skin looking slightly singed here and there.

Chris fell on top of him, trying to detect if there was a pulse. But his own heart was beating so fast and erratically that he couldn't tell.

"Chris! Move!" Jimmy caught Chris's arm and tried to haul him upright. "The fire!"

Chris looked up at his father. "Help me carry him."

In fact, Jimmy did all the work, dragging Dylan's unmoving body until it was a safe distance from the fire. Chris staggered along behind, then fell to his knees at Dylan's side.

His entire world shifted when Dylan opened his eyes.

"Ch-Chris?" Dylan rasped.

Chris could only answer with a throaty sob.

Jimmy kept his head. He went into the house and fetched some jeans and a T-shirt for Dylan. By the time he got back, the bleeding had stopped and Dylan was sitting up, looking woozy and in pain but not in the midst of dying. Chris slumped next to him, so Jimmy helped Dylan put on his clothing.

The little house burned, and sirens sounded in the distance.

"What.... How.... Chris...." Dylan didn't seem able to manage a complete sentence.

Chris lay down next to him. "It's all right. Everything's gonna be all right."

Dylan attempted to smile. "My hero."

COPS arrived, followed shortly by paramedics and firemen. Lots of guys in uniform swarming all over the place, asking a lot of questions.

Dylan was too dazed to answer any of them but flatly refused to be transported to the hospital, no matter how much the paramedics threatened.

It was Jimmy who gave the authorities the most coherent story. He'd been visiting his son, hoping for a reunion, when a truckload of bad guys showed up. They threatened Jimmy and Chris, who took off for refuge in the woods. By the time Jimmy and Chris felt it was safe enough to emerge, the intruders had cornered Dylan in the small house and were about to beat him to a pulp. Chris had run in to help, there had been an explosion—probably somebody's stray cigarette had caught something on fire—and Chris had only managed to drag Dylan out of danger.

The firemen put out the fire eventually. Fortunately, the blaze hadn't spread to Chris's collection of vehicles, but there was nothing left of his house except smoking ruins. They found several charred human bodies inside.

The cops ran the plates on Chester's truck and discovered that he had a long arrest record. They seemed to buy Jimmy's and Chris's stories, which weren't really all that distant from the truth. A couple of detectives promised they'd be following up, but Chris didn't get the feeling there would be any trouble from that angle. Somebody towed away Chester's truck.

It was well past dark by the time Jimmy and Chris helped Dylan up the stairs to his bedroom. "Going to get the sheets dirty," Dylan mumbled.

"We can wash 'em tomorrow, Martha Stewart." Chris helped him undress, then tucked him into bed.

Jimmy made a quick, hearty stew for everyone. He was a good cook. Chris had forgotten that about him. But Dylan was able to eat only a few bites before his energy flagged completely. "Need to call Rick," he sighed.

Chris shook his head. "You sleep. I'll call him."

"Your house is gone. Everything you own."

"Didn't we just decide that *this* is my house now? And everythin' important to me is right here." Chris patted Dylan's shoulder. Dylan smiled even as his eyes fell shut.

Chris stood wearily and began to walk to the door.

"You should sleep too," Jimmy said. "You're all done in."

"After I call Dylan's brother."

"I'll bring you the phone. Then mind if I use it to call Tasha?"

"No. Go ahead."

Jimmy nodded. "How much can I tell her?"

"Tell her everything, man. I don't care."

"She's gonna think I been drinkin' again," Jimmy replied with a dry chuckle.

"Jimmy? Do you mind crashin' here tonight? Couch downstairs ain't bad. I think the three of us gonna need a chat tomorrow."

Jimmy smiled widely. "Guess I could manage that."

While Jimmy went downstairs, Chris slipped out of his filthy jeans and into a clean pair of Dylan's boxer briefs. Then he climbed into bed and, since nobody was a witness, gave his sleeping partner a sweet, tender, girly-girl kiss on the forehead. "I love you, Dylan Warner," he whispered.

Footsteps in the hallway announced Jimmy's return. He waited while Chris made a quick call to Rick and Kay—mostly a whole lot of *Calm down, figured you'd want to know, it's all over now, we'll call you in the morning*—then took the phone when Chris was done. Jimmy turned and walked to the bedroom door.

"Hey," Chris said softly.

Jimmy turned to look at him.

"You were… you were fucking amazing." He took a deep breath. "Thanks, Dad."

His father's answering smile could have lit the night sky.

But when Chris fell back onto the pillow and snuggled up close to Dylan, he realized he owed one more thank-you. He wasn't sure if the recipient was around anymore to hear it, but he had to say it anyway. "Thank you, Uncle Frank," he whispered. "You saved the family."

He couldn't be positive, but he thought he saw, just maybe, a happy little glow blink once out of the corner of his eye.

CHAPTER 23

THE cold November wind sent noisy gusts of rain against the house, but indoors everything was warm and cozy. Candles burned atop the fireplace mantel—unscented handmade soy candles Dylan had ordered from Etsy, but it was Chris who had lit them.

Dylan sat on the couch looking dazed. Chris wasn't sure what was causing the expression on his partner's face: the really satisfying blindfold-and-cock-ring-enhanced sex they'd spent most of the afternoon enjoying; the wrapped birthday gifts piled beside him; or the small crowd gathered expectantly around.

Chris bent down to whisper in Dylan's ear. "You okay?"

Dylan nodded mutely, and Chris squeezed his shoulder. Hell, maybe the expression on Dylan's face was due to the fact that he currently had a nice glass plug shoved up his ass. He'd allowed Chris to put it there before discovering Chris had organized a surprise birthday party for him. Chris was probably going to pay for this later. He was rather looking forward to that.

"You didn't have to do this," Dylan said to him.

"I know. But I had to top what you did for me in September." That had been the first time since he was tiny that Chris had celebrated his birthday. Dylan had bought him the router he'd been lusting after, shoved him into fancy clothes, and taken him into the city for steaks and onion rings. And when they'd returned to the farm, another surprise was waiting, this one delivered by Jimmy while they were at dinner: a shiny new Airstream trailer. Dylan had bundled Chris into the truck and they'd spent a week driving down the coast, camping out, doing little more than screwing, sleeping, and watching the waves.

"But… a party?" said Dylan.

"Family get-together. C'mon. There's pie at the end." Chris was referring to Kay's famous pies, two varieties made with berries from the farm. "Hey, everyone. Present openin' time."

It took a few minutes for everyone to gather. Kay and Rick had been standing near Stender's wife, Rachel, probably discussing the will they'd been working on. Two months from her due date, Kay was round and glowing. Stender had been near the window, closely examining the wooden molding. Mrs. Phillips was sitting in a chair with Tasha beside her; the older woman was admiring the younger one's jewelry. Jimmy, Ery, and Tasha's teenage daughter, Hayleigh, stood together and talked about whether Hayleigh might want to study graphic arts in college. And Matty was huddled very close to Tasha's son, Kevin. Kevin was a dentist, earnest and slightly pudgy, and he and Matty had taken to each other right away.

But all the guests gathered eagerly around and waited for Dylan to open his gifts.

Dylan wiped his hands nervously on his jeans. "This is way too much, guys."

"But we like giving you stuff!" said Kay. "Now hurry up!"

He smiled at her and then reached for the first brightly wrapped item.

Stender and Rachel gave him a small model of the school project, which had broken ground the previous month. Most of Dylan's suggestions had been accepted. Everyone was especially excited about the rooftop garden, and there were plans for the business classes to run the café as part of their schoolwork.

From Matty there was an oversized book about Frank Gehry and a small stack of gay porn DVDs, which made Dylan turn fiery red and everyone else laugh. "Can I borrow them when you're done?" Ery asked with a grin, earning himself a friendly nudge from his grandmother.

Tasha and Jimmy had brought jewelry—a silver wolf-shaped ring that matched the one they'd given Chris back in September, and another ring that had the initials C and D worked together in a clever stylized design. He put them both on right away.

From Ery there was an abstract painting that Dylan vowed to hang over the fireplace. Mrs. Phillips gave him an antique book about spirits. Kevin and Hayleigh had gone in together for a pair of tickets to some band Chris had never heard of and would probably hate, but which made Dylan bounce happily in his seat.

Kay had to send Rick out to the car for their present. He came back looking damp and slightly disgruntled, and Kay grabbed the parcel from him and plunked it onto Dylan's lap. He sniffed at her. "How come you smell like cat?"

Rick answered. "Because we're crazy, that's why. We have a baby on the way, but we adopted a kitten the other day."

"Yeah," added Kay. "He's so adorable! I found him in the parking lot at work. Somebody must have dumped him. Isn't that awful?" She sniffled. The hormones were still wreaking havoc with her emotions. "But now he has a safe home. The vet says he's about four months old, and we named him Frankie."

Chris and Dylan exchanged startled looks. "Frankie?" Dylan said.

"After Chris's middle name, actually." She reached over to pinch Chris's cheek. "Our kitty has these same big blue eyes."

Some things, Chris decided, were better left unexplored. He watched while Dylan carefully peeled the paper off his present—of course Dylan wasn't a ripper—to reveal a large wooden box. Dylan pried that open too. Inside were gardening tools. Hand rakes, trowels, seed starters, and the like, plus lots of little packets of seeds and a couple of gardening how-to books.

Kay smiled. "I know you guys were planning to put veggies in where Chris's house used to be. We thought this way you could plan it out over the winter."

"Thanks, guys. That'll be a lot of fun." A certain gleam in Dylan's eyes meant he was already imagining layout schematics and unnecessarily ornate arbors.

Dylan set the box near his feet and looked at his pile of loot. "Wow. I never expected…. This is a little overwhelming." He smiled around at his friends and family. "Thank you."

But Chris shook his head. "You ain't done yet. Haven't gotten to my presents."

The look of alarm on Dylan's face made everyone laugh. Chris waggled his eyebrows. "Don't worry. I've saved *those* for later. But I got a few things for you that can stand public inspection."

"You've given me everything I could want already, Chris."

Every woman in the room cooed, as did Ery. But although that made Dylan blush, he didn't break eye contact with Chris. Clearly he wanted Chris to know that he'd meant it—but Chris already knew.

"Tough, Dyl. 'Cause there's no refund on these things." From the spot on his bookshelf where he'd hidden them earlier, Chris retrieved four manila envelopes. He'd numbered them so he knew in which order to hand them over.

Dylan shook the first one, shrugged, and carefully tore it open. He stuck his hand inside, then frowned quizzically at what he scooped out. "A passport?"

"Open it."

Dylan did, revealing an incredibly goofy and unflattering photo of Chris. "It's yours."

"I know, genius. Applied for it myself. Thought I'd be ready in case one of these days you wanna whisk me away. We could go to Barcelona, maybe." He grinned at Dylan's somewhat sheepish smile. "Okay, here's the next one."

Dylan set the passport beside him and took envelope two. Everyone waited impatiently while he scanned the papers he found inside. "A bank statement?"

"Savings account. First I ever had. I wanna add your name to it too. And if you wanna drone at me later about a 401(k) or whatever, I'm willin' to listen."

That earned him an ear-to-ear smile. Dylan had been after him forever about planning for the future, planning for emergencies. It just about gave Dylan hives to know that Chris allowed money to flow into his hands and right back out again, with little concern for what-ifs. "Jeez, Chris. That's a really big deal for you. Thank you."

"Ain't done yet. Here."

Envelope three contained more papers, this time a much thicker sheaf. "I'll save you the readin' for now. Rachel and Stender helped me with this part." Chris took a deep breath. "That's a domestic partnership agreement. All fancy and legal and everythin'. I know we said all that crap ain't necessary, but Rachel said it's a good idea for taxes and shit, plus then Stender says I can be covered under your health insurance. But if you don't wanna sign, that's okay 'cause…." He realized he was babbling and shut his mouth with a snap.

This time Dylan looked pleased and maybe just slightly damp-eyed. "I'll sign. I think maybe a little ceremony might be nice, though. I want to see you in a tux."

Okay, maybe deep in his heart, Chris was secretly relieved to learn that Dylan wanted to make a thing out of this. Other than his granddad's funeral, there had really been no formal occasions in Chris's life—no graduations, no friends' weddings, nothing—and he felt as though something as important as this ought to be marked as special. "Okay," he said simply.

Kay and Matty actually squealed, and Kay flew over to give them both hugs that were awkward due to her big belly. "Can I help plan?" she asked.

"We wouldn't have it any other way," answered Chris. "But I got one more thing for you, Dyl."

"Yeah?"

Chris handed over the final envelope. "Rachel helped with this one too."

Dylan pulled out more papers. These had lots of official-looking paragraphs and about ten zillion places for him to sign or initial. "What's this?"

"If we both sign, those papers'll merge the two farms back into one big parcel, and you and me will be.... What's the phrase, Rachel?"

"Tenants in common. That means you both own equal rights to the entire property."

"Oh," Dylan said. It was just a simple word, but the look on his face said it all—he was delighted.

He carefully put all the paper aside, stood, and wrapped his arms around Chris. Chris hugged him back. The embrace was so tight neither of them could breathe well, but Chris didn't care. For a few minutes, the whole world dropped away—jobs, friends, family, property—and they were joined together as one.

Chris buried his face in Dylan's strong shoulder and tried really hard not to cry. He knew life wasn't going to be all rainbows and rose petals. They would bicker about chores and finances and music. Dylan would angst over his work challenges and worry over his wolfish exploits. Chris would feel insecure sometimes and get irritable and snarky. Possibly new supernatural weirdness would occur. But they had loved ones, and they had each other. They'd built a beautiful home and a beautiful life, with strong foundations and a solid structure that would last for years. Everything that mattered was already theirs.

"Come on," Dylan said, pulling slightly away. He looked a little puffy-eyed. "I think we've all earned that pie."

"Yeah," Chris said and patted him firmly on the butt, which made Dylan squirm deliciously due to the plug. "I think we have."

KIM FIELDING is very pleased every time someone calls her eclectic. She has migrated back and forth across the western two-thirds of the United States and currently lives in California, where she long ago ran out of bookshelf space. She's a university professor who dreams of being able to travel and write full time. She also dreams of having two perfectly behaved children, a husband who isn't obsessed with football, and a house that cleans itself. Some dreams are more easily obtained than others.

Kim can be found on her blogs:
http://kfieldingwrites.blogspot.com/
http://www.goodreads.com/author/show/4105707.Kim_Fielding/blog

and on Facebook:
https://www.facebook.com/KFieldingWrites.

Her e-mail is dephalqu@yahoo.com, and she can be found on Twitter at @KFieldingWrites.

Also from KIM FIELDING

GOOD
BONES

KIM FIELDING

http://www.dreamspinnerpress.com

Also from KIM FIELDING

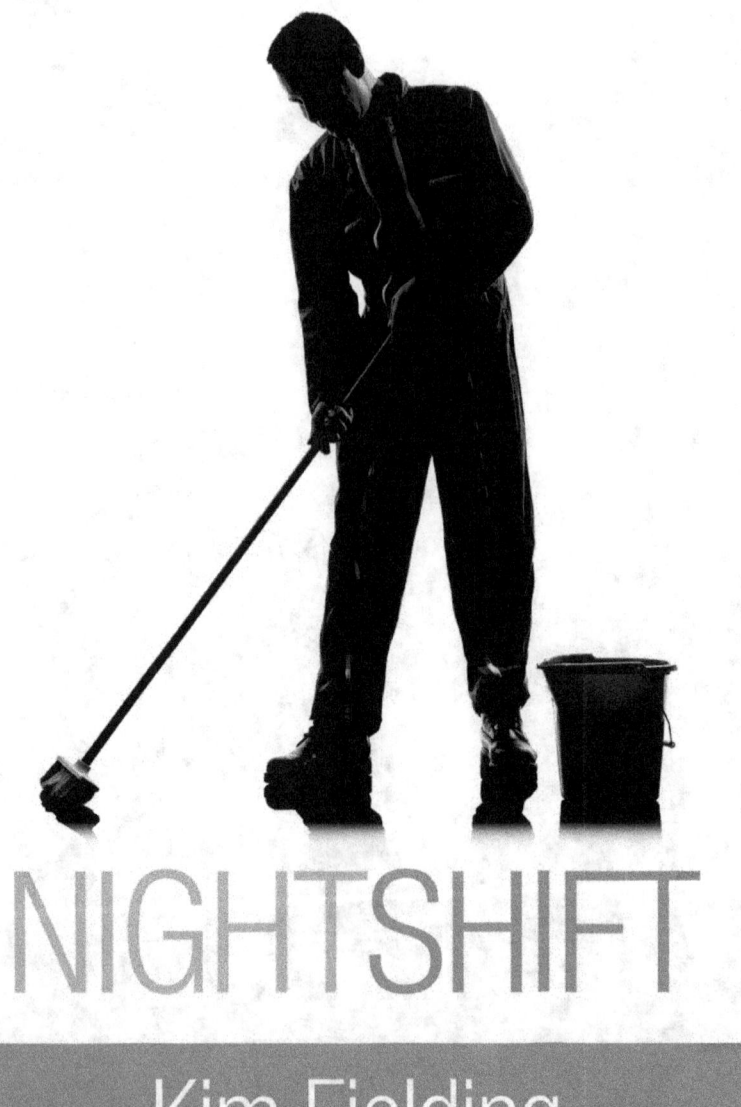

DENYING YOURSELF

Silvia Violet